MURDER
at the
HIGHLAND
CASTLE

BOOKS BY HELENA DIXON

HELENA DIXON

MURDER
at the
HIGHLAND
CASTLE

Bookouture

Published by Bookouture in 2023

An imprint of Storyfire Ltd.
Carmelite House
50 Victoria Embankment
London EC4Y 0DZ

www.bookouture.com

ISBN: 978-1-83790-064-0
eBook ISBN: 978-1-83790-063-3

With love to all my friends North of the Border.

PROLOGUE

December 22nd 1935

Finnglach Castle
The Highlands
Scotland

Dear Sir,

I find I am in immediate need of a private investigator and have been given your name by Mrs Olivia Parsons, a neighbour of mine. She has assured me that your agency is most efficient and discreet, both factors are of paramount importance in this matter.

I have been beset recently by a strange series of events. Taken individually they are minor, indeed trivial; however, I have now come to believe that my life is in danger. I write therefore to beg your most urgent assistance.

If you are able to help me, please reply by telegram to this letter and I shall make immediate arrangements for you and any assistant you may wish to bring to travel to my home here in Scotland by the 30th of December.

You may be assured that I am prepared to be very generous with financial recompense for your trouble and time in dealing with this matter. I look forward to your most prompt attention.

Sincerely,

S Barlas

CHAPTER ONE

Matt read the letter out loud to Kitty before placing it down on the dining table. A weak wintry sun streamed in through the dining room window at their home at Churston, where they were just finishing breakfast. A small pine Christmas tree stood in the corner of the room and wedding anniversary cards stood amidst the festive greetings on the mantelpiece. Bertie, their roan cocker spaniel, was asleep at their feet, his furry tummy full of sausages.

'Well, old thing, what do you think? Shall we take on this chap's case? He clearly expects a rapid reply.' Matt frowned as he looked at his wife.

Kitty poured the last of the tea from the china pot through the metal strainer into her cup. 'It's a most peculiar letter. He doesn't give us any details at all about what this danger to his life might be. However, he does say that my aunt Livvy recommended him to us. I suppose I could telephone her and ask her about him. You know, in case he is rather eccentric and not to be relied upon.'

Matt nodded. 'I think that may be wise.'

Kitty's great aunt Livvy lived in Scotland and since she had given this person their name, then she might be able to provide some background to the case. The tone of the letter concerned Matt. Despite the lack of details, one thing about the strange missive stood out very clearly. Whoever this S Barlas was, he was frightened, very frightened and desperate.

* * *

Kitty finished her tea and placed her linen napkin down on the table before rising to make her call from the telephone in the hall. Her aunt Livvy was her beloved grandmother's younger sister and she and Kitty had always been close. She was certain her great aunt would at the very least be able to provide some background information on this S Barlas person.

The operator took a while to connect the call amidst much crackling on the line. At this time of year, the telephone system to the remote area of the Highlands of Scotland where Livvy resided was not always terribly reliable. The winter weather frequently cut off all communication.

'Hello, Aunt Livvy?'

'Kitty, darling, how are you?' Her aunt's voice was hard to make out over the hissing on the line.

'I'm well, thank you. Aunt Livvy, do you know a Mr Barlas? Matt and I have just received a rather peculiar letter from him. He said you had recommended him to us?' Kitty rushed into the conversation fearing they might lose the connection before her aunt could give her any information on their potential new client.

'Yes, that's right, darling, he lives about forty miles from me. Sir Stephen is Lord Barlas of Finnglach Castle.' Her aunt's voice was barely audible through the noisy line.

'And is he reliable? His letter gave no details on the concerns he wished to consult us about?' Kitty asked.

'I met him last at a pre-Christmas ceilidh. I don't quite

recall how the subject came up, but I mentioned that you and Matthew were private investigators, and he took your card. I had one with me in my purse. He was very keen not to be overheard I thought.' The line cleared temporarily, and the last part of her aunt's statement sounded quite clearly in Kitty's ear.

'He's invited us to Finnglach Castle in time for New Year,' Kitty said.

'Oh, how nice. You'll have a marvellous time. Stephen always goes all out for Hogmanay. He has quite a house party, I believe, at the castle.' The line went dead before Kitty could ask her aunt for any further details about either Lord Barlas or the New Year celebrations.

She replaced the receiver of the black Bakelite telephone on its stand and went back through to the dining room to tell Matt what her aunt had said.

'Hmm, I take it we should accept the invitation then? It's quite a tight squeak if we are to get there for the thirtieth. It's already the twenty-seventh today.' Matt picked the letter up once more and reread the contents.

'It will be rather a rush to pack and it's a very long journey but there is something about his request...' Kitty broke off and bit her lip. The tone of the letter concerned her, and if this Lord Barlas's life was really in danger then she felt they had a duty to respond.

'I'll pop down to the post office and send a telegram. We had better make arrangements to pack,' Matt said. 'And, I agree, there is something about the wording of that letter that is very worrying.'

Matt left to take his motorcycle to the village post office. Kitty picked up the letter and studied it again before going into the sitting room to look for the *Atlas of the British Isles* that Matt kept on the small rosewood bookcase near the fireplace.

She took a seat on the black leather armchair beside the fire and opened the book on her lap. Bertie plodded into the room and settled down once more with a heavy sigh at her feet.

After a moment's searching, she found Finnglach Castle on the map of the Scottish Highlands. Situated in the shadow of the mountains on the edge of a loch it certainly seemed quite remote. The map indicated that a circle of ancient stones was situated close to the castle within the grounds.

Kitty left the book open and set it aside on the coffee table for Matt to see on his return. She then pulled a recent copy of *Debrett's Peerage* from the shelf and looked up the entry for Lord Barlas.

'Lord Stephen Aloysius Malcolm Winston Barlas, fourth Earl of Finnglach.' Kitty traced her finger along the entry as she read aloud. 'Hmm, first marriage to Lady Catherine Ebbs, one child, Ottilie. Oh, how sad, his wife died, now married to Velma Barlas née Weeks of Chicago, Illinois, United States of America. That marriage was only just over a year ago.'

Bertie opened his eyes and yawned, clearly unimpressed by Kitty's discoveries. Kitty smiled at her dog. 'I don't suppose you will be of any assistance with the packing.'

Bertie thumped his tail on the Turkish carpet in agreement.

Matt was soon back from his errand and Kitty dispatched him into the spare room to retrieve their trunks after she had shown him her research.

'I wonder what travel arrangements Lord Barlas will make for us? It is a long way from here to Scotland.' Kitty helped her husband to tug their luggage out onto the landing, hindered by their dog.

'He must have something in mind. Looking at that map you showed me Finnglach appears very isolated, and I seem to recall your aunt saying they are often cut off in that area during the winter with the snow.' Matt blew a small cloud of dust from the top of the trunk causing the ever-inquisitive Bertie to sneeze.

'I think our warmest clothing would seem to be in order. I'm sure I have some lambswool vests somewhere, although they are dreadfully prickly.' Kitty frowned at the trunk.

Matt laughed. 'Sounds just the ticket, darling.'

Kitty shook her head in mock despair. 'I'll start to pack if you can sort out Bertie's things. Thankfully country houses and their owners are well used to having dogs around the place. Grams will happily have Rascal. That cat spends more time at the Dolphin than here anyway.'

Kitty and her grandmother owned the Dolphin Hotel in Dartmouth and her grandmother still lived there. Until her marriage to Matt twelve months earlier Kitty had also lived and worked at the hotel. Since her wedding, however, they had appointed a manager, Mr Lutterworth, to manage the hotel and Kitty had joined Matt as a full partner in Torbay Private Investigative Services.

'Very well, yes, Bertie will be better off coming with us as he's much too naughty to be left with anyone else for more than a day or so. I know your grandmother will jump at the chance to have Rascal. I'll pop out and let Mrs Smith know too.' Matt kissed Kitty's cheek and set off whistling downstairs to make arrangements for their pets and to inform their housekeeper about their trip.

Kitty heard the front door close a few minutes later, followed by the roar of Matt's motorcycle engine. With her husband gone, she turned her attention to her packing.

Thirty minutes later, after pulling numerous items from her cupboards and drawers, she surveyed the chaos and went to make her second telephone call of the day.

She had just finished sorting out Matt's clothing when there was a knock at the front door.

'I came as quick as I could. Lucky I was just in time for the bus. Our Dolly said as you was in a right flap. Your grandmother give me leave to come over here when she heard as you was going to Scotland.' Alice smiled at Kitty as she entered the hall.

Alice was Kitty's dearest friend and worked as a chambermaid at the Dolphin, alongside her younger sister Dolly, who was employed on the management team.

'Oh, bless you. I started to pack but then got in a pickle so I telephoned Dolly hoping you would be at the hotel. Grams said she would take Rascal for me too while we were away,' Kitty explained.

Alice drew off her gloves and hung her coat on the stand in the hall. 'Dolly said as you had to go to Scotland in a hurry. It's not your aunt Livvy, is it?'

'No, it's someone she's referred to us though.' Kitty went into the sitting room to retrieve the letter and passed it to her friend.

Alice pursed her lips as she read. 'It sounds like it might be quite a delicate matter. Not much time for you to get all the way to Scotland.'

'I know, and we've no idea what arrangements Lord Barlas intends to make for our travel. I assume it may be the night train from London,' Kitty said.

'I know you said your grandmother would have the cat but what am you doing with Bertie?' Alice asked, looking askance as the dog sat on her foot.

'He's coming with us. We can't leave him here. Mickey would take him if it were just for a day or so but we can't leave him for too long.' Kitty ruffled the dog's ears affectionately.

'That's true. A right nose for mischief that dog's got. Well, we'd best get to packing then.' Alice followed Kitty up the stairs to the bedroom only to stop in the doorway at the sight of the clothes strewn all over the bed. 'Dear me, this is a fair muddle. Everything will be creased to high heavens if you throw things in like that.'

Kitty went to retrieve some of her stockings only to be shooed out of the way by her friend who promptly unpacked the items she had already placed in the trunk.

''Tis a good thing you sent for me.' Alice quickly and expertly began to sort and pack Kitty's things. 'I assume as you'll need warm things and evening wear as you'll be there for New Year? I've heard as it's a big thing in Scotland. They have them bagpipers and whisky. I saw it in a film a couple of years ago.'

'Yes, you're right. I telephoned Aunt Livvy this morning to try and find out some more about this Lord Barlas. I looked him up in Debrett's too. She said he usually has a house party at the castle for the New Year.' Kitty sat down on the dressing table stool and tried not to get under Alice's feet as she bustled back and forth folding and sorting.

'If that's the case, then I wonder who he is afraid of in that party? Must be someone staying at the castle, or he wouldn't be wanting you and Captain Bryant to be dashing off there right after Christmas,' Alice remarked shrewdly.

'That's true, I hadn't thought of that. But surely if you thought your life might be in danger you would send everyone away, wouldn't you? Or at least those you suspected might have reason to harm you?' Kitty said as she passed Alice her shagreen-covered vanity case ready for her jewellery and cosmetics to be packed.

'Unless he can't, if they happen to be his nearest and dearest. I expect you'll soon see the way of it once you get to Scotland,' Alice said as she placed Kitty's favourite perfume inside her vanity box.

'I hope you're right,' said Kitty to her friend, giving her a warm smile as Alice snapped the box shut.

CHAPTER TWO

Travel instructions and permission to bring Bertie arrived promptly the following morning via a telegram after breakfast.

'We are to take the train to London this afternoon, then berths have been secured for us on the night train into the Highlands,' Matt said as he studied the brief message.

Kitty was quite excited at the idea of sleeping on board a train. It all sounded like a bit of an adventure, even if it would be a very long journey. Matt assured her that they would dine on board and the guard would alert them in time for them to alight at the station closest to Finnglach in the early hours of the morning. Special arrangements had been made for Bertie.

The journey to London went smoothly and Bertie appeared to cope well with the travel arrangements. The night train appeared to be a popular service and the station was busy. There seemed to be quite a lot of passengers intent on travelling to Scotland in time for the Hogmanay celebrations.

The steward showed them to their berths and Kitty was especially enamoured with the small cabin, completed by neatly made bunk beds. She was slightly troubled by how well Matt would cope with the enclosed space, but he assured her that he would probably stay up in the lounge car overnight with Bertie.

Since being confined to the trenches during the Great War, Matt hated being in small spaces. He had witnessed the horrors of men, and even horses, being buried alive in the mud. Even in a car he needed to have a window partly open. This was his main reason for continuing to use his motorcycle as his main mode of transport rather than driving Kitty's car; he liked the open air.

Dinner in the dining car was most delightful with excellent silver service, as they enjoyed tomato soup, pork chops with vegetables and potatoes, followed by lemon syllabub. Kitty marvelled at how the waiter managed to stay on his feet without spilling even a drop of the wine as the train rocketed along in the darkness.

Matt managed to take Bertie out at a couple of the scheduled station stops before everyone began to retire for the night. Instructions were left with the steward in charge of the sleeping arrangements to wake them an hour before they were due to disembark in the Highlands.

'Are you quite certain you will be able to get some sleep?' Kitty asked her husband as he prepared to return to the lounge car, leaving her to go to her bunk.

'Perfectly, old thing, come and find me after the man wakes you up.' Matt kissed her cheek and made his way back along the swaying corridor of the train accompanied by Bertie.

Kitty hoped he would be all right. She felt slightly guilty about him staying in the lounge car while she slid happily between the crisp white-cotton sheets of her cosy bunk bed. The rhythmic rocking of the train and the chunkity-chunk of the wheels on the track soon rocked her to sleep.

Before she knew where she was, the train attendant was tapping at the door of her carriage to wake her and asking if they would like tea and toast. She raised the blind on the carriage window to see nothing but darkness outside. No sparks of light from a cottage, no moonlight, nothing but inky darkness.

Kitty shivered and hastened to dress and get her things together. They couldn't be far away from their destination now.

Matt was dozing in a corner of the lounge car with Bertie snoring at his feet. He opened his eyes as Kitty took her seat beside him.

'Good morning. I've asked the man to serve our tea and toast in here,' Kitty said.

Matt yawned and stretched his arms and legs. A trace of stubble covered his chin. 'Thank you.' He glanced at his watch. 'We should arrive at the station at six a.m.'

'Did you manage to get any sleep?' Kitty asked quietly as she glanced around the virtually deserted carriage.

'Yes, it wasn't too bad at all,' he assured her. 'I took Bertie out again when we stopped at one of the stations,' he continued as the attendant set down a tray loaded with tea things and a chrome-plated toast rack in front of them.

'Your station will be in around twenty minutes, sir, madam. I've been advised that it is icy with some snow,' the attendant informed them. 'Would you care for some hot water, sir, for shaving, in your berth?'

'Please,' Matt accepted the man's offer.

'Is the station far from Finnglach Castle, do you know?' Kitty asked the attendant.

'Finnglach Castle, eh? It's about forty miles, madam, but it may be tricky to get there in this weather. It's a lonely spot and some say as the little folk haunt the glens around there,' the steward said.

'I saw there was a circle of standing stones on the map.' Kitty knew most wild places had similar legends. Dartmoor, for instance, was widely believed to be home to pixies.

'That's right, madam. They say as the stones was once people, flesh and blood like you and me, but they was cursed and turned to stone. Folk do say as they have heard voices and seen them dancing on nights when the moon is full,' the steward informed her.

'Let us hope we don't encounter them during our stay,' Matt said, thanking the man and tipping him generously.

'Gosh, a creepy local legend and bad weather. I hope Alice packed that lambswool vest of yours, darling. I think you may need it.' Matt winked at her as she poured their tea.

There was just enough time to take their refreshments and for Matt to shave before the train came to a halt.

Kitty accepted Matt's hand to alight from the train, while their trunks were unloaded onto the platform. They were the only passengers to disembark at the station. Bertie sniffed the air curiously while Kitty shivered as the freezing air stung her cheeks. She had put on her sheepskin mittens and a warm woollen hat, along with her heaviest winter coat with its large fur collar. Even so, it was much colder than what she was used to. Dartmouth rarely saw any snow and the frosts were relatively fleeting since the sea air and more temperate climate kept the more extreme winter weather at bay much of the time.

The station was tiny and dark with only an oil lamp burning in the station master's office. Kitty looked around for any signs of life as the steam train that had delivered them sounded its whistle and clunked its way out of the station.

'I thought we were to be met?' Matt frowned as he too looked around the empty platform.

The words had barely left his lips when a chauffeur in a heavy greatcoat and peaked cap came towards them.

'Captain and Mrs Bryant? Lord Barlas has sent me to collect you for this part of the journey.'

Matt helped the man to wheel their luggage on a trolley out to the waiting Rolls Royce. Kitty slid onto the back seat, pleased to see there were several thick woollen tartan travelling rugs which she used to cover her legs and feet. Bertie hopped up and settled himself down between herself and Matt.

With the luggage safely stowed, the chauffeur drove the large car off into the darkness. Kitty tried to see through the windows, but dawn was still some hours away. All she could make out were a few cottages and some trees at the side of the roads. There were no streetlights.

'The snow is deeper near the castle, so Lord Barlas has arranged for a horse and cart to take you the last part of the journey when we reach the village,' the chauffeur told them.

Kitty glanced at Matt. Travelling to Finnglach was certainly quite the adventure. It felt as if they had been on the move forever. She hoped Bertie would behave on a cart ride. He was always slightly wary of horses. He had coped with the journey remarkably well up until now.

The first pink and gold rays of dawn had started to lighten the sky when they reached a small group of stone cottages. They stopped at the edge of what Kitty assumed must usually be the green in the centre of the hamlet. The chauffeur announced they had reached the village of Finnglach and asked them to wait while he alerted the man who was to take them on the final leg of their journey.

Even in the limited light, Kitty could see that the snow was heaped up against the walls of the cottages. The car had already slid a few times on the ice before they had reached the village and it had taken all of the chauffeur's skill to keep a steady course.

After some minutes the chauffeur returned, accompanied by a short, ruddy-faced man bundled up in ancient tweed and wool. He prepared the cart and harnessed the sturdy piebald pony that was to pull it, transferred their luggage, and they set off for the castle.

Kitty held tight to the wooden bench and shivered under the thick woollen rugs, as the cart bumped its way along the snowy track towards a pine forest. Matt huddled next to her to give her his support and to keep her warm. Bertie too was snuggled down with just his nose peeping out to sniff the air as they rode along.

Ahead of them as the sky grew lighter, she caught her first glimpse of the grey tile-covered turrets of the castle above the pine trees. The track climbed upwards for a short distance and beyond the castle she glimpsed the vast, silent, frozen waters of the loch.

The woods were quiet as the road dropped down again and the castle was lost from sight as they were surrounded by the tall, blue-green trees. The only sound was the jingle of the horse's harness and the crisp crunch of the frozen snow beneath the wheels of the cart. The pony's breath appeared as a cloudy plume as the animal snickered and tossed his mane.

Kitty pressed closer to Matt, wondering how something as large as the castle could suddenly vanish from sight. They plodded on for another mile or so along the narrow track. After a while, the trees began to thin and once more Finnglach Castle and the loch returned to full view.

The pale-grey fairy-tale structure of the castle was mirrored in the semi-frozen surface of the loch and the light blue and pink streaks of the morning sky seemed to add a silvery, almost magical touch to the scene.

As they drew closer to the castle entrance, Kitty noticed the ring of large grey stones standing on the loch shore not far from the castle. Snow covered and weathered they stood like ancient, silent sentinels. Something about them caused her to shiver and Matt hugged her close.

'Almost there, darling. I hope they have a good fire going,' he said as the cart finally jingled to a halt near the front door of the castle.

Their driver jumped down and pulled hard on the large black cast-iron bell pull beside the vast wooden door.

The door creaked open, and an elderly manservant clad in rusty black stepped forward to greet them. Matt assisted Kitty down from the back of the cart as the driver saw to their luggage. Bertie followed, shaking himself as he looked around the snowy ground, sniffing the air.

'Captain Bryant, Mrs Bryant, welcome to Finnglach. Please come away inside. I hope your journey here has not been too uncomfortable.'

Kitty and Matt followed the man into a huge hall filled with oversized dark oak furniture. The walls were hung with faded banners and sets of antlers. Ancient weapons were also displayed with round shields on the rough stone walls. Kitty was relieved to see a fire blazing away in the vast stone hearth. A large pine tree decked in baubles and silver tinsel strands stood in an old whisky barrel near the fireplace. The air was warm, and the decorations added a festive touch.

'Lord Barlas and his party are at breakfast. If you would care to freshen up after your travels, I shall then take you through to the dining hall. If you wish, sir, madam, John here can take your dog to the kitchens for his breakfast?' the butler offered.

Kitty was glad of the opportunity to tidy her face and hair after the long journey from the station. The offer of breakfast also sounded most welcome as the benefit from the tea and toast they had received on board the train had worn off some hours ago. Bertie too had looked delighted at the mention of food and trotted away quite happily with the manservant.

She rejoined Matt in the hall and the butler led them along a corridor and into a large dining room. A small group of people were already seated at the long polished table, while a man and a woman were helping themselves to food from the silver-lidded dishes that were placed atop the small burners on the sideboard.

'My lord, Captain and Mrs Bryant,' the butler introduced

them to the older dark-haired man seated at the head of the table.

Lord Barlas immediately set aside his linen napkin and cutlery and rose to shake their hands. 'Captain Bryant, Mrs Bryant, welcome, welcome to Finnglach Castle. I trust your journey was not too arduous? Please do come and join us, I'm sure you must both be ready for something hot to eat and drink.'

'Thank you, sir, for your kind invitation. The travel arrangements were very well organised, you were most kind,' Matt replied as he and Kitty both took a seat at the table.

A maid in a black uniform with a white apron quickly stepped forward to set out cutlery and delicate china teacups for them, along with a silver pot of fresh tea.

'Splendid, splendid. Now, please allow me to introduce you.' Lord Barlas had resumed his seat and Kitty was conscious of the open curiosity of the other guests. 'Of course, not everyone is down yet. My wife, Velma, always prefers to take her breakfast in her room. She is looking forward to meeting you both later.'

Kitty smiled politely.

'This is my daughter, Ottilie, and her fiancé, Mr Donald Waterford.' Lord Barlas waved a slightly pudgy hand in the direction of the couple seated at the table.

Ottilie was a dark-haired woman of about thirty, dressed in a heather-coloured tweed suit with a pale-lilac cashmere sweater. Her fiancé was a large, bluff, sandy-haired man of a similar age.

Kitty and Matt duly murmured their hellos and shook hands as the other couple who had been at the sideboard came to sit down.

'And this is Miss Romy Fisher, a friend of my wife's, and her friend, Mr Maxfield Cotter,' Lord Barlas continued.

'Delighted to meet you.' Matt shook hands with Maxfield. 'I

say, are you the racing driver? I've seen you in action on the track a couple of times, exhilarating stuff.'

'Thank you, yes indeed, most kind of you to say so.' Maxfield was a tall, dark-haired man. Kitty thought him good-looking in a dangerous kind of way. She suspected that he probably had a trail of broken hearts behind him.

Miss Fisher was petite, with auburn curls and a snub nose. Her clothing looked expensive, and she had a distinct American accent when she spoke.

'You must have had quite a time getting here. The road was barely passable when we all arrived before Christmas, wasn't it, Maxfield?' Romy looked to her companion for his agreement.

'Yes, and I believe more snow is forecast in the next few days,' Maxfield agreed.

'Oooh, let's hope we have good supplies.' Romy gave an exaggerated shiver. 'It's just too marvellous though, isn't it? Christmas and New Year in a Scottish castle. They'll never believe me when I get back to California.'

'You may rest assured that Finnglach is used to this kind of weather. We have a good supply of food and firewood, an emergency generator and plenty of candles and oil lamps,' Lord Barlas assured her.

'So long as we have plenty of Scotch.' Romy giggled and smiled at Kitty. 'What say you, Mrs Bryant?'

Before Kitty had a chance to respond the sturdy oak door of the dining room flew open and a large, older woman clad in voluminous emerald-green drapery stood in the doorway. Her bejewelled hands were clasped to her heart and her dark, curly hair was almost covered with a vibrantly patterned silk scarf that matched her dress.

Lord Barlas rose to his fee, looking concerned. 'Nettie!'

'Stephen, be careful! My guides tell me that danger is very close to you right now.' She raised a hand and pointed dramatically at their host. Her dark eyes flashed as she glanced about the room, before her gaze settled momentarily on Kitty and Matt.

'Beware, I tell you, death is close at hand.' The woman turned on her heel and departed in a dramatic swish of emerald drapery.

CHAPTER THREE

There was a moment of awkward silence before Lord Barlas sank back down onto his chair. Matt's gaze met Kitty's and he guessed that her thoughts probably mirrored his own. Had they been called to Scotland on a wild goose chase? That some eccentric lady had convinced their host that he was in danger?

The other guests had continued to eat their breakfast and exchange inconsequential remarks about the weather as if the meal had not been interrupted at all. Something which convinced Matt that this sort of event must not be uncommon in the household.

The door to the dining room opened once more and everyone looked to see who was entering. A smartly dressed woman in her late thirties with immaculate dark hair entered the room accompanied by an older, good-looking man with a thin moustache.

'I say, whatever is going on with Madam Fortina this morning? She just barrelled past us in the hall and nearly knocked poor Lynette into the suit of armour at the foot of the stairs,' the man grumbled as he pulled out a chair at the table for his wife.

'It seems she's had another of her visions. It seems that Daddy is in terrible danger again,' Ottilie replied with a shrug. 'I really don't know what has come over Nettie lately. These messages are becoming rather too much.' She gave her father a concerned glance.

The man took a seat beside his wife. 'I say, Stephen, old boy, you look a little shaken. She's not getting to you is she with these wild fancies?'

Lord Barlas did indeed appear a little pale. 'No, not at all. I think we are all used to Nettie by now. Rufus, Lynette, may I introduce Captain Matthew Bryant and his wife Kitty. Captain Bryant, Mrs Bryant, Sir Rufus and Lady Lynette Smythe, old friends of the family.'

Matt and Kitty duly shook hands and answered enquiries about their journey to the castle while they ate their bacon and eggs.

'Who was the lady in green that came in earlier? Nettie?' Kitty addressed her question to Lady Smythe since she was seated next to her.

Lady Smythe rolled her eyes. 'She calls herself Madam Fortina. Velma, Stephen's wife, employs her as a psychic medium. She advises Velma on all kinds of things. Velma is American.'

Matt assumed that Lady Smythe had added the last part as some kind of explanation for Lady Barlas employing someone as a psychic medium.

'Does she often make those kind of entrances? She burst in here to tell Lord Barlas he was in some kind of danger?' Kitty asked.

Sir Rufus chuckled drily. 'Oh, my dear lady, she does all kinds of strange things. Just lately, however, she does seem to have acquired a bee in her bonnet about Stephen's safety.'

'Yes, only last night she snatched a glass of whisky from his hand and poured it away into the aspidistra pot in the library.

Then insisted on getting a fresh bottle opened.' Romy Fisher joined in the conversation.

'Dashed waste of good Scotch whisky and not terribly good for the plant, if you ask me,' Maxfield said.

'Poor Daddy is becoming a nervous wreck.' Ottilie patted her father's hand affectionately. 'But Nettie has always been so accurate, it is quite worrying.'

Matt noted that their host had stayed silent until now on the whole subject of Madam Fortina and her psychic warnings.

'How very extraordinary,' Kitty remarked.

'Accurate my foot! I wish Velma would see sense and get rid of the woman. I mean, there is some amusement to be found in her usually when she holds her readings and things but just lately, well...' Lady Smythe left the sentence hanging.

'Thank you, my dear, for your concern.' Lord Barlas gave his daughter's fingers an affectionate squeeze. 'Madam Fortina means well, I'm sure.'

'But surely you aren't taking any of her nonsense seriously, are you?' Sir Rufus asked as he exchanged a glance with his wife.

Lord Barlas paused just a fraction of a second too long before replying. 'What? No, of course not. Nonsense as you say. Only you know that Velma takes all of this very seriously.'

'Darling Velma is a very spiritual person,' Romy agreed.

Matt noticed Lady Smythe's immaculately pencilled eyebrows raise a little at this statement.

Donald Waterford had been silent until this point. All his concentration had been on solidly eating his way through a laden breakfast plate. 'I think it's all a load of rubbish. Woman is a charlatan, if you ask me,' he remarked as he wiped his mouth with his napkin.

'Darling, you know Nettie has always been very good at delivering messages from the other side,' Ottilie protested.

'Takes a fraud to know a fraud, I say,' Sir Rufus's words

were barely audible and fortunately neither Ottilie nor her fiancé appeared to have heard him.

Matt wondered what had gone on between the urbane older man and Ottilie's fiancé. Clearly Sir Rufus did not approve of Donald Waterford.

Romy and Maxfield had finished breakfast and rose from the table. 'Well, we're going to go outside for a bit of a walk before the mist comes down again. I expect we shall see you all at lunch.' Romy looked around the table.

'Donald and I have some wedding planning to do so we shall be in the library.' Ottilie also stood and glared at her fiancé who was still eyeing the toast rack as if he would have preferred to eat some more food rather than plan his wedding.

'Matt and I should really go and unpack and rest for a while. Travelling so far is quite exhausting.' Kitty glanced at Matt and he picked up on the cue in her expression.

'Yes, indeed, perhaps we could see you before lunch, Lord Barlas?' Matt suggested as he joined Kitty in preparing to exit from the breakfast table.

'Good idea, come to my study at twelve and we can go over that matter I mentioned, and do call me Stephen, we are family after all.' Lord Barlas nodded.

Matt followed Kitty from the room. He had picked up on the sudden interested glance the Smythes had given them when Lord Barlas had made his suggestion for a meeting. The mention of them being family seemed to indicate that this was the cover story Lord Barlas had given his guests to explain their invitation to the castle.

In the hall they found the elderly butler who had greeted them on arrival as they followed the corridor towards the stairs.

Matt enquired about the direction of their room.

'First floor, sir, in the west wing, fourth door as you follow the landing.'

Matt thanked him and he and Kitty made their way up the

grand polished dark-oak staircase. The lime-washed walls of the landing seemed to be lined with portraits of Lord Barlas's ancestors posing with various horses or dead deer. Suits of armour and oak blanket boxes were placed in alcoves.

When they reached their room, it appeared that Lord Barlas's staff had already unpacked their luggage and hung their clothes inside the vast mahogany wardrobe that stood opposite the four-poster bed. A small fire crackled merrily in the stone grate and rich-red tapestries embroidered with gold thread, faded with time, curtained both the bed and the small window.

Kitty prowled about the room, opening and closing the drawers of the armoire and the dressing table, before peering out of the window.

'We have a splendid view of the standing stones.' Her tone sounded slightly doubtful.

Matt joined her at the window. 'We do indeed. You don't like them?' he asked. From this angle, looking down they could see three quarters of the circle. The stones looked bent and almost twisted, and he could see how people thought they might once have been human.

'I don't know. They seem eerie to me.' Kitty frowned as she continued to stare at them. 'I think I'm probably just tired and this whole set up is rather strange, isn't it?'

Matt stared out at the snow-covered landscape. The loch was as still and flat as a millpond. 'Madam Fortina and her dire predictions, you mean?'

'Yes. Are we just here because Lord Barlas has been frightened by her? Do you think he really is in any danger, or is it just something that woman has cooked up? Maybe to extort some money out of him, perhaps? You know, a kind of protection racket?'

Matt looked at his wife and chuckled. 'Is that from that film you and Alice saw at the picture house last month?'

Kitty elbowed him gently in his ribs. 'You know what I

mean.'

'I understand your concerns, but I do think there is something very wrong here. Whether Madam Fortina is a charlatan or not, Lord Barlas certainly appears to me to be a frightened man.' Matt had seen enough in his army days and in his work for the British Government after the war to be able to tell when someone was genuinely scared.

Kitty stepped away from the window and sat down on the red-velvet mahogany stool in front of the dressing table. She picked up her comb from the silver-topped dressing set that had been laid out from her vanity box and started to tidy her hair.

'It will be interesting to hear what he has to tell us when we meet him later,' she said.

Matt sat down on the edge of the bed and slipped off his shoes. 'That business with the whisky glass sounded concerning.'

Kitty paused and turned her head to look at him. 'Yes, I thought that too. I wonder if that is an example of the kinds of incidents he mentioned in his letter.'

'It could be. Of course, if Madam Fortina is hoping just to scare him for some reason, then the contents of that glass may have been perfectly innocent.' Matt picked at a stray piece of thread on the leg of his dark-grey woollen trousers.

'But the glass could have contained something more sinister than Scotch whisky.' Kitty turned back to the dressing table mirror.

'And if it did contain something sinister, then who put it there and why?' Matt's gaze met Kitty's in the mirror's reflection.

'And how did Madam Fortina know about it?' Kitty added as she set down her comb.

The corners of Matt's lips tilted upwards into a wry smile. 'I take it that you don't believe Madam Fortina was warned by her spirit guides?'

Kitty's expression sobered. 'I think it more likely that she either saw or overheard something that made her believe Lord Barlas's drink may have been tampered with, or she staged it to make it seem as if he were in need of her protection.'

'Romy Fisher said that Lady Barlas is a great believer in Madam Fortina's abilities,' Matt said.

'Yet Ottilie's fiancé seems to think that Madam Fortina is a fraud, even though Ottilie herself defended her. It will be interesting to meet Lady Barlas.' Kitty turned around on the stool to face her husband.

'You said that Lady Barlas was Lord Barlas's second wife?' Matt mused.

Kitty nodded. 'Yes, Ottilie's mother died when she was around ten, according to the entries in *Debrett's*. Lord Barlas only remarried last year.'

'Interesting, and Ottilie is engaged to Donald Waterford. Sir Rufus doesn't seem to care for the match.' Matt looked at Kitty.

'Yes, I heard what he said too, he obviously thinks that Ottilie's fiancé is not on the level. I hope Lord Barlas has a good story to give to his house guests about why we have joined the party. It seems as if he has told everyone we are relations.' Kitty had raised her concerns about how to explain their invitation on the train during their journey to the castle.

'He did say in his initial letter that he was looking for discretion,' Matt said.

'A wise decision if it turns out that someone here is trying to kill him. I suppose too that if the others believe we are related, then our being here makes perfect sense,' Kitty agreed as she attempted to stifle a yawn.

'I dare say we shall discover more at twelve o'clock.' Matt lay back on the bed, and patted the coverlet in an invitation for her to join him.

CHAPTER FOUR

A couple of hours later, feeling more refreshed after a nap, Kitty accompanied Matt back downstairs. A maid, dusting in the hall, fetched Bertie for them from the kitchen and then directed them all to Lord Barlas's study.

They discovered Lord Barlas alone in the large square room. Kitty looked around her with interest. A fire crackled merrily in the grate and an elderly black Labrador was snoring on the shabby rug in front of the fire. He looked up at Bertie when they entered the room, then promptly fell back asleep. Two of the stone walls were lined with bookcases laden with books stacked higgledy-piggledy on the shelves. Rolls of documents were pushed into the gaps between the books. It was a cluttered room, but cosy.

Lord Barlas was seated behind a large oak desk similarly covered with books and papers. Behind him stood two large wooden filing cabinets and an old-fashioned substantial green-painted metal safe. The study was clearly a working office and Kitty guessed their host probably spent most of his time there.

'Captain Bryant, Mrs Bryant, please do take a seat.' Lord Barlas had risen to shake their hands as they had entered the room. He indicated towards a couple of battered bentwood chairs placed in front of his desk.

'Please do call me Kitty,' Kitty said as she took her seat next to Matt. She was bursting with curiosity to discover more about why they had been commissioned to come to Finnglach.

'Yes, Kitty, of course,' Lord Barlas agreed.

Bertie wagged his tail before settling at Kitty's feet, clearly happy to share the room with Lord Barlas's dog.

To her surprise, Lord Barlas didn't immediately retake his seat, but instead paced about behind his desk, his hands behind his back and a worried frown creasing his forehead. Kitty glanced at Matt.

'You must both be wondering why I have asked you here and at such short notice.' Their host stopped his pacing as if he had come to a decision as he turned to face them.

'Your letter seemed to imply that you were in danger, sir,' Matt said.

'Yes, that's true. Well, at least I have become convinced that it may be true.' Lord Barlas sighed and rubbed at his face with his hands.

'Perhaps if you begin by telling us what has been happening to lead you to this conclusion,' Kitty suggested.

The older man sat down heavily on his office chair. 'You must understand that even now this seems quite fantastical. It may be that I am wasting your time, and all of this is caused by some kind of paranoia on my part.'

Kitty looked around at the contents of the office, all of which spoke to her of a secure country estate owner, not the type of man who would usually be troubled by ideas that someone was trying to murder him.

She exchanged a glance with Matt. 'Please just tell us what has happened. If there is nothing to fear then at least your mind will be at rest.' Her tone was gentle. It was clear to her that Lord

Barlas was deeply troubled by his worries, whether they had any foundation was another matter.

'Very well, Mrs Bryant, forgive me, Kitty.' Lord Barlas raised his head and looked at her. 'This all began at the start of December. My wife and I, along with Madam Fortina and Ottilie and her now fiancé, had returned here to Finnglach. We had been in London until then and before that in America. I have a number of businesses in the city which require my attention from time to time.'

He paused for a moment as if to gather his thoughts.

'Do please go on, sir.' Matt had taken out a small notebook and pencil from his pocket.

'It's traditional for me to hold a small house party here over Christmas and Hogmanay. I have houses elsewhere, of course, but Finnglach Castle is my ancestral home. The weather here is wintry and company is welcome. Rufus and Lynette are both old friends and, in Rufus's case, my business partner in various ventures for many years, so naturally they were invited. They have been here many times over the years.'

'And the others in the party, sir?' Kitty asked.

'Romy Fisher is a friend of my wife's and is also under contract to me for my theatrical productions. Velma thought she would enjoy a traditional Scottish Christmas and New Year. Since Miss Fisher is an actress and a singer, one hoped that she might also be entertaining as a guest. Maxfield Cotter is her boyfriend. You recognised him I noticed, Captain Bryant?'

Matt nodded. 'Yes, sir, I follow motor sports and have had the pleasure of seeing him race a couple of times.'

'Yes, so naturally he too seemed as if he would be a good addition to the party. Everyone was assembled here by the eighth of December.' Lord Barlas paused again as if still trying to work out what it was that he wished to say.

'I spoke to my aunt Livvy after we received your letter. She told me that she had recommended us to you at the ceilidh before Christmas. I assume that between the house party assembling and the time of the dance there had been incidents which troubled you?' Kitty glanced across at Matt who was scribbling furiously in the notebook.

Lord Barlas blinked. 'Thank you, Mrs... erm, Kitty, yes, that's correct. Everything was fine for the first few days. It seemed as if everyone was enjoying their stay. Then, well, I still don't know quite what happened. I mean, one expects the odd argument or disagreement when a group of people are together for a period of time but, well, this was different.'

'How was it different?' Kitty asked. She was intrigued by the older man's statement. Lord Barlas had not struck her as being a particularly sensitive kind of man so far.

He appeared a typical, solid, countryman, not given to imaginings but grounded in managing his estate and lands.

'I realised there were tensions in the party. For one thing, Rufus dislikes my future son-in-law. You must understand that Ottilie has not had the most fortunate of lives. She lost her mother, my first wife, when she was a child and her first husband, Marcus Tremaine, was also killed a couple of years ago in a climbing accident in the Himalayas. Rufus has always looked out for Ottilie, indeed he has been more like an uncle to her. He is her godfather, so I suppose that's only natural.' Lord Barlas paused once more.

Kitty had heard of Marcus Tremaine, his exploits as a mountaineer and adventurer had been the kind of stuff that made the newspapers. She hadn't realised that he had been married to Ottilie.

'Has Sir Rufus given you a reason, sir, why he disapproves of your daughter's engagement to Mr Waterford?' Matt asked.

'He says he is awaiting proof of something, he has merely hinted that he knows something to Donald's detriment. That Donald is a fortune hunter. Ottilie and Donald did not become engaged until Christmas Eve and the Hogmanay party we have planned is partly to celebrate the engagement in style.'

'But you yourself have no concerns about Mr Waterford?' Matt asked.

'Nothing that I can put my finger on, but I do have doubts about him. And, if Rufus thinks he is a wrong'un, then I must admit I am concerned. I love Ottilie very much and want her to be happy. My daughter is, however, much like her late mother in her character. She is stubborn. I dare not raise any concern about Donald to her without irrevocable proof of a problem or, well, she may marry him out of spite.' Lord Barlas slumped back in his seat. 'It goes without saying that my daughter is a wealthy woman.'

'She has control of her money?' Kitty asked. She knew that many young women in Ottilie's position might well be rich on paper, but beyond receiving a generous allowance their wealth often remained under their father or husband's control.

'Rufus and I manage Ottilie's investments for her, something that was in place before her first marriage, and which has continued. Marcus was a wealthy man in his own right and cared little for material things. On his death, she obviously inherited his estate and requested we manage it for her. She has a generous allowance but until she remarries, or anything happens to either myself or Rufus, then she cannot touch the capital.'

'I see.' Kitty could see his dilemma about his daughter's relationship with Donald, but was unsure how any of this had led Lord Barlas to believe his own life was at risk.

'Madam Fortina is employed by Lady Barlas?' Matt asked.

'Velma believes implicitly in psychic guidance. My wife is a sensitive woman. Before our marriage she was an actress, hence her friendship with Miss Fisher. She also has something of a gift. Madam Fortina led to our meeting in the first place.' Lord Barlas gave a wry smile. 'Not my usual kind of thing, but Ottilie had been feeling rather down and it was the anniversary of Marcus's death.'

'So she consulted a psychic?' Kitty said as she connected the dots.

'Yes, Madam Fortina has something of a reputation amongst the artistic community and Ottilie heard of her talents from Romy. I accompanied her to one of her readings and met Velma.' Lord Barlas sighed and rubbed his eyes once more.

'When did Madam Fortina begin to warn you of a threat to your well-being?' Matt asked.

'She started a couple of days before the ceilidh. I suppose that was just after the first incident.' Lord Barlas shifted uncomfortably in his chair causing it to creak.

'And what happened then?' Kitty had begun to feel that getting information from their employer was like drawing teeth. So far, they seemed to have gone around in circles without getting much of anything, except some personal disputes within the house party.

'My gun went missing.'

Kitty gave an alarmed look at Matt. This sounded much more serious. 'What sort of gun?'

'A small handgun. My shotguns and so on are all in a gun cabinet under lock and key. The one that's missing is my old service revolver. I usually keep it in here.' Lord Barlas pulled open the centre drawer of his desk. 'It's normally locked but I needed some papers from there a few days before the dance and discovered the drawer was open and the gun missing.'

'You've no idea when it may have been taken?' Matt asked. His face was sombre.

'It was in there when we all arrived at the castle. I had opened the drawer then as my spare chequebook was in there and I moved the gun out of the way to get to the book. Naturally I locked it back up again afterwards. I keep the key on my watch chain, along with my safe key, so whoever took it must have picked the dashed lock.'

'May I see the lock, sir?' Kitty asked.

Lord Barlas grunted his consent and scooted his chair back so Kitty could come around to his side of the desk. She bent to examine the brass escutcheon plate surrounding the keyhole and could immediately see a multitude of telltale scratches.

'It's definitely been picked,' Kitty said as she retook her seat.

Lord Barlas moved his chair back into its former position.

'I take it there has been no sign of the gun since? Has the castle been searched? Are the guests aware the gun has gone?' Matt asked.

'I decided not to say anything to avoid alarm, and if the thief did turn out to be one of my guests, I wanted to catch the scoundrel out. No point in prewarning them. My servants here are very trustworthy, Captain Bryant. They were in my father's employ before me, and their family trees extend as far back in this place as my own. They have conducted a thorough and discreet search of the castle but as you say, there is no sign of the gun.' The older man's expression was grim.

'Are your guests still unaware the gun is missing? Did any of them know you had a gun?' Kitty asked.

'My wife and Rufus obviously know I keep a gun in the desk. As for the others, I'm not certain.' Lord Barlas shrugged uneasily.

'Sir, the safe behind you, I take it that is where you store any valuables in the castle, jewellery, silver, money?' Kitty asked as another thought struck her.

Lord Barlas looked a little astonished by her question. 'Yes, and, of course, any important documents, my will, the trust deeds for Ottilie, share certificates and so on, why?'

'It's a key and number combination, isn't it, sir?' Matt asked.

'Yes, both Velma and I know the combination, as does my estate manager. I keep the keys myself on my watch chain as I said. The safe key and the drawer key,' Lord Barlas said. 'What are you driving at?'

'I wondered if anyone had tried to get to the contents of the safe. It may be that whoever took the gun was looking for things that might have greater value, or for information of some kind and stumbled upon the gun during their search of your study,' Kitty explained.

The colour seemed to drain from Lord Barlas's face, and he pulled a slightly grubby white-cotton handkerchief from his jacket pocket and dabbed at his temples.

'My butler thought he heard a noise in here one night as he was doing his rounds to check all was secure. He reported to me that the desk lamp was on, and the door of the study unlocked. There was no one around so thought he had been mistaken. This was after the gun had been taken. He assumed either myself or Velma must have forgotten to turn the lamp off and omitted to lock the door.'

Matt jumped up from his seat and tucked his notebook into his pocket. He crossed the room to examine the safe using a small magnifying lens that he produced from his top pocket.

'I would say, sir, that an attempt has also been made to pick the lock on the safe.'

CHAPTER FIVE

Matt returned to his seat. Lord Barlas's expression was grim.

'So, Madam Fortina warned you that you were in danger just after the gun went missing, but you are certain that no one other than yourself and your trusted servants knew of the theft?' Kitty asked as his lordship's complexion began to return to its normal healthy hue.

'That's correct. She gave her first warning while we were all at dinner. She claimed her spirit guide told her to warn me.' Lord Barlas looked bewildered.

'You hadn't told your wife or Sir Rufus about the gun?' Kitty asked.

'No, no one except my butler who alerted two of the footmen, and they were sworn to secrecy.' Lord Barlas looked slightly affronted that Kitty seemed to be doubting his word.

'And I presume, sir, that apart from the gun there were other incidents which led you to request our assistance?' Matt said.

The older man nodded. 'I take Buster here out every morning via the side door from the boot room. He's an elderly dog now and with the bad weather he doesn't go far. I always follow him out and wait for him before going back inside. I let him out and went to follow him, but stopped when I realised how icy it was underfoot. I stepped back inside to collect my cane. As I did so there was an almighty crash and a ton of snow and ice fell from above, right where I would usually have been standing.'

'Good heavens.' Kitty could see the incident had upset the man.

'Fortunately, it missed me and Buster. I might have thought it merely an accident had it not been for Madam Fortina's warning. Ice does accumulate on the drainage ledge around the castle. I have the servants go around with brooms and poles to clear it. When I looked at the debris, however, I could see there was a large piece of masonry concealed in the snow. I knew then it was no accident. During the summer I had ensured that all the masonry had been made good to withstand the winter. There was no chance that stone had come loose by itself. I had checked the work myself. It had been prised loose and I believe someone pushed it.' Lord Barlas looked at Matt and Kitty.

Matt had resumed his notetaking. 'I see. Has anything else happened, sir?'

'Just one more thing.' Lord Barlas delved into the top pocket of his velvet-fronted waistcoat and pulled out a folded piece of paper.

Matt took it and unfolded it and showed it to Kitty so they could both read the contents. The cheap sheet of lined paper had a message made up of letters which had been cut and pasted on.

'That last was a warning. The next will not miss.'

Kitty frowned. 'The letters look as if they have been cut from an old paper or book of some kind. It seems to confirm your belief that the ice and masonry falling was not an accident.'

'Where did you find this note, sir?' Matt asked.

'It was on my pillow when I retired for the night. Fortunately, Velma didn't see it. I wrote to you the next day.' Lord Barlas leaned forward in his seat. 'I need you to discover who is behind this and stop them. More snow is forecast for the next few days so until Hogmanay is over, and the roads are safe for travel again, we will probably be unable to leave. My life is in danger, Captain Bryant.'

The older man's hands trembled as he spoke.

'Do you have any idea at all, sir, who may be responsible for these events? You know the people here much better than we do.' Kitty fully expected Lord Barlas to have been considering who would be the most likely culprit amongst his guests. She was certain that were she in his position it would have fully occupied her every waking moment.

'None at all,' the man said firmly.

Kitty could see her own surprise at this answer reflected in her husband's expression.

'There is no one amongst your guests or family who you have argued with, or who may bear a grudge against you?' Matt asked.

'No one. Certainly not enough to wish to kill me. That is what makes this business so unnerving.' Lord Barlas leaned back in his seat and Kitty could see their interview was almost at an end. Either the man genuinely could not narrow down their field of suspects, or the person he did suspect was someone very close to him indeed.

'Very well. May I ask then, sir, who would benefit from your death financially?' Matt asked.

Kitty saw Lord Barlas bristle at the question and at first thought he might refuse to answer.

'My wife, Velma, of course, although she is an independently wealthy woman. Her father is Jerome Weeks, the Chicago steel baron. She would, however, still gain property and more money. Ottilie would take control of her trust fund, although when she marries Donald there is a substantial sum settled both upon her and any future children she may have. Beyond that, there are bequests to my staff and the controlling shares in two of my companies would go to Rufus. That is the theatre company and my new film production business. He already is a partner in the companies, and this would give him outright control.' Lord Barlas's eyes narrowed. 'It is of course ridiculous to suppose that any of those bequests would provide a motive to harm me.'

Kitty forbore to mention that many murders were committed for sums which were a great deal less than the ones that must be involved here.

'Thank you, sir, that's most helpful. Perhaps, sir, you may consider changing the combination to your safe?' Matt tucked his notebook away, carefully enclosing the anonymous note inside its pages.

The man nodded, and gave a grunt of assent.

'One last thing, Lord Barlas,' Kitty said as their host began to shuffle the documents on his desk. 'What story are we to give to your guests for our presence in the castle? You referred to Matt and I as family at breakfast. I assume you do not wish it to be known that you have sent for private investigators?'

The man paused. 'No, you are correct, Kitty. If the culprit were forewarned, they may be made desperate, or even worse would cover any tracks they may have made. In which case they could try again at some point. That is why I decided against involving the police at this time. I think it best if everyone assumes you are here for pleasure. Distant relatives seemed to be a plausible reason to me. Ottilie knows very little about the family, so neither she nor my wife will question the connection.'

'Very good, sir.' Matt rose and Kitty followed suit. It seemed they would learn little else from their host before lunch. 'We shall report anything we discover to you.'

'You have my blessing to go anywhere you wish within the castle and its environs. You will find that Finnglach is an interesting building. There are many myths and legends about the castle, the loch and, of course, the standing stones.'

Kitty and Matt thanked him and left the study with Bertie trotting behind them.

Kitty maintained a tactful silence until they were well away from the closed oak door and she was certain they could not be overheard. 'Well! What did you make of all that?' she asked.

'I don't know. It's very worrying. If I were Lord Barlas I would be very afraid. That incident with the falling ice was clearly no accident,' Matt said thoughtfully.

They had paused in the great entrance hall beside the fire. To a casual observer it would appear they were admiring the landscape painting above the fireplace while availing themselves of the heat from the blaze in the hearth.

'I thought the same thing. Perhaps after lunch we should attempt a walk outside and see if we can spot anything out there,' Kitty suggested.

'We need to be careful. There is something very strange at play here and someone in this castle has possession of Lord Barlas's gun.' Matt rubbed his chin and frowned at the orange flames leaping in the vast hearth of the fireplace.

'Did they take it to harm him? Or to prevent him from defending himself? I wonder what they were looking for in the study? They must have attempted to pick the lock on the safe after getting into the desk drawer,' Kitty said.

'You make a good point about the gun. I can't see what good picking the safe lock would have done without the combination, however.' Matt looked at Kitty.

'Then you think whoever did it knows the combination already?' she asked.

'I suspect it is possible. Lord Barlas clearly keeps the key with him at all times so they would have no other option except to try and pick the lock, but they still couldn't open it without the combination. Unless, of course, they were already a skilled safebreaker,' Matt suggested.

One of the maids entered the hall to strike the large brass gong near the foot of the stairs.

'It's time for lunch, let's see what else we can discover. We may even meet Lady Barlas, our new relative,' Kitty said with a grin as she tucked her hand in the crook of Matt's elbow and followed Ottilie and her fiancé who had emerged from the library.

Kitty found herself seated between Matt and Maxfield Cotter at the dining table. Matt had Romy Fisher on his other side. Bertie tucked himself discreetly under her chair. Lord Barlas entered to take his place at the head of the table closely followed by a very beautiful younger woman with sleek dark hair, dressed in an exquisitely cut navy wool frock trimmed with red tartan.

'Ah, Velma, my dear, may I present Captain Matthew Bryant and his wife, Kitty, a distant cousin on my grandfather's side. I don't believe you've met before.' Lord Barlas made the introduction as the rest of the party arrived and were seated.

'No, I don't think we have had the pleasure.' Lady Barlas's gaze flickered over Kitty's neat tweed suit and pale-blue woollen sweater.

'Matthew and Kitty live in Devon, not much chance to see snow there, eh?' Lord Barlas was clearly intent on getting their cover story established.

'Not unless one ventures onto Dartmoor, sir, no,' Matt agreed.

'Your visit here will prove quite an experience then. We do

have lots of opportunities at Finnglach for winter sports,' Ottilie said.

'I don't think I've ever tried any winter sports before,' Kitty remarked amiably as soup dishes containing what smelled like vegetable soup were placed in front of them.

'You don't ski? Or ice skate?' Lady Barlas looked surprised.

'No, it's very temperate in Dartmouth. We have sea bathing and sailing,' Kitty explained.

'Oh, I see, well, you could always try snowshoeing or sledding. That can be quite fun especially around the edge of the forest. What about you, Captain Bryant?' Lady Barlas asked.

'I have done some skiing in the past, and please, do call me Matt.'

More questions followed from the rest of the group about where they lived.

'And what do you do for a living?' Sir Rufus asked looking at Matt as the now empty soup dishes were collected.

'I work for the government, sir, and Kitty's family own a hotel in Dartmouth.' Matt's answer seemed to satisfy, and Kitty breathed a small sigh of relief at her husband's quick thinking.

It was not a lie either since they were often asked to take on cases by Matt's former employer, Brigadier Remmington-Blythe, who headed a small and secretive department in the heart of Whitehall.

'I don't believe I've ever visited Dartmouth, although I have been to Torquay once or twice,' Maxfield remarked as plates of roast beef were set before them.

'Perhaps you should visit some time. It is a most delightful place,' Kitty said politely as roast potatoes and Yorkshire pudding was added to her plate.

'I went once. It is quite nice, but I must admit I prefer the French Riviera. It's a little more chic, and, of course, the weather is more dependable abroad.' Romy waved away the offer of potatoes.

'We had thought we might like to go to France in the spring. Is there anywhere you would recommend?' Kitty decided to ignore Romy's slight towards her Devon homeland and focused on flattering the girl's ego by listening to her suggestions.

The American girl was clearly well travelled and knowledgeable. Maxfield's conversation skills appeared rather more limited, although Matt did manage to get him talking about racing and motor cars by the time the dessert of rice pudding with raspberry jam was served.

Madam Fortina was seated next to Lady Barlas and Kitty noticed that she remained silent throughout the meal. Although Kitty suspected that the woman was listening to everything going on around her. Sir Rufus and his wife were deep in conversation with Lord and Lady Barlas.

'We thought we might wrap up after lunch and venture outside for some fresh air,' Kitty said to Romy. 'The standing stones are very intriguing.'

Ottilie caught her conversation. 'There are quite a few stories about the stones. They go back hundreds of years, long before the castle was here, I believe.'

'How fascinating,' Matt said.

'One story says they were used for pagan sacrifices. There's a vast slab of rock like a table in the centre of the circle and it has these strange brown stains that the local villagers say are blood. Nonsense, of course,' Lord Barlas joined the conversation. 'Much more likely that it was some kind of calendar or temple, similar to the stones at Stonehenge. There are several books in the library about the stones.'

'Another village story says the stones were once all humans and they displeased the local priest by dancing on the Sabbath, so he cursed them, and they were all turned to stone.' Ottilie giggled. 'And, of course, the circle is in the fairy glen, so look out for the little folk.'

'The steward on the train said there were stories about the stones coming to life,' Kitty said.

'Yes, one must keep on the good side of the guardians,' Lord Barlas remarked with an amused smile.

The rest of the table joined in, telling more stories about the origin of the circle and its invisible, mythical inhabitants. Kitty was left wondering if she was the only person that found the stones silent presence unnerving.

CHAPTER SIX

After lunch had ended, Kitty donned her fur-lined winter boots and thick woollen coat with the warm fur collar. Matt pulled on his heavy black leather gloves and adjusted the bright-blue scarf around his neck, tucking the ends inside his own winter over-coat. Bertie had a smart red-felted coat that Alice had made for him for Christmas.

'Well then, my dear, are we all set to brave the elements?' His blue eyes twinkled as he asked the question.

Kitty secured her fur hat over her ears and smiled back at him. 'Yes, some fresh air will be welcome, even if it is rather chilly.'

They walked out of the castle, exiting through the small arch-topped side door of the boot room, which their host had assured them was closer to the stones. This was also the door Lord Barlas had used when the ice had fallen from the roof. Several large frost-covered pieces of fractured grey stone had been stacked neatly against the castle wall. A glance upwards revealed the area from where they had fallen. The icy air stung Kitty's cheeks and a sharp breeze was blowing across the frozen landscape.

Presumably the staff had cleared the stones from the path and placed them to one side. Kitty could see that they would have landed directly on their host if he had followed his usual morning routine. Stepping back inside at the last minute had assuredly saved his life.

The faint sound of gramophone music and laughter drifted through the closed leaded pane windows of the castle as they rounded the corner and set off in the direction of the stone circle. The frozen snow crunched beneath their boots as they followed the barely visible pathway. It was an incredibly beautiful scene, but Kitty continued to feel uneasy, especially after what their host had told them.

The stones stood in a small clearing, surrounded on one side by tall pine trees, their dark-green branches laden with snow. Rooks called hoarsely to one another, invisible in the dark woods, as if to announce their approach. The ground at the far edge of the stones sloped down to the gravel shore of the loch where the water rippled in, driven by the wind.

The breeze blew directly in their faces as they reached the edge of the circle. Close up, Kitty could see the stones were much larger than she had anticipated, standing a good couple of feet higher than the top of her head. Snow was piled in drifts around the bases of the rocks leaving clumps of the rough, tussocky grass exposed to the elements.

'They seem to be made of some kind of granite.' Matt examined the surface of the closest stone as Bertie sniffed at the floor.

'It must have taken a lot of work to get them here, and to carve them.' Kitty shivered and wasn't sure if it was just the cold air or the brooding presence of the rocks that had sent a chill through her bones. The slabs seemed roughly hewn and twisted, almost as if over the years they had tried to hunker down into the soil beneath them.

She held on to Matt's arm as they continued to walk on into the centre of the circle. Once inside the breeze appeared to stop and the air grew still. Kitty could no longer hear the hoarse calls of the rooks, everything was silent. The central stone slab they had been told about was now directly ahead of them.

Kitty had expected to see a layer of snow on its top but instead the smooth grey stone surface was bare, revealing deep rust-brown streaks. She could see how the stories had started that this had been a place of pagan sacrifice. The red marks did look like blood when contrasted with the colour of the stone. None of the other rocks in the circle appeared to have red markings.

'This one doesn't look as if it has fallen over. It must have been placed that way, like a table,' Matt remarked.

'Or an altar.' Kitty tightened her grip on Matt's arm. The eerie atmosphere in the ring unsettled her.

He glanced down at her, his expression concerned. 'You don't like it in here, do you?'

Kitty shook her head. 'I don't know what it is. It's almost as if we're being watched, like the stones are listening to us. I know it's fanciful, but I can see how the stories we were told about over lunch were started.'

Matt looked around. 'Well, we know that we can be seen from the castle, at least from the upper floors, so someone could watch from there.'

'Like the view we have from our window,' Kitty agreed. 'I know, it's silly. I think it's probably all the stories we heard and then Lord Barlas's experiences that's making me feel uneasy.'

Matt placed his gloved hand on top of hers where it was resting in the crook of his arm and gave it a pat. 'Come on, old thing. Let's get back inside the castle and warm up.'

They turned around to follow the path back the way they had come.

Ahead of them, Bertie halted suddenly, one front paw raised, and his gaze fixed on something at the edge of the stones near the trees. The small hairs on the nape of Kitty's neck prickled as she tried to see what had spooked her dog. Was there someone watching them from the treeline?

'Someone has built a snowman.' She hadn't noticed the snowy figure on their way into the circle. She gave herself a mental shake for being so fanciful.

It had been built to the side nearest the forest, between two stones, half hidden in the gloom of the woods. It stood almost as tall as Matt with small, black pieces of gravel marking its eyes and mouth. A carrot had been placed as a nose, a dark-green tartan scarf was around the neck and a battered trilby topped its head.

Kitty wondered who had constructed it. She supposed it could have been some of their fellow guests, or perhaps the children of the castle servants. She shivered again. It seemed an odd thing to do, somehow out of place and almost disrespectful. She would have thought a better place for a snowman would have been near the front entrance to the castle.

'It's a good thing we're here in daylight. I suspect our snowy friend could give you quite a turn if you were here at dusk,' Matt said and gave Bertie's leash a tug to get the spaniel moving once more.

Kitty gave the snowman a final glance and quickened her steps, eager to be out of the circle and back inside the warmth of the castle.

Matt and Kitty left their outdoor boots and attire in the spacious cloakroom area of the boot room in the section that was clearly used for guests. They had left their house shoes there earlier when they had donned their boots while sitting on the long wooden bench. Kitty tidied her hair in the small, speckled glass mirror on the wall above the bench.

They hadn't taken much notice of the rest of the room when they had been preparing to go out. Now, Kitty saw that it appeared to double as a repository for all the equipment anyone could wish for in order to pursue a range of outdoor activities.

Wooden skis of various sizes were stored on racks along with metal ski poles and walking poles. A random collection of snowshoes had been stacked in a large tea chest and various gaberdine waterproof mackintoshes were hung above a selection of boots. Tennis, golf, quoits and croquet equipment were also stored in boxes arranged tidily on the red quarry-tiled floor. Ice skates of various sizes were also neatly placed in a rack beside a large box which seemed to contain costumes of some kind.

* * *

Matt could see Kitty still appeared pale and unnerved by their visit to the stone circle.

'Shall we go to the drawing room? We can warm up by the fire, and I daresay we will be able to get a pot of tea?' he suggested.

'Good idea, then after that we could explore the layout of the downstairs a little. The castle is such a large place, I'm afraid of getting lost,' Kitty agreed.

The drawing room proved to be another large space. Dark wood panels covered the walls, giving it a slightly cosier and more intimate feel than the lofty grandeur of the great hall. The carved white-marble fireplace was of a similar scale and bore what Matt assumed must be the Barlas coat of arms in a shield in the centre of the mantelpiece.

Silk-shaded lamps had been switched on all around the room giving off golden pools of light to offset the gloomy afternoon. Lord Barlas's elderly dog lay snoring peacefully on the hearthrug in front of the fire and Lady Barlas and Madam Fortina sat on either side of the fireplace on a pair of old-fashioned tapestry covered armchairs.

'Oh, I'm so sorry, are we disturbing you?' Matt asked. The two ladies had been conversing in low tones when he and Kitty and Bertie had entered the room, stopping abruptly when they realised the door had been opened.

'No, not at all, Captain Bryant, do please come in. Have you just returned from your walk? You must both be quite frozen.' Lady Barlas had a soft, well-modulated voice with a distinct American accent.

'Thank you, and please call me Matt.' He and Kitty made their way to a large, dark-green leather, button-backed sofa covered with tartan wool rugs. Bertie joined the other dog in front of the fire.

'And do please call me Kitty,' Kitty added as she sat next to him.

'I was just about to ring for tea.' Lady Barlas stretched out a slender white hand to pull on the embroidered bell pull beside the fireplace.

'Tea sounds lovely, thank you. It is frightfully cold outside,' Kitty replied as a maid entered the room in answer to the summons.

Lady Barlas smiled graciously and instructed the maid.

With the maid dispatched about her mission Lady Barlas settled back in her seat. 'And what did you think of the standing stones?'

Kitty glanced at Matt. 'I must admit they are quite atmospheric, aren't they? I hadn't realised quite how large and imposing they were until we were up close to them.'

'Oh yes, indeed they are. I must admit I don't care for them at all. Even in summer they always give me the chills.' Lady Barlas gave an exaggerated shudder. 'Stephen, however, adores them. He says they give Finnglach a sense of purpose. That his family history is entwined with the stories of the stones. I don't see it myself but then I guess he grew up with them.'

'I think your husband said you were from Chicago originally?' Matt asked.

Lady Barlas beamed. 'Do you know it? We go back to

America quite often but, of course, Stephen's business interests keep us here for a large part of the year.'

'I have been there, yes, many years ago now. It's a thriving city,' Matt said.

He caught Kitty's faint look of surprise. He knew that she was aware of many of the places he had travelled to in the years following the war when he had worked for the government. However, he couldn't recall if he had ever said that he had spent time in that part of America. Kitty's disreputable father, Edgar Underhay, also currently lived in America, but mainly resided in New York.

The door of the drawing room opened, and the maid reappeared pushing a small gilt and marble trolley laden with crockery and silverware. She parked it next to Lady Barlas and dispensed tea to everyone and offered around a small, tiered stand of mince pies and shortbread fingers. Once everyone was served the girl left, leaving the trolley behind.

Madam Fortina had remained silent since their entry to the room, although Matt had been conscious of her sharp, dark gaze resting first on Kitty and then on himself.

'Lord Barlas said that you were a distant relation?' Madam Fortina asked, looking at Matt over the brim of her cup.

'Yes, somewhere on his grandfather's side of the old family tree. It was frightfully generous of him to invite us to Finnglach for Hogmanay.' Matt did his best to sound casually cheery.

'I've always been interested in seeing Scotland in winter. My great aunt Livvy is a neighbour, of course. Her house is about forty or so miles away from here,' Kitty said.

'Mrs Parsons? A most delightful lady. Yet you have never visited here before?' Lady Barlas asked.

'No, not since I was a child. I'm afraid my work at the hotel always kept me quite busy until recently. Aunt Livvy often comes to us now as she finds the milder climate better for her since she has grown older,' Kitty responded with a smile.

'Stephen told me you were recently married?' Lady Barlas took a sip of her tea.

'Yes, we just had our first wedding anniversary on Christmas Eve,' Matt explained.

'How romantic to have had a Christmas wedding,' Madam Fortina observed.

'Stephen loves Christmas, although, of course, Hogmanay with all these quaint Scottish traditions is the biggest celebration.' Lady Barlas's gaze fell on the large Christmas tree situated by the window on the far side of the room.

Madam Fortina's cup and saucer clattered as she set them down abruptly on the low oak side table next to her chair. Her plump body began to writhe in an alarming fashion and her eyes closed.

'Oh my goodness, is she all right?' Kitty asked in alarm as Madam Fortina began to groan.

Lady Barlas held up an imperious hand to stop them from moving as Matt went to rise, ready to summon help.

'Don't worry, it's just the spirits moving through her. We must listen carefully as they often have a message.' Lady Barlas leaned forward towards the medium, an eager expression on her pretty face.

'Beware, there is danger. Death is at hand.' Madam Fortina's voice had changed into a deep growl.

'Who? Who is in danger? Me? Stephen?' Lady Barlas was on the edge of her seat, her heavily kohl-lined eyes bright with excitement.

'Danger.' The woman seemed to lurch forward and then fell back on her chair, panting heavily, her eyes still closed.

CHAPTER SEVEN

Madam Fortina lay motionless in her seat, her head now lolling to the side and her turban slipping over one eye. Kitty looked at Matt uncertain of what they should do. Lady Barlas settled back in her chair and picked up her cup and saucer to finish her tea.

'Forgive me, Lady Barlas, but does this happen often? Is she quite all right?' Kitty asked as Madam Fortina's breathing became more stertorous. She found this exhibition by the medium to be quite alarming and was concerned for the woman's health.

'Oh yes, she is quite all right. It happens when the spirits use her as a vessel to pass on an urgent message. One never quite knows what they will have to say.' Lady Barlas sighed. 'It would be helpful if they were more specific sometimes, of course. Poor Nettie, she will be absolutely exhausted when she comes around. It takes a lot of energy from her.'

'I see. How very extraordinary. That's twice now that she has said someone is in danger. When we first arrived, she said that your husband might be harmed,' Kitty said.

Lady Barlas frowned as she set down her empty cup. 'Yes,

she has expressed her concern to me, and I know she has warned Stephen. She has received several messages saying the same thing, it's very worrying. I suggested that his doctor be called in case, you know, it might be his health, but Stephen pooh-poohed me. He says he is as fit as a fiddle and dear Nettie is talking nonsense.'

Matt glanced at the seemingly sleeping medium. 'And Madam Fortina has never given warnings like this before?' he asked.

'Gracious me no, not really. She usually has excellent advice financially and if I am undecided on a course of action, she has been most helpful in reading the cards or my palm. And, of course, helping dear Ottilie. You know Ottilie's first husband was killed in an accident not long after they were married? Well, Nettie was able to reach him on the other side and reassure her that he was at peace. Such a comfort to the poor girl.' Lady Barlas looked fondly at Madam Fortina.

'Has your husband not taken her warnings seriously then? I think I should be quite afraid if it were me.' Kitty could see both from Lady Barlas's words and her body language that she seemed to hold Madam Fortina and her abilities in high regard.

Lady Barlas's forehead creased into a worried frown. 'No, I fear Stephen does not take Nettie's concerns as seriously as I do. Yet, I don't know, I can't help feeling as if something is wrong. I'm very sensitive to these things myself. I've always had a very spiritual nature, right from when I was a child.'

'Then let us hope that on this occasion that the spirits are mistaken,' Matt said.

'One can only hope so. I mean there was that accident with the ice, but really, what kind of danger could Stephen face here?' Lady Barlas asked as Madam Fortina began to stir in her chair, slowly opening her eyes to blink at her surroundings.

Madam Fortina slowly pushed herself upright in her seat

and straightened her emerald-green sateen turban. 'Oh, I'm so sorry.'

'Nonsense, my dear, I shall ring for refreshments.' Lady Barlas tugged the bell pull once more and instructed the maid who responded to fetch Madam Fortina something to eat and drink.

'Nettie always requires some fresh fruit and a glass of iced water when the spirits have visited her,' Lady Barlas explained as the maid departed on her errand.

Kitty glanced at Matt relieved to see that he, like her, was managing to appear suitably poker faced during this nonsense. It was not that Kitty completely dismissed mediums, but she had seen and heard enough from her father to make her very aware of how easy it could be to fool people.

'I'm afraid the spirits come upon me without warning at times.' Madam Fortina held her head in her hands.

'Who was it that came this time?' Lady Barlas asked the medium. 'She has several guides that speak through her,' she turned and explained to Kitty and Matt.

'It was Claudius and he was most insistent,' Madam Fortina murmured as the maid set a glass of iced water and a bowl of chopped up apple pieces on the side table, before wheeling away the tea trolley.

'Oh, Claudius is her main guide. He was a roman centurion who died in battle.' Lady Barlas sounded impressed.

Madam Fortina picked up her glass with a shaking hand and sipped at the water. 'What did he say?' she asked, looking around at Kitty, Matt and Lady Barlas.

'More warnings of death and danger,' replied Lady Barlas. 'He didn't say who the warnings were for. I can only assume he must mean Stephen since you've had a couple of similar messages recently.' Lady Barlas looked troubled as she clasped her hands together on her lap.

Madam Fortina set down her glass and picked a slice of

apple from the bowl. 'Yes, I suppose that must be the case. I feel so weary.'

'We should leave you to recover in peace,' Kitty suggested as she called Bertie to her.

'Yes, of course, you must take some quiet time,' Matt agreed and rose from the sofa picking up on Kitty's cue.

* * *

'Well, what was all that about?' Matt asked in a low tone once they were safely outside the drawing room and the heavy oak door had closed behind them.

'I don't know. In my opinion though it's all "a load of hooey" as my father would say. Either Madam Fortina is the person who means to harm Lord Barlas, or she knows something.' Kitty looked at her husband.

'I agree,' Matt said. 'I've seen a lot of these mediums in action. Just after the end of the war it was almost a cottage industry. So many widows and bereaved people desperately seeking comfort or reassurance about their loved ones. And so many men who never came home.' He shook his head, his mouth set in a grim line.

'Yes, I fear Lady Barlas and her stepdaughter are probably being taken advantage of. Madam Fortina seems to have found herself a comfortable berth,' Kitty said. She had found it particularly interesting that the medium apparently gave Lady Barlas financial advice.

'We should spend some time exploring the castle, get our bearings. That wretched gun is missing, and someone has clearly got Lord Barlas in their sights. It would be good if we were at least familiar with the layout of the place,' Matt said.

'Best to be prepared,' Kitty agreed. She could see her husband's point. If they were to discover who wished to harm their host, they needed to identify both potential risks and possible culprits as swiftly as possible.

They now knew where the dining room, Lord Barlas's study, the boot room and the drawing room were situated. Kitty was fairly confident that the door next to the drawing room must therefore be the one to the library.

She pushed the door open and peeped inside. The library was a long narrow room lined with bookshelves from floor to ceiling. A long oval-shaped mahogany table ran almost the length of the room with chairs around the sides. Green glass-shaded reading lamps were placed at strategic intervals and a small fire crackled in the stone grate at the far end of the room.

A small group of high-backed armchairs were grouped near the fireplace. Sir Rufus was seated in one of them near the fire, a pile of papers spread out before him on a low rosewood table. He looked up as they entered the room.

'Oh, begging your pardon, Sir Rufus, we didn't mean to disturb you. We were just trying to find our way around the castle,' Kitty apologised, since it seemed Sir Rufus was working and had probably hoped he would not be disturbed.

'Oh no, not at all, my dear. Do come in.' The older man gathered up his papers and slipped them inside a black leather document case. 'I was just reading through some of my correspondence. The post has been rather haphazard lately with the weather and, of course, the telephone connection is not always reliable. I had a bundle of letters I had not responded to from just before Christmas, but the light is fading now, and my eyes are not what they were.'

Kitty stepped further into the room with Matt and Bertie following behind her. 'This looks a marvellous collection of books. We were with Lord Barlas earlier and he had another large selection in his study.' Kitty gazed at the books on the shelves. There were lots of titles about fishing, game, birds and natural history on the first bookcase. The second one had books on ancient civilisations and art.

'Yes, Stephen is a great reader, like his father. The family has amassed this collection over time. Some great houses, you know, used to buy books in bulk and never read them. Just placed them on the shelves for decoration to make themselves look good.' Sir Rufus winked at her and chuckled. 'Not like Finnglach.'

'You've known Lord Barlas for a long time, sir?' Matt asked.

'Oh yes, since we were boys. My father was a friend of his father,' Sir Rufus said. 'Stephen said you were a distant cousin?'

'Yes, on his grandfather's side of the family tree. It's most kind of him to invite us for Hogmanay,' Matt said.

'Yes, Stephen always holds a big celebration. Lots of traditional activities, first-footing, of course, to bring good luck to the house and, of course, the pipes.' Sir Rufus leaned back in his chair.

'We were wondering, sir, about this odd business with Madam Fortina. We were just with Lady Barlas in the drawing room and, well, there was another warning. Do you think Lord Barlas is in any danger?' Matt asked.

'Stephen, in danger? Good lord, no. Who would want to harm Stephen? Especially here in his own home? Poppycock, that's what that is. The woman is a fraud, if you ask me. Velma won't hear a word against her though, and neither will Ottilie, for that matter.'

'There was that accident though with the ice falling from the roof and bringing down some of the stonework.' Kitty glanced at Sir Rufus as she spoke.

'An accident, my dear, and not unexpected with a house as old as Finnglach and the extremes of weather here. Please don't worry your pretty little head about it, Mrs Bryant. I know how you ladies can be. That accident was probably what gave that charlatan the idea in the first place.'

Kitty gritted her teeth and tried to retain a pleasant smile. 'You are probably right, Sir Rufus. It was quite unsettling when Madam Fortina spoke with her spirit guide's voice. We thought she had collapsed into some kind of fit at first. It was fortunate that Lady Barlas was present and could reassure us.'

'Humph, yes, it is a real performance. If you ask me Stephen should have signed Nettie Fortina up for an acting contract instead of Romy Fisher. I suspect she has the greater talent, although Romy does have a decent singing voice, I suppose,' Sir Rufus said.

'Is Miss Fisher to star in one of Lord Barlas's productions?' Kitty asked.

'She is under contract for the next five years.' Sir Rufus smiled as he spoke.

Matt let out a low whistle. 'Five years. He must think very highly of her talents, that's a long contract isn't it, sir?'

'Well, if she wishes to get out of it, I dare say Stephen will make quite a financial killing. I understand that the film industry in America wishes to sign her, but Stephen is holding out. He has acquired a studio himself, you know. That's a sore point, of course, with Velma.' Sir Rufus rose from his seat and collected up his leather case.

'Oh?' Kitty asked.

'Yes, Velma was a bit of an actress before they were married. That's how she became chummy with Romy. Between you, me and the gatepost she wants to star in the movies herself.' Sir Rufus gave a wry chuckle and patted the top of Bertie's head.

'And Lord Barlas disapproves?' Matt guessed.

'Velma Barlas couldn't act her way out of a paper bag. But Stephen is not about to tell her that, is he now?' Sir Rufus tapped the side of his nose with his forefinger, then collected his papers and left the room.

CHAPTER EIGHT

Before Kitty could say anything to Matt about the information they had just learned from Sir Rufus, Lady Smythe opened the library door.

'Oh, I beg your pardon. I was expecting to find my husband here.' Lady Smythe eyed them suspiciously.

'Sir Rufus has just left,' Matt explained.

'Thank you.' Lady Smythe turned to go, then swivelled on the heel of her brown leather brogue shoe. 'By the way, was he here alone?'

Kitty was surprised by the question. She wondered who Lady Smythe thought may have been with her husband. 'Yes, he was. I rather fear we may have inadvertently interrupted his work.'

Lady Smythe gave a mirthless smile. 'Don't worry, my dear, so long as that was all that you interrupted. My husband is easily distracted.' She disappeared as quickly as she had entered, no doubt in search of Sir Rufus.

'I wonder who Lady Smythe expected to find in here with Sir Rufus?' Matt's question mirrored Kitty's thoughts.

'I suspect a woman. Lady Barlas, Ottilie, or perhaps Miss Fisher?' Kitty mused.

'A jealous wife, you think? Or maybe she has cause for her suspicions.' Matt looked at Kitty.

A chill ran along Kitty's spine. 'There are so many undercurrents here. I can't imagine it was a particularly happy Christmas. Keeping Lord Barlas safe from harm, while trying to work out who may wish to kill him and why, is growing more complicated by the minute.'

'Let's carry on exploring the castle. We have a little time before we need to go and dress for dinner. It would be useful if we could speak to the others and get a view of them.' Matt opened the library door and stood aside for Kitty and Bertie. 'I can hear gramophone music again, let's go and see who is in the music room.'

They followed the sound of the music until they came to a door standing slightly ajar. The sound of jazz emanated from inside the room, so Kitty pushed the door open further.

The volume on the gramophone had been turned up and Romy Fisher was dancing with Maxfield Cotter. The Turkish rug had been pushed aside and they were giggling and laughing as they twirled on the exposed parquet floor.

'Mrs Bryant, Captain Bryant, come and join us,' Romy called breathlessly as she spotted them enter the room.

The girl's cheeks were flushed pink, whether from exercise or from the contents of the empty cocktail glass on the side table Kitty couldn't be certain. Her auburn curls were in disarray and her shoes had been kicked to one side.

The record crackled to a stop and the racing driver left his dance partner to lift the needle and place it back on the rest.

'I do believe I need to catch my breath for a spell, or I shall have stitch.' Romy pressed her hand to her side before half-collapsing onto one of the tapestry-covered chaise longues beside the gramophone.

'We wondered who was playing the music. We heard it earlier when we were outside on our walk,' Kitty said. 'This is a lovely room.'

The music room had a white ornate plaster ceiling, different from the other rooms that they had seen so far in the castle. A black, baby grand piano stood at the one end of the room next to a large, gilded harp. The stone walls were hung with tapestries portraying hunting scenes and above the fireplace was a large picture of a majestic stag.

'It's rather fun, isn't it? Pre-dinner drink, anyone?' Maxfield was at the polished modern oval-shaped cocktail cabinet, the silver shaker in his hand.

'Thank you, that would be super.' Kitty sat herself down beside Romy.

Matt went to join Maxfield at the cocktail cabinet to fix himself a whisky and soda.

'Another one for you, Romy, darling?' Maxfield asked as he rattled the ice in the shaker.

Romy beamed and held out her empty glass towards him. With her glass refreshed with the contents of the shaker and a fresh glass for Kitty, Maxfield came to sit opposite them. Matt joined him with his own drink.

'Chin chin! Here's to a fabulous Hogmanay.' Maxfield raised his glass and the others followed suit.

'It must have been a splendid Christmas here. The decorations on the trees are wonderful,' Kitty said as she admired the small sparkle-covered tree near the piano.

'Oh, it was, darling. Such delicious food. I swear I shall have to get my dressmaker to let out a couple of seams on some of my gowns when I get back to London.' Romy giggled.

'Nonsense, sweetie.' Maxfield shook his head and smiled at his girlfriend.

'Will you be appearing in a new show in the New Year?' Kitty asked the girl.

Romy's mood immediately seemed to alter at Kitty's innocent question. Her shoulders stiffened and the smile died from her lips. 'I'm not certain what's happening, to be honest. I'm under contract to Stephen for a revue but I've been approached for a new movie in America.'

'Goodness, how very exciting for you,' Kitty said.

Romy swallowed a large gulp of her cocktail. 'Well, it will be if I can get to go. Stephen is being an absolute nightmare over releasing me from my contract. We shall see. I can be very persuasive.'

'And I presume that you will be keen to see the start of the racing season?' Matt turned to Maxfield as if he sensed that the mood in the room had taken a slight downward shift.

'Yes, we're kicking off in Pau in France on March first. I've picked up a drive in one of the Alfa Romeo's so should be in a good spot this year. Of course, it would be far better if I could get my own team together,' Maxfield said.

'I felt you were a tad unlucky last season with those mechanical issues,' Matt sympathised.

'Exactly, so a more reliable car should see me right this season at least,' Maxfield explained.

'You are not concerned though about what has been happening politically in Italy recently?' Matt asked.

Kitty knew her husband was referring to the Blackshirts and the continuing unrest in Europe. It had to be a little risky for Maxfield, choosing to race for an Italian team.

Maxfield shrugged. 'Politics have never been my thing, old boy. I just drive the cars.'

Romy downed the rest of her cocktail and stood her glass back on the table. 'Enough about your boring old motor cars, darling, put another record on.' She smiled winningly at Maxfield.

'Your wish is my command, my precious.' Maxfield jumped up and picked out another record from the huge collection in the rack beside the gramophone. Once the needle was in the groove, he held out his hand to Romy who squealed with laughter as she leapt up from her seat.

The sound of big band music filled the room as Maxfield gathered Romy into his arms and they began a lively quickstep around the room. They made a handsome couple. Kitty smiled at Matt and raised her glass. Bertie's tail thumped with excitement at the sudden movement.

They hurriedly finished their drinks and escaped from the room just before the record ended, leaving Romy and Maxfield to continue entertaining themselves. Once back in the corridor leading to the great hall Kitty heard the sound of raised voices up ahead.

She pressed her hand on the sleeve of Matt's tweed jacket in silent warning and together they continued slowly and quietly along the corridor to see who the participants were. Bertie trotting happily alongside them.

'It sounds like Ottilie and Donald,' Matt murmured in her ear as they grew close enough to hear what was being said, but staying out of sight of the antagonists in the hall.

'I've told you before, Donald, Daddy and Rufus look after my investments. Once we are married then we can do as we please, but until then they have my money locked up tight. The capital can't be touched, and I have already given you most of my allowance. I really don't see what the problem is.' Ottilie sounded as if she was on the verge of tears.

'I know, darling. I understand all that but surely if you speak to your father and just explain what a great opportunity this would be for us, he would loan you the money, or agree to advance you a sum ahead of our wedding.' Donald's tone was smooth and persuasive.

Kitty pursed her lips not caring for what she had just heard.

'No, I've told you, it can't be done. Anyway, there will be other opportunities. Our wedding is only a few months away now. Perhaps your bank will have sorted itself out by the time we return to London and then you can use your own funds,' Ottilie suggested.

'It's not that simple, sweet pea. My money is tied up in long-term investments for our future. The amount I can raise once they've sorted that business of the missing cheque out won't be sufficient.' Donald sounded frustrated now.

'Look, why don't you ask Rufus? Explain this to him, maybe he can help,' Ottilie said. Her voice sounded a little fainter and Kitty wondered if she was walking away from her fiancé.

'You know he doesn't care for me. It would be better coming from you, you're his goddaughter.' Donald's voice also sounded further away, and Kitty heard the creak of one of the stairs.

She gave Matt's arm a gentle squeeze and they moved forward again along the corridor arriving in the great hall in time to see Ottilie and Donald disappearing up the stairs.

'Oh dear, that did not sound good,' Kitty murmured to Matt as they paused by the fireplace to allow Ottilie and her fiancé to reach the landing.

'No, it sounds as if Donald Waterford has some financial difficulties and is keen to get his hands on Ottilie's money,' Matt agreed. 'Perhaps Sir Rufus was right when he warned Lord Barlas about Donald.'

Back along the corridor a door banged shut and was followed by the staccato tap of heels marching briskly towards them. Lady Smythe emerged into the hall and ignored them completely as she headed for the stairs.

'Lynette, darling, don't be so ridiculous,' Sir Rufus called after his wife as he hurried along behind her and up the stair-case in a vain attempt to catch her up.

'Gracious, whatever is going on this afternoon?' Matt asked.

'Whatever it is let us hope they have all recovered their

health and tempers in time for dinner.' Kitty glanced at the ornate French bronze ormolu clock on the sideboard. 'We had better go up and bathe and change ourselves before all the hot water is gone.'

'You have a point.' Matt accompanied her as they made their way back to their room.

To Kitty's relief, the curtains had been drawn against the cold, the bed turned down and the fire banked up. Bertie made himself comfortable near the hearth.

'They must be anticipating problems with the electricity,' Matt said. 'Look, a couple of oil lamps have been placed on top of the dresser.'

'I thought they had a generator? I'm sure I heard Lord Barlas mention it at breakfast.' Kitty sat on one of the small fireside chairs and took off her shoes, wriggling her stocking-clad toes with pleasure in front of the fire.

'Even with a generator I doubt it would be enough to power the whole castle, this place is too large. I expect this is a precaution in case the power does go out.' Matt crossed to the window and peeled back the heavy velvet curtain to peer outside at the inky blackness. 'The wind sounds as if it's picked up since we went out this afternoon and there is more snow forecast.'

Kitty shivered as he dropped the curtain back into place. 'Brr, at least the castle seems well prepared.'

'True. My main concern though is that if the weather does deteriorate, we will be trapped here with no way to get out and a possible murderer in our midst armed with Lord Barlas's stolen gun,' Matt said.

CHAPTER NINE

Dinner was to be a quiet affair and there was little opportunity to discover anything meaningful either at the table or afterwards. Their early start and lengthy journey led both Kitty and Matt to retire early.

'What are our plans for today? Do you think we learned anything meaningful yesterday?' Kitty asked as she finished combing her hair and applying her rose-pink lipstick ready to go downstairs for breakfast the following morning.

Matt paused from where he was putting on his shoes as he sat on the edge of the bed. 'I don't know. I still can't work out why a possible murderer would wish to prewarn his intended victim.'

'But it seems to be Madam Fortina who has given the warnings so far. Is she the potential murderer? And if so, why?' Kitty asked.

'Perhaps to ensure that Lady Barlas keeps her on. She might not push it as far as murder. She's made herself very comfortable with the family. If she drums up this idea of a threat and saves Lord Barlas, then it may add credence to her role,' Matt suggested.

'But do you think she wrote that note? And levered that lump of stone to fall?' Kitty could see what her husband meant but it didn't convince her.

'It's all very peculiar, I agree.' He glanced towards the narrow, leaded pane window where Kitty had drawn back the curtain to allow in the daylight. 'The weather has definitely worsened overnight.'

Outside the castle the wind was whipping around the ancient building and flurries of snow smattered against the glass. The stone circle was barely visible in the grey gloom.

'We need to try and dig out who might have a reason for wishing to harm Lord Barlas before there is another attempt on his life.' Matt sat up straight. 'Who left him that note if it wasn't Madam Fortina? And why does she keep warning him? If she is not the potential murderer there must be something that has led her to believe he is in danger, and I don't believe in all that spirit guide hokum.'

'I don't believe in it either. Let's go downstairs and see what else we can find out, tomorrow is New Year's Eve so time is marching on if another attempt might be made. Perhaps we should split up today and see if anyone says anything useful,' Kitty suggested giving her appearance a last quick check in the dressing table mirror. 'Lady Barlas said something at dinner last night about playing some games today in the hall. Perhaps we may learn more if people are relaxed and having fun.' She wasn't quite sure what these games would entail but the rest of the party had appeared enthusiastic at the suggestion.

Matt stood, ready to follow her out of the room. 'Good idea. Perhaps if you try to get to know more about Madam Fortina, I think I'd like to know more about Donald Waterford.'

When they entered the dining room they discovered Lord Barlas, Ottilie and Donald were already at breakfast.

'Good morning, did you sleep well? The gales were dreadful last night, and I hear the road to the village is fast becoming impassable even with the horses, thanks to the snow.' Lord Barlas set aside his newspaper as they took their seats at the table. 'Even this dashed paper is yesterday's. Apparently today's delivery didn't get through on the train, neither did the mail.'

'We were so tired after travelling, I think we would have slept through a hurricane.' Kitty smiled as she greeted her fellow guests.

'Velma is keen on having an indoor games day today. I doubt anyone will wish to venture outside.' Lord Barlas signalled to the maid waiting nearby to bring more tea and fresh toast.

'The quoits in the hall were such fun last time,' Ottilie said brightly. 'And we played musical statues too. That was a hoot. The dressing-up box is still down from the attic so perhaps we can put on a skit later this evening too.'

Kitty noticed that Donald didn't look terribly enthusiastic about any of the suggestions his fiancée was putting forward.

'That sounds delightful. Miss Fisher and Lady Barlas must be great assets in a performance.' Matt helped himself to porridge.

Kitty decided to go straight for the bacon and eggs, she had heard that the Scots preferred their porridge with salt rather than sugar and the idea did not appeal to her.

'Romy has a lovely singing voice and Sir Rufus plays the piano very well, so she may be persuaded to entertain us after dinner this evening,' Ottilie said.

'Does Lady Smythe have a theatrical talent too?' Kitty asked, picking up her cutlery.

Ottilie laughed and her father suppressed a snort. 'Lynette can be very theatrical when she wishes,' Lord Barlas said, attempting to keep a straight face.

After the scenes they had witnessed yesterday Kitty could

guess what they were alluding to and thought it prudent not to say anything further.

'Velma may wish for Madam Fortina to hold another séance this evening,' Donald said. 'She's very fond of that sort of thing.'

Kitty noticed Ottilie's shoulders stiffen slightly at the suggestion and Lord Barlas's expression grew wary.

'Surely not,' Ottilie said. 'I mean, I suppose she could if she wanted to...' Her voice trailed off.

'Hmm, Velma was saying that this time of year is the optimal time to hold a reading,' Lord Barlas replied.

'The walls between this world and the next are thin at the close of the year. A most excellent suggestion, your lordship.' Madam Fortina had entered the room right at the end of the conversation and had clearly heard what was being said.

She was dressed today in black satin with a matching turban. A peacock feather was secured to the side of her head-dress with a diamanté clasp. She seated herself at the table and piled toast onto her plate.

'In fact, I shall discuss it with Velma after breakfast. You would all take part, of course?'

Although the medium framed it as a question Kitty was left in no doubt that it was an instruction.

Donald's expression grew sulkier. 'I'm not sure, Nettie. I only mentioned it as a bit of a lark.'

'Talking to those who have gone before is not something I take lightly, Donald, as well you know. Ottilie, my dear, in the light of your recent engagement, perhaps if your former husband were to come through and give you his blessing on your remarriage it would make a nice start to the New Year?' Madam Fortina began to apply butter to her toast.

'And if he disapproves? What then?' Sir Rufus entered the room and took his place opposite the medium.

Ottilie bit her lower lip and looked distressed.

'I'm quite sure that Marcus would only ever have wished for

Ottilie's happiness, as do we all.' Lord Barlas gave both Madam Fortina and Sir Rufus a look that was clearly intended to quash any further discussion.

'Well, there is no guarantee on who may wish to come through and communicate with us. Or what messages or warnings those dear ones that have passed over may wish to send.' Madam Fortina cast a suddenly sharp glance in the direction of Lord Barlas.

'I suppose that is true. With the warnings you have received recently regarding Lord Barlas, perhaps more information may be forthcoming if you hold a séance,' Matt suggested.

Romy and Maxfield arrived at the table as Matt spoke. Kitty had been a little taken aback at first by her husband's idea, but if they wished to flush the potential murderer into the open then she could see the merits of his suggestion.

'What's this? A séance, eh? We might get that chap come through that you got last time, Nettie. What was his name? Julius Caesar or something?' Maxfield said cheerily.

An expression of deep distaste passed across Madam Fortina's face. 'Claudius Maximus was a roman general, as well you know.'

Maxfield gave a slight shrug of his shoulders as he helped himself to smoked kippers and a poached egg. Romy gave a slight shudder at the contents of his plate and contented herself with picking at a triangle of toast lightly smeared with marmalade.

Lord Barlas tapped his forefinger on the edge of the table as if considering Matt's suggestion. 'You know, Captain Bryant, you may have hit on something. Yes, perhaps a séance tonight might give more information about why you have started to receive these warning messages.' He looked at Madam Fortina.

The medium looked smug. 'Very well, I have no objection but only, of course, if those taking part take the matter seriously.' Her words were clearly aimed at Maxfield.

The conversation moved on to the games that Lady Barlas wished to set up to entertain them all for the day. Kitty was left feeling faintly uneasy and not at all certain that she wished to attend a séance. Especially one that seemed to be designed to flush out a potential murderer.

Madam Fortina finished her breakfast and declared that she would go and make preparations for the evening with Lady Barlas.

'Honestly, Stephen, I don't know why you are pandering to that ghastly woman. You know she's a fake. Even her name.' Sir Rufus spoke up as soon as Madam Fortina had left the room.

'Please don't say that. Nettie has a marvellous gift. She was very good to me when Marcus was killed. I don't know what I would have done without her.' Ottilie rose from her chair and fled from the room with Donald hard on her heels.

An awkward silence fell across the table.

'Sorry, old man, I forgot that Ottilie believes in all that stuff.' Sir Rufus made a clumsy attempt at an apology.

Romy dropped the last remnant of her toast down on her plate. 'It doesn't matter what anyone thinks. I introduced Nettie to Velma and Ottilie and I've seen first-hand how good she is. I agree with Captain Bryant, these messages Nettie has been passing on should be taken more seriously. That accident with the falling ice was frightening. I know it really upset Velma.'

'Quite so, my dear. Whatever is happening is most unsettling. Perhaps this séance might put an end to it all in time for tomorrow night's celebrations.' Lord Barlas placed his linen napkin on the table and picked up his newspaper as he left.

Sir Rufus sighed and helped himself to another cup of tea as his friend left the room. 'I suppose holding a séance would be pretty harmless. That incident with the ice and then Nettie snatching that drink from his hand the other night definitely has Stephen rattled. Those ridiculous warnings too.' He shook his head. 'Dash it all the man is in his own home, surrounded by his friends and family. Why would Stephen of all people be in any danger?'

'I know I mentioned this before but are you certain that you don't know of anyone here with a wish to harm him, sir?' Matt asked in a mild tone.

Sir Rufus looked up from his breakfast and snorted. 'No, of course not, man, don't be ridiculous. I told you, everyone here is very fond of Stephen. This is his home, his family, his friends.'

'I don't know,' Romy said as she went to leave the table. 'If he doesn't release me from my contract soon, I might be tempted to kill him.' She gave a wry smile. 'And no, I didn't try and drop a lump of ice on his head.'

'I suppose if Nero or Brutus or whatever his name is shows up this evening then, perhaps, we'll find out.' Maxfield grinned and followed his girlfriend out of the room.

Kitty and Matt left Sir Rufus to finish his meal alone.

'A séance?' Kitty said as soon as she was certain that no one would overhear her.

'A little pressure on whoever left that note and sabotaged that masonry might bring them into the open,' Matt said.

'Or get Lord Barlas killed,' Kitty responded.

The rest of the day passed uneventfully and pleasantly with Lady Barlas leading various games in the entrance hall. Quoits and skittles on the tiled floor, followed by charades after lunch in the library. Matt took Bertie out for a very quick walk as the weather continued to deteriorate. Lord Barlas had declined to join the games, stating he would be working all day on urgent estate matters.

'Nettie has kindly agreed to hold a séance after dinner this evening. I've proposed that she use the library. Now if anyone doesn't wish to attend then you are, of course, at perfect liberty to retire to another room, and we shall come and join you afterwards. It is most important that there is no negative energy in the room at the time,' Lady Barlas announced at afternoon tea.

Kitty glanced around at her fellow guests but there were no dissenters. It seemed that everyone intended to be in the library after dinner.

CHAPTER TEN

Matt opened their trunk after donning his evening suit.

'What are you doing? The servants already unpacked all of our things.' Kitty twisted round on the dressing table stool where she had been fastening some small ruby droppers to her ears.

Matt opened the lid and slid out the top tray before reaching right to the bottom of the interior. He felt with his thumbnail for a small hidden notch that opened a secret compartment.

'Not quite everything,' he remarked grimly as he took out his trusty small handgun and concealed it inside his jacket.

Kitty's eyes widened as he fastened the trunk back up and returned it to the luggage rest. 'Are you expecting something to happen tonight?' she asked.

'I just don't know,' Matt replied. But with Lord Barlas's gun still missing, he intended to be prepared.

Dinner took place amidst an atmosphere of suppressed anticipation. Bertie had been dispatched to the kitchen for the evening with Lord Barlas's dog. Matt took the opportunity to observe his fellow guests discreetly as they worked their way through the various courses.Lord Barlas was quiet and reserved, his face solemn as he ate. Matt noticed that he barely answered Sir Rufus whenever he spoke to him, and he wondered if something had happened between the two men. Lady Smythe darted sharp glances about the table as she picked at her food, snapping at her husband whenever he spoke to her.

Lady Barlas dressed in dark-green velvet talked animatedly to Romy Fisher who shimmered in a silver-filigree evening gown. Maxfield joined the conversation seemingly intent on amusing Lady Barlas. Donald Waterford appeared to be overly attentive to his fiancée as if concerned about what might lie ahead. Ottilie herself kept glancing anxiously first at her father and then at Lady Barlas.

Madam Fortina had not joined them for dinner. Lady Barlas informed them that the medium was unable to eat before a séance as she needed to rest and conserve her energy for the evening ahead.

Kitty, he knew, was not entirely sold on the idea of a séance. He could sense her tension even as she ate the delicious mincemeat tart and cream dessert. Her delicate features were pale as she made polite conversation with Sir Rufus who was seated on her other side. The reassuring weight of the gun concealed within his jacket comforted him as they finished their coffees and port, before adjourning to the library ready for the séance.

The oval mahogany table had been draped in a dark-red cloth and the room was now dimly lit by candles, which flickered in huge brass, glass-shaded sconces. The green-shaded library lanterns that had been there previously had now been removed. This created pools of darkness within the room and eerie shadows moved on the walls as everyone took their seats.

A Ouija board marked with the letters of the alphabet, numbers, and a red and black yes and no section stood beside a glass of water in the centre of the table before a vacant seat. Matt assumed that this was for Madam Fortina. Lord Barlas took his place at the head of the table. Lady Barlas sent a maid to tell the medium that they were ready.

'Before dear Nettie joins us, I must implore you all to take this séance seriously. You must follow any instructions implicitly or the circle will break, and the energy will dissipate and the connection to the spirits will be lost.' Lady Barlas gazed sternly around the table to ensure that everyone was paying attention.

As she finished speaking, Madam Fortina made her entrance. Matt had been expecting the medium to be dressed in her usual bright colours, but instead she was clothed once more entirely in plain black. Her short dark curls held back by ebony combs, and she was entirely devoid of jewellery.

Beneath the table, Kitty slipped her hand into his and he gave it a brief reassuring squeeze as the medium took her seat.

'Good evening, everyone, I presume Velma has explained to you the serious and delicate nature of what we are about to attempt?'

There was a murmur of assent mingled with the clearing of throats.

'Then we shall commence. Please remain silent unless I or any of the spirits request you to speak. Keep your hand loosely clasped in that of your neighbour's at all times.'

Madam Fortina placed her fingertips on the wooden planchette of the Ouija board as the rest of the group linked hands on top of the tablecloth. Her other hand was taken by Lady Barlas who was seated at her side. Matt's pulse quickened. The medium closed her eyes and began to breathe deeply for several seconds before she spoke. Her voice sounding unusually loud in the quiet of the room.

'I call upon those who have departed this realm for the next. Is there anyone there who wishes to speak to us this evening?' Madam Fortina asked.

The planchette moved abruptly onto the yes section of the

board. Matt heard Ottilie gasp. The medium opened her dark eyes and moved the marker back into the centre of the board.

'Are you connected with someone here tonight?' Madam Fortina asked. Again the planchette moved sharply into the yes section.

'Who is with us?' Madam Fortina asked.

The planchette remained still for a moment under her fingertips then began to move swiftly across the letters of the alphabet to spell out 'a friend'.

In the gloom, Matt could just make out a puzzled expression on Lady Barlas's face. This was clearly something that had not occurred before.

'Do you have a message for us?' the medium asked and the planchette moved to the yes section once more.

'Who is the message for?' Was her next question.

A log slipped in the grate, the crackle sounding loud in the stillness of the room as a shower of sparks shot up the chimney. Outside the thick castle walls the wind moaned.

B-A-R-L-A-S

All eyes turned to Lord Barlas as the Ouija board spelled out his name.

'Lord Barlas?' the medium asked.

Again the board answered with a yes.

'What is your message, spirit friend?' Madam Fortina asked.

Matt tensed, waiting for the inevitable warning that he expected the medium to provide. Instead, however the planchette began to move erratically across the board, not stopping on any letters long enough to leave any form of recognisable communication.

Outside in the corridor a door banged and as everyone looked toward the door, the candles guttered and went out throwing the room into virtual darkness.

'What the devil?' Lord Barlas's voice called out.

'Get the lights,' Lady Smythe cried.

The room was suddenly flooded with light. Maxfield was at the brass light switch beside the door. His face pale in the bright illumination from the overhead electric lights.

'Stephen, you're bleeding! Are you hurt? What on earth?' Lady Barlas had her hand over her mouth as she gazed at her husband.

Lord Barlas was clasping his hand and Matt could see he had obviously nicked his knuckle on something sharp. The item responsible was sticking ominously out of the top of the table. A small dagger of the kind Matt had seen tucked in the socks of Scotsmen when they were dressed in their regalia.

Impaled under the dagger's blade was a piece of paper. Matt could see that words had been cut out and glued in the same way as the one Lord Barlas had given him on their arrival at Finnglach.

A babble of voices broke out as everyone stared at Lord Barlas and the knife.

'What happened, sir?' Matt was on his feet, and he swooped on the knife, holding it carefully with a clean pocket square from his jacket to tug it free of the tabletop. He carefully extricated the note from the blade taking care not to tear the paper.

Lord Barlas looked shaken, his face ashen as he wrapped his own handkerchief around his injured hand to stop the bleeding.

'I don't know, bally lights went out and I let go of Ottilie's hand, then I felt a sharp pain on my knuckle. The lights came on and the dirk was there, and my hand was cut. It must have skimmed me as it landed.' Lord Barlas looked at Matt.

'What does the note say?' Ottilie had placed her arm around her father's shoulders.

'*You were warned. No more chances,*' Matt read it aloud.

There was a gasp from around the table, followed by the sound of slow handclaps from Sir Rufus. 'Well, I have to hand it to you, Nettie, that was the best piece of dramatics I've seen in quite a while.'

The medium hadn't moved from her seat, her dark eyes were fixed on the note in Matt's hand. 'I have no idea what you mean, Sir Rufus. This was none of my doing. I am merely the channel through which the spirits work.'

'Well, if this was someone's idea of a prank, it's really not funny.' Romy gave a shiver.

'I agree.' Ottilie's tone was fierce.

'Perhaps we should all go to the drawing room, and have a drink?' Kitty suggested. 'This has been most disturbing.'

'Yes, indeed, I for one could use a brandy, come, Rufus.' Lady Smythe rose from her chair and went towards the door. The rest of the party moved to follow her as if they too would be glad to leave the room. Lady Barlas and Maxfield supported Madam Fortina who appeared shaky and stumbled as she walked.

Lord Barlas reassured his daughter and his wife that he would be along in a moment. Everyone else left, leaving Kitty and Matt with their host.

'Did you see anything, sir? Anything at all that could indicate who did this?' Kitty asked once the door had closed.

Lord Barlas shook his head and ran the tip of his tongue over his lips.

'No, Mrs Bryant, Kitty. Nothing. I had Ottilie on my one side and Miss Fisher on the other. Both of them were holding my hands until the candles were extinguished.' Lord Barlas lifted his handkerchief to see if the bleeding had stopped on his hand.

'Do you recognise the knife at all?' Matt asked.

'Yes, it's my own. A ceremonial dirk. I intended to wear it tomorrow night for the New Year celebrations. As you may be aware it is traditional that I wear my kilt on Hogmanay.' Lord Barlas got somewhat shakily to his feet, picked up the knife and put it in his jacket pocket. 'I had better go and join the others, my wife and daughter will be anxious.'

'Of course, sir.' Kitty stood aside to allow him to exit the room.

'By the way, I think we should follow Rufus's lead. Play this off as a prank for now.' Lord Barlas turned back to face them, his hand on the door handle. 'Ottilie is very sensitive, and this business is worrying Velma. Just hurry up and get to the bottom of whoever is doing this.'

'As you wish, sir, but I urge you to be very careful. Whoever played this trick tonight has nerves of steel and is unafraid of taking risks,' Matt said.

Lord Barlas nodded and went to join the rest of the group in the drawing room.

'We should follow,' Kitty said as Matt placed the note carefully in his jacket pocket.

'Let's quickly look at the candles and the board first, just to see if there is anything that could have been rigged up for tonight,' Matt suggested.

Kitty went to the Ouija board and examined the planchette and beneath the table for any sign of tampering. Matt checked the candle sconces.

'Nothing, no magnets or wires,' Kitty reported.

Matt stooped and picked up a small piece of pink rubber from the floor under the edge of the tablecloth. There seemed to be a thin piece of wire attached to the end.

'What's that?' Kitty asked curiously.

Matt turned the rubber fragment between his fingers. 'I'm not sure.'

'It looks like a balloon,' Kitty said. 'Do you think someone had concealed a balloon in order to make it bang during the séance to scare everyone?'

Matt frowned. 'Possibly, but I think it more likely that this could have been the cause of the candles being extinguished.'

He saw enlightenment dawn on his wife's face. 'It was rigged so that the air could be released like a gush of wind to cause the blackout? Madame Fortina herself, perhaps?'

'Exactly that. Whoever is doing this has it worked out. It sounded as if they had all attended one of Madam Fortina's séances before, so they would have known what to expect. It could have been her or any of the others,' Matt said.

Kitty watched him add the rubber fragment to the contents of his pocket, alongside the letter. 'I agree, the odd thing is I don't understand why Lord Barlas is being warned that he is in danger if the person doing this is the person intending his murder. Surely they would simply kill him? Why frighten him?'

'If they are one and the same person, of course. The warnings so far have seemed to be via Madam Fortina, with the exception of the note on his pillow and now this one.'

'You don't think she was responsible for tonight? She was the one who set everything up? Why would she not have left the notes?' Kitty asked.

'I don't know. I would have thought perhaps she was the one who had this rigged up but it's on the far side of the table from where she was seated. Also, the notes are threatening Lord Barlas, whereas Madam Fortina seems to be issuing warnings to protect him,' Matt said.

'The balloon could have travelled as the air was expelled, or she could have operated it from her side of the table, but she may not have expected the dagger,' Kitty suggested.

Matt was greatly troubled by the whole affair. 'None of it makes sense. Let's go to the drawing room and see what's happening there,' he suggested. The sense of danger that had been present ever since they had arrived at Finnglach seemed to have been stepped up a notch this evening.

Now he was even more concerned that Lord Barlas's life was genuinely in danger, but why? What last chance had he been given and why would he not tell them about it when they had met with him yesterday?

CHAPTER ELEVEN

Kitty's mind was busy as they hurried along to the drawing room. She was keen that their absence should not be noticed.

They slipped quietly into the room to discover Lord Barlas was now seated beside the fire with Ottilie pressing a large crystal-glass of brandy into his uninjured hand. A dressing had been applied to the cut on the knuckle of his other hand. Madam Fortina sat in a far corner of the room away from the others. Her eyes were closed, and her skin appeared unnaturally pale against her dark clothing.

Lady Smythe and Sir Rufus occupied one of the sofas and Romy Fisher was perched on the arm of one of the chairs, while Maxfield took the seat. They nearly all had drinks. Donald Waterford stood beside the Christmas tree as if surveying the room as Lady Barlas fluttered around pressing drinks on everyone who hadn't received one already.

Matt went to the cocktail trolley and secured a drink for himself and Kitty, while Lady Barlas resumed attending to her husband, examining the dressing on his hand.

'Well, I do think that whoever did this was quite infantile. It was a most unfunny joke. Stephen could have been really hurt.'

Lady Barlas took a seat in the other fireside armchair once satisfied that her husband had not been badly injured by the dagger.

'Absolutely. It was in most terribly bad taste,' said Lady Smythe.

'At least we are all agreed that it was not a message from some malevolent spirit,' Donald Waterford looked at Ottilie as he spoke.

'There was definitely a human hand behind this, and it had to be someone present in this room. Is anyone going to own up?' Lady Barlas looked around at her guests.

'Maxfield?' Donald suggested, looking directly at the racing driver.

'I say, old man, don't go throwing accusations at me. Why would I want to spook Lord Barlas?' Maxfield sat upright in his seat. His handsome face flushing with indignation.

Romy placed a restraining hand on his arm and glared at Donald. 'Of course Max had nothing to do with this. Perhaps you are trying to deflect, Donald. After all, you were worried about the séance in case the spirit of Ottilie's husband came through. Perhaps you wanted to cut the whole thing short.'

Kitty watched in fascination as the tips of Donald's ears turned pink and his hand tightened around his crystal whisky glass.

'How dare you. My only concern was that raking over the past distresses Ottilie and I don't like to see her upset. I certainly would not pull a stunt like this and I certainly wouldn't wish to harm my future father-in-law.'

Ottilie sprang up to dash to Donald's side and placed her arm around his waist. 'Of course Donald wouldn't do such a thing. You might just as well accuse Romy. She is an actress after all and the whole thing was so theatrical. It smacks of the theatre.'

Romy rolled her eyes at this suggestion. 'Really, Ottilie darling, and why would I do such a thing? It's nonsense. If you ask me, the person most likely to be behind all of this is Madam Fortina. She was the one who organised it all.'

Everyone looked at where the medium was seated quietly in a corner of the room.

As if suddenly aware that everyone's attention was upon her, Madam Fortina opened her eyes.

'Contacting those who have gone before us is a very serious matter. I do not play pranks or tricks. My previous warnings to Lord Barlas were from my spirit guides. I have no control over the messages I receive. I am a professional.' Her tone was weary.

'Someone was out to play a prank, though.' Matt produced the fragment of pink rubber from his pocket. 'I found this on the floor as we left the room. It looks as if a balloon was used to produce the gush of air that extinguished the candles. Whether that was designed to be an effect of the séance, and then someone used the opportunity to place the dagger, or if the two things were planned together, I don't know.'

Kitty watched everyone's reactions to this revelation of Matt's trying to see if she could detect anything that might give a clue to who was responsible. A ripple of gasps and shocked murmurs ran around the room. She thought that Lord Barlas, like herself, seemed keen to see if anyone betrayed any sign of guilt.

'I don't expect anyone to own up. However, I do expect this nonsense to cease. I should like to think this is a Christmas jape that has now run its course. Tomorrow is New Year's Eve, and I would like us all to have a good Hogmanay before we go back to London in a few days' time.' Lord Barlas looked around at his guests.

'I can assure you, that I had no part in this. I am not responsible for that childish party trick. Now, if you will all excuse me. Tonight, has been most upsetting and exhausting.' Madam Fortina levered herself up from her seat and left the room with

Lady Barlas hurrying after her. Kitty assumed this was presumably to ensure the older woman was all right.

Donald lifted back the heavy velvet curtain from the window beside the Christmas tree and peered out into the night. 'It's a veritable blizzard out there. I don't think anyone will be going anywhere for a while.'

Lord Barlas stood and placed his empty glass down on the small, polished wood side table beside his chair. 'There is plenty of time for that to change. The villagers and my staff are adept at clearing the roads to make them passable. Now, if you will all excuse me, I intend to retire for the night. I am sure none of you will take it amiss if I spend tomorrow in my office. There are several documents which still require my attention. I shall see you all tomorrow evening for the celebrations.'

There was a ripple of polite farewells and goodnights.

Ottilie flung herself down on the chair her father had just vacated and buried her face in her hands. 'Poor Daddy, what an awful trick to play on him. I wish Madam Fortina had not come here with us after all, then perhaps none of this would have happened.'

Donald moved to place his arm around her shoulders to comfort her. 'There now, darling.'

'It's a nasty business and has gone far enough in my opinion. The sooner Madam Fortina, or whatever her real name is, packs her bags the better. She's the one behind all this, if you ask me. With her pseudo warnings.' Sir Rufus glowered round at them all as if daring anyone to disagree with him.

'I agree.' For once, Lady Smythe appeared to side with her husband.

'What do you think, Captain Bryant? You have been very quiet on the matter,' Maxfield asked.

'Kitty and I don't really know any of you terribly well. My correspondence with Lord Barlas was limited until he invited us to experience a Scottish Hogmanay here at the castle so I must bow to your judgement on this affair.'

Kitty thought that her husband had given both a tactful and truthful reply.

With that everyone finished their drinks and drifted off to their respective rooms for the night. Kitty couldn't help wondering, as she carefully applied cold cream to her face later in the privacy of their room, what the following day might bring.

The blizzard that had begun the previous evening continued throughout the night. Kitty gasped when she drew back the curtains the next day to see how high the drifts were against the trees and walls. Even the standing stones had snow piled against them on the one side where the wind had blown. It seemed the New Year would be off to a chilly start.

For now, however, the snow had stopped, and a weak winter sun was making the still waters of the loch sparkle. In the distance the blue range of mountains had white peaks, and the pine trees glistened under their snowy capes. A couple of men were already outside, wrapped up against the cold and clearing the pathways around the perimeter of the castle.

'It's quite beautiful, isn't it?' Matt observed as he came to stand behind her. 'Under other circumstances this would have been a most delightful holiday. New Year's Eve tonight.'

There was no one else around at breakfast and they saw very little of anyone else all day, except at lunchtime. Madam Fortina had remained in her room and taken her meals on a tray. Romy had been practising her singing in the music room, whilst Maxfield had been playing billiards with Donald. Their altercation of yesterday seemingly forgotten.

Lady Smythe and Lady Barlas were in the drawing room with Ottilie discussing her wedding plans. Sir Rufus had taken himself off to the library again. Kitty and Matt decided there was little more they could do during the day so wrapped up warmly and went outside for a spell with Bertie to marvel at the snowy landscape.

The servants had cleared the path around the castle perimeter and where the wind had blown the snow the way to the stone circle was also clear. They walked as far as they could in the direction of the loch until the snow grew too deep to continue and they turned back.

The exercise helped to clear Kitty's mind and did much to raise her spirits before they returned to their room to dress for the evening ahead. Her aunt Livvy had always told her a great deal about the Scottish celebrations and, despite the events of the previous evening, she was quite looking forward to the party.

Alice had packed Kitty's favourite cherry-red satin evening dress with matching shoes. Lunch had been a light affair since the meal that evening was to be a full seven courses, followed by music and dancing. Kitty was relieved that their excursion outside the castle had given her an appetite.

She assisted Matt with his cufflinks before he donned his evening jacket.

'Are you taking your gun downstairs again tonight?' she asked.

He shook his head. 'I would like to, but it might cause a problem if someone realises that I am carrying a weapon in the middle of a reel.'

A chill ran along Kitty's spine. 'I hope nothing happens this evening. Perhaps last night was the last throw of the dice from whoever is trying to scare Lord Barlas. After all, everyone is alerted now and will be watching one another.'

'I wish that was the case about it being the last act, but we are no further forward in finding out who might want to harm him and why. I can see why some of them might wish to perhaps frighten him a little, but I can't work this case out at all.

We must hope no harm befalls him before everyone leaves for London in the next few days.'

The party assembled in the drawing room for pre-drinks before going into dinner. Lord Barlas was dressed in his full regalia, comprising the dark-green Barlas family tartan kilt with sealskin sporran. The silver-handled dirk of the previous evening was safely stowed in its leather case strapped to his leg over his cream knee-high socks. Lady Barlas was resplendent in silver lamé with a sash of the family tartan draped over her shoulder and secured with a large diamond brooch.

Ottilie too had a similar sash, although hers was pinned to her dark-blue silk dress with a sapphire and diamond clip which matched her earrings. Romy was in a form-fitting bias-cut gown of pale-blue satin and Lady Smythe was attired in a gold sheath dress. The rest of the men were dressed like Matt in formal evening attire.

Madam Fortina was the last to join them. Tonight, she had chosen to wear a dark-purple gown overlaid with black lace and silver clips in her hair adorned with curled ostrich feathers.

Once everyone was present, Lord Barlas's butler circulated around the room bearing a silver platter with sherry for the ladies and small glasses of whisky for the gentlemen. The wireless was on low, playing big band music, and the fire crackled merrily in the hearth. If it had not been for the feeling of tension, the atmosphere in the room would have been convivial and celebratory.

Several other platters followed containing delicious hors d'oeuvres before the signal was given that they should proceed to the dining room. Lord Barlas took his seat at the head of the table with Lady Barlas as his side, followed by Sir Rufus and Lady Smythe. Ottilie and Donald sat on his other side, while the rest of the party, including Kitty and Matt, took their places further down the table.

The white tablecloth was pristine, and the chandelier overhead sparkled and shone on the array of silverware and cut-glass crystal. Kitty noticed, however, that the oil lamps were still in place around the room. The large silver candelabras on the table with the scarlet candles had also been lit, so she assumed there was still a risk of power failure.

The soup course was swiftly followed by the fish course and the atmosphere in the room improved as more wine was consumed along with the food. Venison was served for the main course with side dishes of vegetables and Kitty breathed a sigh of relief when a small palate cleansing dish of sorbet followed. Even with her healthy appetite she was feeling rather full.

By the time the party had enjoyed the cheese course and fresh fruit, Kitty was happy to adjourn back into the drawing room for coffee and cognac. The volume on the wireless had now been turned up and an area of the room cleared for dancing.

Everyone appeared to be enjoying the evening now the meal was finished. Kitty sank down on the end of the sofa with her coffee and watched as Sir Rufus danced with Romy, while Lady Smythe took a turn with Lord Barlas. Donald stood somewhat stiffly to one side as Lady Barlas accepted Maxfield's offer to partner her. Ottilie was deep in conversation with Madam Fortina.

'Care for a dance, Mrs Bryant?' Matt asked, his eyes twinkling with amusement as he murmured his invitation in her ear.

'Why not? Thank you, kind sir,' Kitty accepted, and they joined the group on the dance floor. Time seemed to pass quite quickly and there was a great deal of laughter and merriment as the evening wore on. The tension Kitty had sensed earlier had almost dissipated. Even Lord Barlas appeared more relaxed as he mingled with his guests.

At five minutes to midnight the butler reappeared bearing glasses of champagne.

'Oh my dears, it's almost time for the bells!' Lady Barlas

urged them all into a circle as they waited, glass in hand for the chimes of midnight on the wireless. Once the bells sounded, the toast was drunk to the New Year and from the hallway came the approaching skirl of the bagpipes and 'Auld Lang Syne'.

One of the footmen dressed in full regalia entered the room with the pipes and the group sang and toasted together before applauding. Several other tunes followed, including 'The Skye Boat Song' and 'Loch Lomond' before the man departed, having received a healthy tip from Lord Barlas for his services.

Once the piper had gone, Romy sang, then the gramophone was pressed into service and the dancing resumed. Kitty lost track of who was where as various people left and re-entered the room, no doubt to use the bathrooms and to refresh themselves.

'Lord Barlas is missing,' Matt murmured in Kitty's ear as he twirled her around the dance floor once more. 'He's been gone for a few minutes.'

Kitty looked around. 'I thought Lady Barlas said something about first-footing. He may have gone to do that,' she suggested.

Her aunt Livvy had always said that in order to bring good luck for the year ahead a dark-haired man bearing a piece of coal and a libation of whisky must be the first person to step over the threshold. The first-footing custom was a big part of the Hogmanay tradition.

As she spoke, Lady Barlas lifted the needle from the gramophone record and clapped her hands to attract everyone's attention.

'Darlings, let's all go to the hall, Stephen is due to enter the castle for our first-footing.'

They all dutifully set down their drinks and followed Lady Barlas to the hall where a fresh tray of whiskies awaited them near the front door. The clock on the mantelpiece chimed one o'clock and Kitty noticed that Lady Barlas had a worried frown on her forehead.

'You're right, Matt, something is wrong.'

Matt made his way to Lady Barlas's side, and she saw him murmur something in her ear.

Lady Barlas gave a brief nod and Matt slipped away from the group to head down the side corridor to the boot room. Kitty was torn between remaining where she was or following her husband in order to see what was going on.

No one else appeared to be aware of a problem as they were talking and sipping their drinks while they waited for the front door to open.

'I say, Velma, Stephen is dragging this out a touch, isn't he?' Sir Rufus was the first to comment as the minutes ticked by without the expected knock at the great oak door.

'Captain Bryant has gone to see what's keeping him,' Lady Barlas said. 'He may have slipped on the ice.'

A loud knock sounded on the door as she spoke, and her face lit up in relief. However, when the butler opened the door, it was Matt alone who was in the doorway, flashlight in hand, with a grim expression on his face.

A gust of icy wind swirled in with him as he stepped over the threshold. 'Lady Barlas, I'm afraid everyone should return to the drawing room. There has been a most terrible accident.'

CHAPTER TWELVE

Lady Barlas's face paled and she swayed on her heels. Maxfield swiftly stepped forward to support her before she crumpled. 'Stephen? Something has happened to Stephen?' She glanced wildly around at the circle of concerned faces surrounding her.

Matt's gaze met Kitty's. 'Perhaps if some of the menservants could come and assist you?' she suggested.

The butler quickly appeared to recognise that the situation was very wrong. 'I shall send the gardener and one of the footmen out immediately, madam.'

'Thank you.' Matt turned and went back into the dark. He pulled the door closed behind him, leaving a small pile of melting snow from his shoes on the mat.

'What's going on? What did he mean by a terrible accident? Where is my father?' Ottilie rounded on Kitty.

'We should go back to the drawing room. No doubt Matt will be along shortly to tell us what has happened,' Kitty said. From the look on Matt's face, she knew that Lord Barlas had to be dead, but what had happened to him?

'Yes, my dear, Mrs Bryant is right, come.' Donald placed his arm around Ottilie's waist, and the group made their way to the drawing room.

Lady Barlas collapsed weeping on the end of the sofa, while Maxfield attempted to comfort her, and Lady Smythe pressed brandy upon her. Ottilie sat beside the fire, her back ramrod straight.

'What kind of accident? We should go out there.' Ottilie rose from her chair.

'You cannot go out in this weather in your evening gown. Let Captain Bryant and the servants see what is afoot. They will be back to tell us soon enough.' Sir Rufus looked shaken as he stood in front of the fire which had dwindled now to a small, flickering pile of ash and bits of charred wood.

'Lord Barlas is no longer in this world.' Madam Fortina's voice rang out clearly from her seat in the far corner of the room. 'The warnings have come to pass.'

Her pronouncement caused Lady Barlas's sobs to increase and Ottilie looked as if she were about to faint.

'No, no, I won't believe it.' Ottilie's tone was fierce.

'Darling...' Donald tried to speak but she pushed his hand away from her shoulder.

Romy was sitting in the other fireside chair, her face as pale as Ottilie's.

From outside in the hall came the sound of male voices. Sir Rufus sprang into action and hurried out of the room.

'Donald, go after him and find out what's going on,' Ottilie commanded.

The door reopened, however, before Donald had a chance to move and Sir Rufus came back inside, followed by Matt.

A babble of questions broke out and Sir Rufus held up his hand to get them to stop. He glanced at Matt before speaking. 'I'm sorry to tell you all that Stephen is dead. He was late coming in for first-footing and Captain Bryant here, realising that Velma was concerned, offered to go outside to look for him.'

'Yes, he was supposed to enter the house at one o'clock with the coal and the whisky.' Lady Barlas burst into another bout of sobs making her words hard to understand.

'I learned from the servants that Lord Barlas had put on his outdoor things and collected the items for first-footing and set off from the boot room. I couldn't see any sign of him on the perimeter path, so I searched around with my torch and caught a glimpse of something inside the stone circle.' Matt paused and looked about the room before continuing. 'Lord Barlas was lying on the ground near the stone slab. As I drew nearer it was clear he was dead.'

'Dead? How is he dead? What happened?' Ottilie demanded.

'He was shot, apparently at close range. A single bullet and no sign of the gun. There were no footprints visible near the body as the wind is scouring the snow from the frozen ice under the surface,' Matt said.

'Shot? You mean someone murdered him?' Lady Smythe asked.

'I'm afraid so.' Matt glanced at Sir Rufus. 'The servants have carried him back into the house and I am informed that the telephone lines have failed at present so we cannot send for the police just yet.'

The lights in the drawing room flickered as he spoke, and it seemed to Kitty that the electricity might not be far behind the telephone lines in failing.

'Murder, but that's impossible.' Donald looked aghast at the suggestion.

'I'm afraid it's true and as the road to the village is impassable right now, I can only assume that the killer is still at the castle,' Matt said.

Another babble of voices started up at this. The lights flickered once more and one of the servants entered the room and lit the oil lamps that stood near the fireplace. This proved to be timely as they had no sooner finished than the electricity failed completely.

'Then there is nothing further we can do right now. Velma, my dear, and Ottilie, I am so very sorry.' Sir Rufus's voice was kind.

'I can't believe it. I kept hoping those warnings and what happened at the séance last night was all just a stupid prank that had gotten out of hand.' Lady Barlas dabbed at her eyes with her lace-edged handkerchief, making sooty kohl marks on the white linen.

'Murdered?' Ottilie seemed to be talking almost to herself as if she were struggling to comprehend that her father was dead.

'The warnings were clear. The spirits spoke.' Madam Fortina had moved from her seat to stand closer to the centre of the room. Her face mask-like in the soft yellow light of the oil lamp.

A shiver ran down Kitty's spine. Logically she knew the talk of spirits was nonsense, but here in the darkness of the ancient castle such talk was surprisingly plausible.

'There must be something we can do? A search for the gun, perhaps?' Romy asked. 'There is a murderer on the loose with a weapon.'

'The servants are searching, both the boot room and this floor of the castle. Lord Barlas's gun was taken from his desk a few days ago and I suspect that is the firearm that has been used,' Matt said.

'Stephen's gun was taken? But how? He keeps all his guns locked in a cabinet.' Sir Rufus looked in bewilderment at Matt.

'This one was in a locked drawer of his desk. It was stolen when his office was searched. At the same time, it seems that someone attempted to get into his safe.' Matt looked and sounded weary, Kitty thought.

'You seem to know an awful lot on the matter, Bryant? How

do we know that you are not behind all of this?' Donald suddenly asked.

'Lord Barlas told me about the gun and the attempt on the safe the day I arrived,' Matt explained.

'Besides, he wasn't here when that great lump of ice and masonry almost landed on Stephen's head.' Sir Rufus gave Donald a scathing glance.

'It could be one of the servants,' Donald suggested. 'Someone with a grudge or needing money.'

'In other words, old chum, you would prefer that it was not one of us,' Maxfield drawled. He leaned back in his seat and took out a cigarette from a silver case before offering it around.

'You think someone in here, did this?' Ottilie stared in horror as Maxfield tucked the case back inside his jacket pocket and calmly lit his cigarette.

'Of course, Ottilie. Come on, you saw what happened at the séance last night. That's what Captain Bryant thinks, isn't it?' Maxfield blew out a thin blue plume of smoke and looked at Matt.

'I think if you examine the facts of what has happened over the last few weeks the conclusion is inescapable,' Matt said.

Kitty's heart thumped as the rest of the group looked around at each other in the dim light as if realising for the first time that they did indeed have a murderer close at hand.

'Stop, stop it, all of you. I can't bear it. Stephen is dead, murdered.' Lady Barlas burst out sobbing once more.

'This discussion can wait until daylight. Velma, my dear, you need to rest. You too, Ottilie, this has been a terrible shock.' Sir Rufus offered Lady Barlas his arm in support to escort her upstairs.

There was a muted murmur of agreement from the rest of the group and Ottilie accepted her fiancé's arm to follow her stepmother from the room.

'Well, I for one shall be keeping the door of my bedroom

firmly locked tonight,' Kitty heard Lady Smythe mutter as they all prepared to retire for the night.

The servants had been busy setting up lamps to ensure that they could navigate their way safely through the darkened corridors. Kitty kept close beside Matt as they made their own way up the stairs and into the corridor leading to their bedroom.

The room was dark and cold where the fire had almost gone out. Matt used his cigarette lighter to light the oil lamp. Once she could see, Kitty added more kindling to the fire from the brass scuttle beside the grate. She stirred the embers with a poker until the fire blazed more strongly, throwing heat back into the room.

At least the curtains had been drawn against the cold coming from the leaded glass in the window. She also discovered when she drew back the covers on the bed that a copper warming pan had been applied at some point so at least the chill was off the bedclothes.

Matt turned the key in the lock of the bedroom door as Kitty started to remove her jewellery to change ready for bed.

'For once I agree with Lady Smythe. We should keep the door locked.' Matt stood before the made-up fire and warmed his hands.

'Matt, we failed in our efforts to protect Lord Barlas.' Kitty shivered as she slipped out of her evening gown and hastily donned her warm flannel nightgown.

'Whoever killed him was a ruthless and determined individual. I doubt we could have protected him; this chain of events was in motion before we arrived at Finnglach. Our job now is to discover who killed him and why.' Matt moved to sit in one of the fireside chairs while Kitty finished preparing for bed.

'Do you think the telephone lines will be restored by tomorrow?' Kitty asked as she carefully removed the warming pan from the bed.

'I spoke to the servants after I found Lord Barlas. They said the line usually goes down when it gets this icy and they were expecting it to get even colder tonight. For now he is at rest in one of the cellars until the police can come. The road to the village is currently impassable, even with horses. A large tree came down in the forest and there are large drifts.' Matt started to take off his cufflinks, dropping them back inside a small, padded leather case.

'So, we may not get any official assistance for some time?' Kitty hopped into bed and pulled the sheets and blankets up over herself.

'It certainly seems doubtful. It also means that whoever did this is trapped here too.' Matt hung his jacket inside the vast wardrobe and took off his bow tie.

'And whoever killed Lord Barlas is still in possession of his gun,' Kitty said.

'That, I'm not so certain of. The gun has done its job and our man will not wish to be caught with it, so my guess is that it's been stashed somewhere inside the castle.' Matt changed quickly into his pyjamas and climbed into bed beside her.

'Lord Barlas said they searched the castle when it first went missing and couldn't find it.' Kitty snuggled closer to her husband.

'Now that Lord Barlas is dead though, we may discover more of everyone's true natures and motivations.' Matt yawned as he spoke.

'Should we reveal that we are private investigators?' Kitty asked, she had been giving the matter some thought ever since Matt had discovered the murder.

'Not just yet. I believe that if whoever killed his lordship thinks he may have given us information that could lead to his capture, then we could find ourselves next on his list to be killed. Once someone has crossed that line to commit murder once, it is so much easier to repeat the offence.' Matt leaned out of bed and turned out the oil lamp plunging the room into virtual darkness save for the glow of the fire in the hearth.

Kitty felt the weight of Matt's arm as he rested it loosely across her and her eyes closed. At least with Matt by her side and the door locked they could sleep safely tonight.

Kitty woke with a start early in the morning. The room was still completely dark, and the castle was quiet. The fire was almost out in the grate, so she quickly hopped out of bed to try and get it going again.

Her thick red-felt dressing gown was a welcome barrier against the cold as she raked out some of the ash and added more kindling until a satisfactory blaze burned once more in the grate.

Once she was satisfied that the fire was going well, she used a rolled paper spill from the china spill jar on the mantelpiece to relight the oil lamp. Matt was still asleep, oblivious to her activities.

A peep through the window revealed nothing except darkness and a spatter of snow against the pane. It was clear that the weather had not lifted and more snow had followed the ice storm.

Kitty let the curtain fall back in place and seated herself beside the fire. She wished she knew what had woken her. The castle seemed quiet enough, and despite the snow the wind outside the walls was not unduly noisy.

Matt muttered and stirred in his sleep. She was glad that he had so far not been troubled by any of the recurring nightmares which plagued him. She had taken care with the bed to ensure the curtains were fastened well back so he would not feel enclosed.

Not for the first time on this adventure, Kitty wished Alice had accompanied them. She could have used a nice cup of tea, some hot buttery toast and a good natter with her friend. She hoped all was well back in Devon and that Bertie was not pining for them downstairs in the castle kitchens or misbehaving.

A glance at her small leather-cased travel clock on the bedside table told her it was six o'clock. No doubt the servants would be up and about downstairs. She was tempted to ring the bell and request some tea but was reluctant to wake Matt. At the back of her mind, a stray thought nagged at her. Something about the missing gun and the picked lock on the desk drawer.

She knew she would be unable to sleep if she returned to bed. Instead, she decided to dress and go in search of refreshment. A cup of tea might help to settle her mind. She scribbled a note for Matt, splashed cold water from the rose-patterned china basin onto her face and combed her hair. Satisfied that she looked respectable, she unlocked the door of the bedroom and slipped out into the corridor.

CHAPTER THIRTEEN

The corridor was dimly lit by another oil lamp situated on one of the dark, heavily carved wooden blanket chests which stood in the passageway. Kitty headed downstairs in search of a servant who might oblige her with a cup of tea.

The drawing room had been tidied and the fire re-laid in the fireplace. A young auburn-haired maid wearing a black armband on the sleeve of her uniform was just fastening back the curtains at the French window. The girl reminded her of Alice, increasing her feeling of homesickness.

'Excuse me, please, is there any chance I could get a cup of tea?' Kitty asked as the maid turned around.

'Yes, madam, of course.' The girl had looked a little startled when she realised that she was no longer alone in the room and Kitty wondered if the staff too were concerned about a murderer being inside the castle.

Kitty settled herself beside the fire and waited for the girl to return. All around her she could hear the sounds of the castle coming to life. The clatter of fire scuttles being filled, carpets being brushed and china clinking as trolleys were taken to the dining room to prepare for breakfast.

The girl returned bearing a small tray with a tea setting for one. 'There you go, madam, will you be wanting anything else?'

'No, thank you. I hope I haven't held you up in your work,' Kitty said and smiled at the girl.

'No, madam.' She turned to leave.

'By the way, I don't suppose the telephone lines are restored yet?' Kitty asked as she placed the metal strainer over her cup ready to pour her tea.

'No, madam, the men are outside now bringing down the icicles from the walls so I expect it will take a while to get the power and the telephone back,' the girl said.

'I was afraid you might say that. Thank you.' Kitty added milk from the tiny china jug to her tea and settled back in her seat.

Sure enough, after a minute she heard the sound of male voices and turned to see a couple of men outside the window. They were warmly bundled up in scarves and gloves and carried brooms and long poles. This activity was followed by the sound of falling ice smashing onto the pathways. No doubt they were keen to avoid any further accidents from falling ice.

She had almost finished her tea, when Lord Barlas's elderly dog, accompanied by Bertie, wandered into the room. Bertie bounded towards her, wagging his tail. Kitty fancied the elderly Labrador accompanying him looked disappointed when he realised that it was not his master who occupied the chair.

'Poor old boy.' Kitty set down her cup and called the other dog to her, fussing him and patting his silky coat. Bertie nudged his nose into her knee as if to remind her that she was his mistress.

The memory of what had been bothering her at the back of her mind returned. 'That was it. When we were in the study the other day, the key,' Kitty muttered.

The dogs looked at her questioningly.

She wondered if Matt had noticed if the key to the safe that Lord Barlas kept on his watch chain was still with him when he died, or had the killer taken it? Whoever had tried the safe before had attempted to pick the lock and they had assumed they must have known the combination. What if that person now had the key to the safe and had been to Lord Barlas's study? Was whatever was inside the safe the key to the murder?

Kitty jumped up, startling both dogs who had been preparing to settle at her feet. She couldn't really go down into the cellars in search of the late Lord Barlas. Besides, she was sure that door would be firmly locked, and her presence would be hard to explain. No, her best option was to head for Lord Barlas's study and see if anything looked out of place.

A swift peep out into the corridor showed no sign of either the servants or any of her fellow guests. With luck most of the house party would still be asleep and the servants' efforts would be mainly concentrated on the breakfast preparations.

Kitty left the dogs behind and walked swiftly along the corridor towards Lord Barlas's study. If anyone saw her trying the door, she could always claim she was lost and looking for a different room. Since she had only been at the castle for a few days this should be completely plausible.

There was still no one in sight, however, as she placed her hand on the door handle. She paused for a few seconds to listen in case someone might already be inside the room. When she heard nothing, she opened the door and slipped inside, closing it quietly again behind her.

She wasn't really sure what she was looking for or what she expected to see. A glance around showed the room to be pretty much as she remembered it when she and Matt had been interviewed by Lord Barlas on the day they had arrived.

She picked up the receiver of the black Bakelite telephone on the untidy desktop and tried dialling. The maid had been correct when she had said the lines were still down as no reassuring purr or crackle reached her when she placed it to her ear. Kitty replaced the receiver and looked around the desk.

Most of the documents appeared to be invoices, mainly for feed for the rearing of game birds and bills that were concerned with the maintenance of the castle. There was also a large stash of documents which seemed to be correspondence about Romy Fisher's contract. Kitty read the letters as quickly as she could whilst listening out for any sign that someone might be approaching the office door.

It was clear from the correspondence that Lord Barlas was refusing to release the actress from her contract. A copy of a letter had been attached to the latest request stating that Lord Barlas had plans that involved the starlet, and he was unable to accept the offer to release her from her commitments. A quick search revealed no sign of the contract itself and Kitty wondered if that might be one of the documents inside the safe.

The safe was still shut, although she supposed it could have been opened and relocked since Lord Barlas's death. Kitty tried the various desk drawers but found nothing of interest in any of them.

Frustrated, she looked around the room for anything else that might be of interest. The servants had not yet been in to clean and the ashes from the previous days fire were still in the grate. A fragment of partially burnt paper caught Kitty's attention and she bent to examine it more closely, extracting it from the ash.

The paper was creamy, thick and of good quality. She blew on it gently to remove the thin layer of grey film obscuring the words.

'*Last Will and Test...*' Kitty murmured softly. 'Gosh.'

She tucked the paper away safely inside the front pocket of her navy serge dress. She was about to escape the study when she saw the door handle move. Without stopping to think she darted to the floor-length brocade curtains at the rear of the room and secreted herself behind one of them.

The door clicked open, and she heard the tread of feet as someone entered the room. She kept as still as she possibly could and hoped the large wooden filing cabinet as well as the thickness of the curtain material were providing effective concealment.

Whoever had entered was not a servant, as she heard none of the sounds of the grate being cleared or of tidying and polishing. Instead, she heard the faint rustle of papers being moved and guessed that whoever had entered was looking at the documents on the desk in the same way she had done. She heard the sound of the person opening and closing desk drawers, followed by a faint metallic noise which she guessed was a futile attempt to see if the safe was unlocked.

There was a moment's silence and Kitty wondered if she dared risk a quick peep around the curtain to see who was in the office. Before she could act, she heard the unmistakable sound of one of the filing cabinet drawers being opened.

Hardly daring to breathe, she pushed herself back against the castle wall as far as she could and prayed she was not making a noticeable bulge in the curtain. After a few seconds she heard the drawer being closed again, followed by the click of the study door handle.

She let out a breath and risked a quick peek out in time to see what looked like the tall, distinguished figure of Sir Rufus exiting the office. Once he had gone, Kitty scrambled out of her hiding place, her heart hammering against her ribs.

She crossed to the door and opened it carefully to take a look outside, hoping Sir Rufus would have gone. To her relief the corridor was empty once more and she slipped out, ensuring the door was closed behind her.

'That was a narrow squeak, Kitty,' she muttered to herself as she made her way back towards the main hall. She collected Bertie on her way, eager to get back to her room to see if Matt was awake so she could tell him what she had seen.

* * *

Matt was just finishing shaving when Kitty arrived back in their bedroom. He could tell from her flushed cheeks and bright eyes that she clearly had something of importance to tell him.

He listened carefully as she recounted her adventures. 'So, Sir Rufus was poking about in the office, was he?' Matt said thoughtfully.

'I wonder what he was after?' Kitty asked.

'I don't know. Lord Barlas had said he had a number of financial documents he wished to review. Perhaps it was something to do with those,' Matt said.

'And then there is the key. That's what woke me up this morning. I had this horrid nagging feeling there was something we hadn't thought of,' Kitty said.

'Yes, you're right. I hadn't thought about the key to the safe being on Lord Barlas's watch chain. Lady Barlas will need the key if she is to access the safe. After all the will is probably in there.' Matt frowned.

'Is it though?' Kitty produced a scrap of paper from the pocket of her dress and handed it to him.

Matt's brows raised and he released a slow whistle. 'It looks as if Lord Barlas or someone else burnt a copy of his will in the grate yesterday. But who and why? Good work, Kitty.'

Matt had asked the servants to place their late master in a cold unused cellar and to keep the door locked until the police were able to be summoned and could evaluate matters. They had placed his lordship on a trestle and covered him with a sheet. Many of the servants had been visibly upset since they had known the lord all their lives.

He had noted that Lord Barlas had still been wearing his heavy gold signet ring with the family crest and that his gold watch chain was still present across his waistcoat. He hadn't thought though to look to see if the small key to the safe was still attached to it.

'I suppose someone will need to retrieve the key at some point. I wonder if the will that was destroyed was a recent one or an old one? Lord Barlas said that Lady Barlas knew the combination to the safe,' Kitty said.

'True. Perhaps Sir Rufus thought the safe might have been unlocked and he merely needed the combination part this morning in order to access the contents. I wonder if he knew about the will or was searching for it? That is, of course, assuming Lord Barlas ignored our advice about changing the combination. It may be that no one can access it without forcing it open.' Matt pulled a knitted Argyle sweater over his head and picked up his tweed jacket.

'It's all very suspicious. Did you notice anything else last night when you went to search for Lord Barlas?' Kitty asked.

'Not much, the wind had whipped the top surface of the snow and there were no footprints visible, not even those of Lord Barlas. When I returned to the boot room, I did spot a pair of the boots had been recently worn. They were wet and there was a small pool of water on the tiles. I also saw a pair of the snowshoes looked as if they had been used. Probably by the same person.' Matt had checked them both discreetly when the servants had not been observing him.

'Did you manage to look at the coats?' Kitty asked.

Matt nodded. 'One of the gaberdine overcoats was wet on the shoulders. One of the scarves had drops of water on the wool too. But there was nothing to determine who could have taken them. I presume the scarf had been used to protect their head and the coat was of a size that could have fit anyone.'

'Surely though, it must have been one of the men that killed him? All the ladies were wearing expensive evening gowns. It would have been difficult for them to dress in boots and snow-shoes in order to slip out of the castle to murder him?' Kitty's forehead creased in concentration.

'The dressing-up box was still there. They could possibly have slipped on something from the chest in order to venture outside,' Matt suggested.

'I suppose so, but it seems very unlikely.' Kitty's frown deepened.

'I agree, but if it was one of the men, were they working alone or in partnership with one of the women?' Matt suggested.

'Madam Fortina?' Kitty prepared to follow him downstairs to breakfast.

'We need to discover the real source of those vague and mysterious warnings she kept providing. I'd also like to know if she was the person behind the anonymous notes.' Matt opened the bedroom door and they headed for the dining room accompanied by the faithful Bertie.

Sir Rufus was seated at the dining table when they entered the room. He raised his head and greeted them sombrely as they took their seats. Like Matt he wore a black tie in respect to their late host.

'The telephone lines are still down and there is no way to get a message to the village. One of the gardeners tried an hour or so ago and couldn't get through the woods. This is a bad business, Bryant,' Sir Rufus said as he added more sugar to his tea.

'I agree, sir. Poor Lady Barlas must be devastated.' Matt nodded acceptance to the maid to supply them with fresh toast.

'I made enquiries to her maid this morning and she is remaining in her room today. I doubt if we shall see much of Ottilie either. She was devoted to her father. The poor girl has had so much tragedy in her life.' Sir Rufus shook his head in a gloomy fashion.

'Have you any ideas, sir, on who could have been responsible?' Matt was curious to hear what Sir Rufus might suggest.

'It sounds terrible, but I do wonder if Donald Waterford might be the man. He's a shady character if ever I saw one and Ottilie is a wealthy young woman. The only way he could get his hands on her money though is either by marriage or, well, Stephen's death,' Sir Rufus confided in a conspiratorial whisper.

'Lord Barlas said Ottilie's money was held in various trusts and investments.' Matt applied himself to his boiled egg and tried to keep his tone casual. He knew that Kitty was also paying close attention to the conversation despite appearing to be preoccupied with buttering her toast.

'He told you that, did he? Hmm, well yes. After Ottilie's first husband died, she was in a terrible state. The girl has little financial knowledge and would have been easy prey for the fortune hunters. She agreed with her father that it would be prudent if he, and I, resumed the management of her affairs. She receives a generous allowance and her capital is invested.' Sir Rufus dabbed at the corners of his moustache with his napkin.

'It was very fortunate for Ottilie that you and Lord Barlas were able to assist her,' Kitty said as she passed one of her sausages to Bertie under the table.

Matt knew his wife well enough to know that statement was probably the exact opposite of her true thoughts on the matter.

'Yes, well, Ottilie is my goddaughter, as you know. I would always want to look after her best interests.' Sir Rufus smiled approvingly at Kitty.

'Do you know how she and Donald met?' Kitty asked.

'Some nightclub in London, I believe. Some of her friends had suggested an evening out to try and lift her spirits. I think he was a friend of a friend.' Sir Rufus's smile vanished.

Matt wondered if he would say more but the dining room door opened and the gentleman in question appeared, bringing the conversation to a close.

CHAPTER FOURTEEN

Donald greeted them all affably and went to the sideboard to help himself to bacon and eggs from the silver platters that were being kept warm with small spirit burners.

'Ottilie is having her breakfast in her room. Poor girl is in a dreadful state after last night.' Donald joined them at the table bearing a substantial plate of food.

The recent demise of his future father-in-law had clearly not affected his appetite.

'I'm not surprised. She was very close to her father, as you know.' Sir Rufus raised his eyebrows as Donald dug into his breakfast.

'Is Lady Smythe joining us?' Kitty asked.

'No, not this morning. She too was very upset so she is taking her breakfast on a tray,' Sir Rufus said.

'It's a dreadful state of affairs. The sooner the police can get here the better. I still think it would be wise to look at the servants.' Donald looked meaningfully at the young maid who was tending the dining room.

'I think it far more likely that Lord Barlas's killer is amongst our fellow guests,' Matt replied mildly.

Donald chewed and swallowed his bacon. 'Dash it all, Bryant, that's a bit rich, don't you think? Why would any of us have wished to kill him. Neither Ottilie nor I have any motive to have wished him ill.'

'No? Well, Ottilie is now a very rich young woman. She inherits this castle for a start,' Sir Rufus responded.

'Finnglach is Ottilie's home, and she has her own money anyway.' Donald glared at Sir Rufus.

'Indeed, and now she can access her money herself. No doubt you will now try persuading her into investing in one of those madcap schemes of yours.' Sir Rufus took a sip of his tea.

'That's rich considering that you too will benefit from Lord Barlas's death. Ottilie told me that her father had set up his will to leave the controlling interests in his theatre and film businesses to you.' Donald's voice rose slightly.

'So you were enquiring about the terms of Stephen's will, were you? Interesting.' Sir Rufus smiled smugly at the younger man.

Kitty noticed Donald's grip tighten around his utensils as the tips of his ears turned pink.

'I refuse to lower myself to your odious insinuations,' Donald hissed.

Maxfield entered the room just in time to hear Donald speak. 'Well, good morning, all. I see that we are already eyeing one another with suspicion,' he remarked as he ladled porridge into a bowl before joining them.

'We were merely exploring who amongst us may have had a motive for murdering Stephen,' Sir Rufus said.

Maxfield gave a careless shrug of his shoulders. 'I don't think I have a motive.'

Kitty wondered if this were true. However, she had to admit that she couldn't think of one unless it was to assist his girlfriend out of her very restrictive contract.

Sir Rufus promptly echoed her thoughts. 'Unless you

wished to get your lovely lady friend out of her contract so she could strike it rich in California,' Sir Rufus said. 'I heard a whisper that you yourself had been scouted for a possible film role. I also heard that they only wanted you if Romy came as part of the package.'

'It's true that I have been approached by the same studio that are interested in Romy. However, I can't see Romy tripping outside in a blizzard in her evening gown armed with a gun to shoot Stephen, can you?' Maxfield asked in an even tone as he stirred his porridge.

'But you could have done it,' Donald said looking at Maxfield.

Maxfield shrugged again. 'I could have, but I didn't. Like I said before I had no motive. The contract is Romy's problem, not mine. I am exploring the film avenue as a possible career once my driving adventure ends. I had no tie to Lord Barlas or his studio plans. Also, it may be that Romy would be settled here in England too as Lord Barlas had told her she would get film opportunities at the new studios near London.'

'Is Romy all right, this morning?' Kitty asked. She felt the conversation was in danger of taking a very ugly turn and she intended to keep it on a productive track.

'She has a bad headache. Too much champagne and whisky, combining with murder. I daresay she will surface in time for lunch,' Maxfield said.

'I should go and check on Lynette as she is very distressed by all of this. I shall see you at luncheon,' Sir Rufus excused himself and left the room.

'Pompous old fool,' Donald muttered as soon as the older man had gone.

'Steady on, old chum. I know he can be annoying, but he really seems to have caught a nerve,' Maxfield observed as he pushed his now empty porridge bowl to one side and loaded up his side plate with toast.

'Making disgraceful insinuations,' Donald continued to mutter as he scowled at the butter dish.

'Oh, I see, he has you in the frame for murder, does he?' Maxfield chortled.

'I fail to see the amusement in being accused of murder,' Donald said stiffly.

'Well, somebody killed our host. It definitely wasn't suicide was it, Captain Bryant?' Maxfield looked at Matt.

'The gun is missing, and he was shot by a third party. No, suicide is not a possibility,' Matt confirmed.

Kitty had finished her breakfast and she could see that Matt too was almost ready to leave the table. She was keen to discuss everything with him so they could go over what they had learned over breakfast.

'The sooner the police can come and sort this out the happier I will be. Ottilie and I can return to London where it's safer.' Donald looked around the table as if daring them all to disagree with him.

'If they let anyone leave before they catch whoever did this.' Maxfield stood and stretched. 'Better prepare for a longer stay in Scotland, old boy.'

Once Maxfield had gone, Donald looked at Kitty and Matt. 'What's your assessment on this, Bryant? Is he right? Could they keep us here?'

'Well, they will have to complete their investigation, and someone here has to be responsible for Lord Barlas's death,' Matt said.

Donald nodded. 'I've told you what I think already. The servants,' he added in a stage whisper.

'Lord Barlas told me that his staff have all been with him for years. They have served both him and his father before him. Their connections with Finnglach go back as far as that of the Barlas family. I sincerely doubt that any of the serving staff would wish to murder their master,' Matt said.

Kitty thought she detected a faint look of relief on the face of the serving maid that someone was standing up for the staff.

Donald appeared disgruntled that Matt had failed to agree with his suggestion.

'Who do you think it might be, if not the servants?' Kitty asked.

Donald blinked. 'Um, I don't know. I suppose Sir Rufus would be the obvious choice. Ottilie said that he would get the controlling shares in the theatrical business and the new film studio. That all has to be worth a few bob and Lady Smythe likes money.' He scraped back his chair from the table. 'I'd better go and see how Ottilie is, try and cheer her up a bit.'

Once the dining room door closed behind him, Kitty leaned back in her seat. 'Phew, that was all rather intense.'

Matt grinned at her, the dimple quirking in his cheek. 'It was rather. Shall we head for the library and find ourselves a quietish corner?'

Kitty smiled back. 'My thoughts exactly, my head is spinning.'

* * *

The library was empty and quiet. It had been restored to its pre-séance state with the lamps back on the table. A good-sized fire was burning in the grate and Kitty sank down on one of the leather armchairs with a sigh. Bertie flopped down beside it.

'There are so many books in here, and in Lord Barlas's office. I wonder if any of them provided the words that were pasted into those two warning notes,' Kitty said as she studied the laden shelves.

'Unless you intend checking each one, I doubt we will find out,' Matt said as he took his place opposite her.

'What do we do now?' Kitty asked. 'It seems that Sir Rufus benefits financially from Lord Barlas's death. So does Ottilie, and therefore by extension, Donald. Lady Barlas must also inherit something, presumably money or shares.' Kitty frowned.

'Lord Barlas said she was a wealthy woman in her own right remember? So she is unlikely to have a financial motive for wishing her husband dead. I also can't see how she could have gone outside to kill him.' Matt crossed his legs and smoothed the material of his trousers, brushing away a piece of lint.

'Why was Lord Barlas inside the stone circle? Did he go to meet someone?' Kitty asked. 'It was a terrible night, and no strangers could have come to Finnglach. Surely if it was a meeting, he would have seen them in his study or some other place within the castle.'

'Perhaps he was lured there? He could have seen or heard something that made him pause and go and investigate. When I found him, he was lying in the snow, the piece of coal and the whisky glass he had been carrying were nearby and he had a small silver hip flask of whisky in his coat pocket.' Matt sounded thoughtful.

'Unless then there is a tradition which we are unaware of?' Kitty suggested. 'A twist on the first-footing?'

'You mean he had to placate the guardians of the stone circle before bringing good luck for the year to Finnglach? I suppose Ottilie might know. We can try and find out when she comes downstairs.'

Kitty jumped up and scanned the bookshelves. 'The train steward said there were lots of stories connected with the castle and the circle. Here, this might tell us.' She extracted a slender burgundy bound volume entitled *Myths and Legends of Finnglach*. She seated herself once more and began to flick through the pages.

'Yes, look here. It says that on New Year's Eve the master of Finnglach must offer a toast to the guardians of the circle before re-entering the castle or ill luck, and often a death, will follow.'

Kitty pointed out a paragraph below a line drawing of the stones.

'I wonder how widely known this superstition was?' Matt closed the book and placed it on the table.

Kitty sighed. 'Amongst the guests you mean? From the way they were talking when we first arrived, I imagine they would all know. Sir Rufus and Lady Smythe have been here before and Ottilie would know anyway. It's so difficult trying to sort out who could have had a reason to kill him though. Maxfield is adamant that he had no reason for killing Lord Barlas.'

'Apart from wishing to extricate his girlfriend from her contract. And possibly if he wanted a film contract himself more badly than he's letting on. Didn't someone say he wanted his own race team?' Matt added.

'Is that a strong enough reason?' Kitty asked. She had her own very nebulous thought about Maxfield, but she wondered if perhaps she was imagining things.

'Go on, I can see you have something on your mind.' Matt smiled as he spoke.

'I know this sounds ridiculous, but well, I wondered if perhaps Maxfield is a little fond of Lady Barlas? He was very attentive to her last night, at Romy's expense. He hardly gave her a glance. And a couple of times I've thought I've caught him looking at Lady Barlas in a particular way,' Kitty said.

'She is a wealthy woman and a very pretty one. Lord Barlas was considerably older than her. She and Maxfield did make a handsome couple when they were dancing together last night. Maybe he thought she might fund his racing dreams.' Matt ran his hand through his hair.

'It was just an idea,' Kitty conceded, though she was usually quite perceptive when it came to sniffing out love affairs.

'Do you think Lady Barlas has any feelings towards Maxfield?' Matt asked.

Kitty shrugged. 'I don't know. She certainly appeared happy

enough in her marriage, but I suppose she might have been flattered by the attention.' Matt had posed an interesting question. She didn't think that Lady Barlas had particularly encouraged Maxfield, but she had certainly bestowed plenty of smiles upon him. She had partnered him for several of the games during the afternoon. Sir Rufus had partnered Romy after Lady Smythe had bowed out pleading a headache.

The library door clicked open, and Madam Fortina entered the room.

'Oh, I'm so sorry, am I disturbing you?' She stopped short when she noticed them.

She was wearing an unusual outfit of burnt orange and black. A black chiffon scarf was draped around her throat and Kitty assumed this must be her mark of respect to Lord Barlas.

'No, not at all, please come and join us,' Kitty said.

The older woman made her way a little unsteadily to where they were seated in the corner. Kitty thought she looked tired and as if she had almost aged overnight. Madam Fortina seated herself heavily on one of the leather armchairs.

'How are you feeling this morning?' Kitty asked. 'Last night was so awful, poor Lady Barlas.'

Madam Fortina nodded her head gravely. 'I must confess, I am exhausted. I feel so guilty. I failed to save him you see, despite all the warnings the spirits gave me.' The woman's lip trembled.

'I doubt there was anything more that you could have done,' Matt assured her. 'How is Lady Barlas this morning? Have you seen her?'

'Poor dear Velma. I went to her and to Ottilie. As you can imagine, they are both completely distraught.' Madam Fortina sighed and closed her eyes as she rested her head back on the chair.

'I can imagine,' Kitty said sympathetically.

'It is all so very extraordinary. Have you ever received these kinds of messages before, madam? Messages warning someone that they are in peril?' Matt asked.

The medium opened her eyes and looked at him. 'No, never. Usually, my guides bring messages from those who have gone beyond the veil. Those messages usually comfort those left behind.'

'Have you any idea who would have wished to harm his lordship?' Kitty asked. She was pretty sure that these so-called messages from the spirit realm probably had their roots in something that had occurred in the present world.

'I only pass on the messages I am called to relay, my dear. I know of no one within Stephen's party that would have wished him ill.' Madam Fortina's dark eyes were shrewd.

'Have you been with Lady Barlas for some time?' Kitty was curious about the medium's relationship with the family.

'I have known her for about eighteen months and have travelled with the family exclusively for the last four months at Velma's insistence,' Madam Fortina said.

'She must find your support very helpful. Lord Barlas told us your guides had given her some financial advice.' Kitty tried to keep her tone light and innocent.

Madam Fortina's gaze sharpened. 'Darling Velma asked some questions during some of our readings. I am but the messenger for the spirits, my dear. I have no personal knowledge of financial matters.'

Kitty was tempted to say that she thought it unlikely a long-deceased roman general would know much about the stock market but bit her tongue. It wouldn't be helpful to antagonise the medium if they wished to obtain information.

'What took you to America? I understand you met Lady Barlas out there? I notice that you have an English accent. My father resides in New York, and I am always curious about what leads people to travel.' Ever since Sir Rufus had mentioned that

Madam Fortina was an assumed name, Kitty had wondered about the woman's background.

As Matt had noted, at the end of the Great War there had been a huge rise in the numbers of women claiming to be able to reach those who had passed over during the conflict. But all these years later, it was no longer as popular.

'I have possessed the gift ever since I was a small child. I was married once...' Madam Fortina paused and turned a narrow gold band on her wedding finger. 'Then the war came along and my husband, like so many others, perished. I was left alone with my young son to raise. You understand this, I suspect, Captain Bryant?'

Matt nodded. Kitty thought that no doubt Madam Fortina's husband had been older than Matt when he had gone to war. Matt had been very young, and he too had lost his first wife and child during those terrible years.

'Those years were very hard for me. Afterwards I found other women, like me, who had lost those they loved. They had no grave here at home to mourn at. Some had no answers at all. Their loved ones were still missing. My calling became more insistent and I wanted to try to help those women.' The medium stopped.

'And so you adopted the name Madam Fortina?' Matt asked.

'It was not so far from my maiden name. I had my child to think of, you see. Other children were not kind to him. He was teased at school, told his mother was a witch.' Madam Fortina sighed. 'We moved around a lot and then I had the opportunity to travel to America. My son was older by then and independent. He remained in England, and I moved abroad. I was fortunate enough that my talents had been noticed by a lady from Chicago.'

'Is your son settled now in England?' Kitty asked.

The woman's expression closed and became guarded. 'I

believe so. We do not correspond these days. He would prefer not to acknowledge my profession.'

Kitty felt quite sad for the medium. She could imagine that it must have been a difficult life.

'I'm sorry,' Kitty said.

Madam Fortina bowed her head. 'Thank you. I understand he is happy with the path in life he has chosen, even if he does not wish to acknowledge me.'

The library door opened as Madam Fortina finished speaking and Lady Smythe appeared. Unlike Madam Fortina, Lady Smythe was dressed in darkest navy from head to toe. 'I don't suppose any of you have seen my husband? He's usually in here at this time of day.'

'No, we haven't seen him since breakfast,' Matt replied. 'Can we help you with anything?'

Kitty thought that Lady Smythe appeared on edge, her gaze skittering around the room as if she half suspected Sir Rufus might be hiding behind a bookcase.

The woman came further into the room. 'I just wondered where he might have gone.'

'You are welcome to join us if you like. I think everyone is feeling rather unnerved after last night,' Kitty said.

'It is probably safer to be in company,' Lady Smythe agreed and moved closer to the group. 'Now Stephen is dead it makes one wonder who may be next.' She glanced disparagingly in Madam Fortina's direction. 'I, for one, am taking no chances.'

CHAPTER FIFTEEN

'Do you feel that you are particularly in danger, Lady Smythe?' Matt asked. 'Have you received any threats or warnings?'

Kitty noticed Madam Fortina shift uncomfortably in her chair at Matt's questions. Had Madam Fortina been the person who had left the note on Lord Barlas's pillow and the one that had appeared at the séance?

'No, of course not, but someone in this castle murdered Stephen and apparently the murder weapon has not yet been uncovered.' Lady Smythe shivered dramatically.

'Who do you think may have wished to kill Lord Barlas?' Kitty asked.

'I have no idea, that is what is so unnerving. I mean, if Stephen had argued with anyone or something then perhaps, in the heat of the moment, one could understand but this... this is simply impossible. All those dramatic warnings that he was in danger.' She looked at Madam Fortina. There was a hint of scorn in her tone.

'I merely relay the messages the spirits pass on to me,' Madam Fortina replied.

Lady Smythe shrugged. 'So you say. I mean, that nonsense with the dagger at the séance.'

'I know nothing about what happened that evening.' Madam Fortina rounded on Lady Smythe, her tone fierce. 'That dagger was nothing to do with me. The spirits do not harm people.'

'Even so, Lady Smythe does have a point. Someone gave Lord Barlas a warning or rather a threat using his own dirk. If you say that wasn't you, Madam Fortina, then who was it?' Matt asked.

'I have no idea who it could have been. I thought we had agreed that it was someone's idea of a practical joke,' Madam Fortina said.

'It wasn't the first note that Lord Barlas had received, however. A similar message had been left a few nights earlier on his pillow. He showed it to Kitty and me when we arrived at the castle.' Matt looked at Lady Smythe and Madam Fortina.

Kitty could see that both women appeared astonished by this revelation.

'There was another note?' Lady Smythe said.

'Yes, the same style of message, words cut out and pasted onto paper. Possibly from one of the books in this very room.' Matt glanced at the bookshelves.

Lady Smythe shuddered. 'Ugh, how beastly. It's as if whoever killed him wanted to torture him by letting him know he was in danger. I suppose as well that business of the falling ice bringing down the masonry was planned too?'

'I rather think that's probably the case, yes. I know Lord Barlas didn't think that was an accident and now he is dead. Are you certain that neither of you can think of any arguments or disagreements in the party? Any undercurrents that you may have picked up on that all is not as it seems?' Matt's voice was sterner this time.

Lady Smythe's shoulders sagged. 'We all felt strange

through Christmas. Nothing definite, nothing that one could say was wrong.'

'But?' prompted Kitty.

'There has been a tension in the atmosphere. Rufus has been rather, well, absent, as if he were worried about something. Not that he has confided in me, as usual.' Lady Smythe sounded rather bitter about that. 'Romy, of course, has had several discussions with Stephen about his plans for the film studio and her contract. She was keen to be allowed to go back to America so some of those were rather heated. She is a redhead after all. Maxfield seemed to encourage her one minute and then backtrack the next. Most peculiar really. Velma has been taking every opportunity to try and showcase her own theatrical skills, so I rather think she envisaged a return to the boards. That would be a huge mistake in my opinion.'

'Lord Barlas did not share her enthusiasm to return to her stage career?' Kitty asked.

'Oh, dear me no.' Lady Smythe gave a little laugh. 'No, Velma's talents are not sufficient to mark her out for stardom. He was quite forceful on the issue, insisting she rethink. Oh, he said it nicely, of course. And then Maxfield has seemed a little off too. He and Romy have been arguing a lot, although I think their relationship is quite volatile anyway. He has been paying a lot of attention to Velma again. They knew each other before her marriage to Stephen.'

'Do you feel that what Lady Smythe has described is accurate?' Matt asked Madam Fortina.

The older woman blinked as if her mind had been elsewhere. 'Yes, I think so.' She fidgeted again with the black scarf around her throat. 'If you'll excuse me, I think I have something of a headache coming on.'

Kitty watched as the medium left the library. She couldn't be certain, but she was sure that under the scarf she had noticed ugly reddish blue bruises around Madam Fortina's neck. Had someone attempted to strangle her? A chill ran through her at the thought. Was Madam Fortina being threatened by someone? The same someone who had killed Lord Barlas?

'If you ask me, that woman is the one behind it all. I wouldn't have put it past her to have slipped out and murdered Stephen. I know for a fact he resented the influence she had over Ottilie and on Velma.' Lady Smythe barely waited for the library door to close.

'You are convinced that she is a fraud? I know your husband has made his feelings on the matter clear,' Matt said.

'Of course. Spirits my eye. If you ask me, there are several people here who are not quite what they seem. Madam Fortina is one and Donald Waterford is another. I have caught him out in several untruths. Not that Ottilie will listen to a word against him, of course.' Lady Smythe adjusted the edges of her navy wool jacket and admired her diamond brooch.

'What kind of untruths?' Kitty's curiosity was aroused.

'Oh, claiming to be one of the Waterfords from Ireland. I know them very well and I can assure you that Donald is definitely not related to them at all.' Lady Smythe sniffed. 'A social climber of the worst kind, dreadful. Then there are his various mentions of employment and his so-called business pursuits. I know for a fact that some of those are not as he has presented them. Indeed, I have it on good authority that he was asked to leave at least one place due to financial impropriety. It was all hushed up, of course, as he was involved with the owner's daughter at the time.'

'Oh dear,' Kitty said. 'And Ottilie is unaware of this?'

'Rufus naturally passed the information on to Stephen. He was awaiting the arrival of some documents that would give proof to the allegations. The intention was then for them to both speak to Ottilie and make her aware of her fiancé's background. Now, well, with Stephen's death, I don't know what will happen. If she will listen to Rufus even.' Lady Smythe sighed.

'Poor Ottilie,' Kitty said. 'She does seem to be most unfortunate. Her husband being killed and now her father is murdered, and her fiancé may well be a fortune hunter.'

'At least she has Velma. Velma may be her stepmother and closer to her in age than one would normally feel is appropriate, but Velma is very kind-hearted. I mean, look how she puts up with Romy,' Lady Smythe said.

'I thought Lady Barlas and Miss Fisher were good friends?' Kitty was intrigued.

'Oh my dear, Romy Fisher is quite a minx. She will befriend anyone who she feels might be able to be of use to her. She got in with Velma as she wanted to spend time in England and thought a contract with Stephen to appear in the West End and then his films would make her famous. When she discovered she was not getting the biggest parts and that the studio side of things was not yet up and running, well, she wanted out. She managed to get a big studio in California interested in her through Maxfield, but she now can't get out of her contract with Stephen. Or, rather she couldn't. I imagine his demise may make things easier for her.' Lady Smythe nodded meaningfully. 'And, of course, she is man mad.'

Kitty looked at Lady Smythe. 'I don't follow you.'

Lady Smythe leaned forward conspiratorially and lowered her voice. 'She will go after anything in trousers. If I were you, I would keep a close watch on your husband around Miss Fisher.' She leaned back with a satisfied smile on her lips.

Kitty wondered if Romy had been the cause of the argument between Sir Rufus and his wife the other day. It certainly sounded as if that might be the case. Sir Rufus had certainly appeared to enjoy being partnered with Romy for the games afternoon when Lady Smythe had claimed a headache.

'I see. I hadn't realised,' Kitty said.

Matt appeared to have been pretending he hadn't heard any of the conversation by busying himself with adding more wood to the fire. Bertie yawned and stretched in satisfaction at the renewed blaze.

'I think the emergency generator is still running but even with the fires it's still quite cold,' he said as he retook his seat.

'I shall be glad when the power and the telephone lines are restored. The generator really is only sufficient to run the kitchen area. The sooner the police can arrive the better.' Lady Smythe gave a dramatic shiver. 'Do you think they will find out who is behind this?' She looked at Matt.

'I certainly hope so. It's a most uncomfortable position to be in right now,' Matt said.

Kitty agreed. Their position was uncomfortable in more than one way. Their fellow guests had no idea that she and Matt had been invited to Finnglach by Lord Barlas because he had feared for his life. Now he was dead, and they were trapped in the castle by the weather with his killer. There was no way to escape or to summon assistance.

'At least Stephen always ensured that Finnglach has a good supply of food and fuel,' Lady Smythe said.

'Have you been here before during the winter when this has happened?' Kitty asked.

'Some years ago, when Ottilie was married to Marcus. The snow was very bad, and we were cut off. Stephen was a widower then and the house party was smaller with Ottilie's former governess, a Miss Ravenhurst, and some cast members of a revue Stephen had running in London at the time. It took three days before the power and telephone were restored and anyone could get through to the village,' Lady Smythe said.

'Let us hope it takes less time for things to be resolved this time.' Kitty hoped the telephone at least might be restored before too long.

'I think I shall go and try to find Rufus. I wonder where on earth he has gone. It really is most inconsiderate of him. He knows that I am quite on edge right now.' Lady Smythe excused herself.

'That was illuminating.' Matt smiled at Kitty once Lady Smythe had departed.

'Very,' Kitty agreed. 'Are we any further forward, do you think?'

'We know more about Madam Fortina, and Lady Smythe was very forthcoming about her fellow guests.' Matt leaned back in his seat and frowned.

Kitty quickly told him of her observations regarding Madam Fortina's choice of attire.

'You think the scarf is to hide bruising?' Matt immediately sat forward once more. 'You think she was attacked? Or threatened? But why would she not say anything?'

'I don't know, but I'm sure she has bruises on her throat.' Kitty too was worried about the implications of those marks.

'We need to keep a close watch on her, she could be in danger.' Matt met Kitty's gaze and she could tell his thoughts mirrored her own.

* * *

Matt was thoughtful as Kitty rang the bell for the servants to request a tray of tea. She had scarcely retaken her seat when one of the maids appeared, followed by Maxfield Cotter. The request was given to the maid as Maxfield flung himself down carelessly onto a vacant chair.

'Tea, eh? Topping idea. The first refuge of the English nation in times of trouble,' Maxfield said as the girl disappeared to prepare a tray.

'You've just missed Lady Smythe and Madam Fortina. They were both here earlier. Lady Smythe is looking for her husband. I don't suppose you've seen him anywhere, have you?' Kitty asked.

'Sir Rufus? The poor man was hiding out in the music room. You may have noticed that his good lady wife likes to keep a close eye on him,' Maxfield replied laughingly.

'Does she have a reason to watch him?' Kitty asked.

Maxfield grinned at her. 'He does have quite an eye for a pretty face, old Rufus. He's very pally with Romy at the moment.'

Kitty's brow raised. 'Does that bother you at all?' she asked as the maid reappeared pushing a small marble-topped gilt cart laden with tea things.

Maxfield's smile widened. 'No, not really. Romy and I are chums but it's nothing serious for either of us.'

The maid parked the trolley close to Kitty's chair and took her leave when Kitty assured her that she would serve the tea herself.

'I wonder when the telephone lines will be restored?' Kitty said as she poured out the tea and passed around the cups.

Maxfield straightened himself up in his seat and helped himself to a shortbread biscuit from the trolley. 'I don't know. I asked the butler chappie and he said that they were still down. He's been trying them every half an hour.'

'There were certainly some large icicles that the gardeners had knocked down this morning from the walls of the castle,' Matt said. 'If the same kind had formed on the power and telephone lines it's little wonder that we are cut off.'

'Poor old Stephen, he dodged one possible fatality when that whacking great ice lump came crashing down, only to go and get himself shot.' Maxfield took a bite of his biscuit and chewed thoughtfully.

Bertie had edged closer to the trolley when he had realised that biscuits might be in the offing. He positioned himself close to Maxfield, looking at him with large, begging eyes.

'And now everyone is eyeing up everyone else in case they might be next,' Matt replied. He found Maxfield an interesting character. Of all the people in the castle he seemed the one least bothered by the murder. Was it because of his career? Perhaps dying held less fear for him when he confronted risk and the possibility of death every time he ventured onto the racetrack.

Maxfield brushed the crumbs from the front of his dark-green tweed jacket. 'Who is your money on then, Bryant? You and Mrs Bryant must be outside bets as the murderers since the accident with the ice and the warnings from our resident medium all started before you arrived.'

'I don't know. It all seems quite peculiar. I mean why would you warn a person if you intended to kill him? For that reason, I am disinclined to think that Madam Fortina had anything to do with it,' Matt said.

'Interesting. You see, my money would have been on the old bird. She has her hooks into Velma. Both she and Ottilie both pay very close attention to everything Madam Fortina and her hokey roman spirit guide say.' Maxfield drained his tea and selected another couple of biscuits. He passed one to Bertie.

'And why does that give Madam Fortina a motive?' Matt asked. He was curious to hear Maxfield's reasoning.

'Well, old Stephen didn't like it. He would have liked to give our Velma's spiritual advisor the old heave ho. He was quite strait-laced really. He disapproved of anything that didn't fit his ideas. One of his oldest friends had an affair with one of the dancers Stephen employed and he sacked the girl and cut his pal off. Never spoke to him again. Any kind of dishonesty really wound him up.' Maxfield leaned back and munched on his biscuit.

'I wonder that he fell for Madam Fortina then,' Kitty said. 'He must have known from his theatrical experience that she was not on the level.' She guessed that Lord Barlas had tolerated the medium to humour his wife.

Maxfield appeared to consider Kitty's statement. 'I think he overlooked it because she brought a great deal of comfort to Ottilie at a time when nothing and no one else could help her. Then, of course, he met Velma and so he sort of tolerated her presence.'

'Sir Rufus and Lady Smythe seem to believe that Donald Waterford is also not all he seems,' Matt said.

Maxfield grinned. 'Yes, Sir Rufus seems to make a point of needling dear Donald, as indeed do I. A bad trait, I must confess, but his ears do turn a delightful shade of pink when he is annoyed.'

Kitty choked on her tea and Matt had to pat her on her back. 'Steady on, old thing.'

'Oh dear, Donald does get riled up quite easily. Lady Smythe said she had proof that he was a fortune hunter,' Kitty said when she had recovered herself.

'Not that Ottilie is likely to listen to any criticism of her darling fiancé,' Maxfield said.

'Apparently Sir Rufus was awaiting written proof, then he and Lord Barlas had intended to talk to Ottilie,' Matt said.

'Interesting stuff. That would seem to put dear old Donald in the frame then. He will be in for a juicy payout when he marries Ottilie. If her father had put a stop to the wedding, then that would definitely give him a very strong motive, don't you think?' Maxfield said.

Matt privately agreed that the racing driver had a good point. It did seem as if Donald would have had a great deal to lose if Lord Barlas had convinced his daughter to break off the engagement. He also wondered what would have happened if Ottilie had refused to end her relationship.

CHAPTER SIXTEEN

Several guests were absent from the lunch table. Lady Barlas remained in her room, as did Ottilie. Romy put in a slightly late appearance, her face white and strained. She apologised as she took her seat at the table just as everyone was finishing their first course.

'There is no need to apologise, my dear,' Sir Rufus assured her, earning himself a sharp look from his wife.

Madam Fortina was silent throughout the meal, seated beside Donald. Kitty noticed that her scarf was now wound even more closely around her neck. There was no more news about the telephone lines or the power being reconnected.

Outside the castle the weather appeared grey and dull with no indication at present of a possible thaw. At least the wind appeared to have dropped and no further snow had fallen. Kitty would have dearly liked to have wrapped up and ventured outside for a closer look at the area where Lord Barlas had been found.

Given the thick layer of ice that glistened on the paths whenever a weak ray of winter sun forced its way through the cloud, she decided it would be prudent to remain indoors. At least for now, frustrating though it might be.

When lunch was concluded the party all drifted together to the drawing room where at least the fire made a cheerful blaze. The remaining gay decorations from Christmas seemed to make a hollow mockery of the events of Hogmanay. Festive cards with pictures of jolly robins and the tinsel-clad tree appeared out of place.

The ladies settled themselves on various chairs. Matt joined Kitty on the sofa and Sir Rufus was commandeered by Lady Smythe into assisting with a jigsaw. Donald stood near the Christmas tree looking glum, while Maxfield paced restlessly about the room. Lord Barlas's dog watched him warily from his place near the hearth. Bertie lay beside him.

'Dash it all, there must be something we can do!' Maxfield turned on his heel and glared at his fellow guests.

'What do you suggest?' Sir Rufus asked. 'The lines are down, there are snowdrifts that the horses cannot get through and the servants say a tree has fallen blocking the road to the village.'

'Surely we can at least try. There are skis and snowshoes in the boot room. I can't stay cooped up in here much longer,' Maxfield said.

'Are you proposing trying to get through to the village?' Matt asked.

'Yes, why not? At least if I've given it a go, I'll feel as if I've done something. I'm going to see what I can find.' Maxfield tilted his chin belligerently as if expecting Matt to argue with him.

'Do you have experience in these kinds of conditions?' Sir Rufus asked.

'Enough to give it a bash,' Maxfield said.

'Then I'll come with you.' Donald's unexpected agreement with Maxfield's proposal took everyone by surprise.

'Donald, are you certain about this? It sounds like madness.' Lady Smythe gaped at him.

'Maxfield is right, we owe it to Stephen to at least try. I've done a fair bit of winter sports. I think we could do it.' Donald sounded determined.

'It should be two people in case there is a problem,' Matt said thoughtfully.

Maxfield's face lit up in an impish grin. 'Come on then, Donald old son, let's see if we can get some help.'

The two men left the room together.

'Do you think this is a wise idea?' Sir Rufus asked Matt as the door closed behind them.

'Probably not, but they sounded as if they were set on the idea. At least they can try,' Matt said.

Kitty thought it unlikely that they would make it through the forest, but perhaps if the villagers had started to try and clear from their end it might be possible. It also occurred to her that if one of them were Lord Barlas's murderer then they would be unable to escape if someone else were accompanying them.

'Max won't settle unless he has made an attempt,' Romy said quietly. 'He thrives on adventure. He is a first-class skier.'

'There are only a few hours of daylight left and it's a dark day as it is. I hope they remember to take torches.' Lady Smythe glanced at the window.

Madam Fortina had remained silent throughout the exchanges. She had seated herself in her customary spot away from everyone else on the edge of the room. Kitty wished there was some way she could get the woman by herself. She wanted to know about the bruising she thought she had seen around the medium's neck.

Romy picked up a magazine and flicked idly through the pages. She seemed unconcerned that her erstwhile boyfriend was engaged on a hazardous expedition through the forest. It seemed to add weight to Maxfield's claim that he and Romy had a loose relationship.

The afternoon wore on and the servants arrived to light the oil lamps.

'I wonder how Maxfield and Donald are getting on.' Kitty crossed to the window to peer out into the gathering gloom. 'I do hope they are safe.'

'The whole exercise is ridiculous. They could get themselves into real trouble if they get stuck in the forest in the dark.' Sir Rufus had risen from the jigsaw table and joined her to peer outside.

'I hope they have either reached the village or had enough sense to turn around and come back,' Romy agreed as the trolley for afternoon tea was brought into the drawing room.

Kitty looked at Matt. If anything had happened to the two men, then no one would know. If the telephone was still down, there would be no way they could call the castle to say they had arrived safely at the village. Similarly, if they were in trouble in the forest the castle couldn't send a search party out in the dark.

They had just poured the tea when Ottilie joined them. Her eyes were rimmed with red and she looked tired and drawn.

'Oh, my dear, come and sit by the fire. Let me get you some tea.' Lady Smythe bustled forward to look after her.

'I was hoping to find Donald. Do you know where he might be?' Ottilie asked as Lady Smythe pressed a china teacup and saucer into her hand.

Madam Fortina, who had moved closer to the fire during the course of the afternoon, broke the momentary awkward silence.

'He and Maxfield have set off to try to reach the village to get help.'

Ottilie's cup rocked in its saucer spilling some of her tea. 'What? They have gone into the forest in this weather? Did no one try to stop them?' She looked around until she caught Sir Rufus's gaze. 'Did you not say anything?'

'Now, now, my dear, we all advised them against the venture, but they wouldn't be swayed. I am certain that if they cannot reach the village they will turn back and will return soon,' Sir Rufus soothed.

'And what if they fall and break an ankle? The forest is full of tree roots and pitfalls that get hidden by the snow and it's so dark out there. I know Donald is a good skier but he has no idea what the forest is like. I lost Marcus on a day like this. I couldn't bear to lose Donald too.' Ottilie gazed wildly at the now curtain-covered window.

'Have no fears, they are safe. The spirits have assured me,' Madam Fortina spoke confidently in a calm voice.

Ottilie burst into a flood of tears as Lady Smythe rescued her teacup and saucer and looked on helplessly.

'Pshaw, piffle, spirits indeed,' Sir Rufus muttered under his breath.

'Ottilie, I am sure they will be all right. Maxfield is an experienced skier and Donald seems a sensible man. You said he was a good skier too. They won't take any risks, and they are together.' Romy knelt on the floor beside her and took her hand in hers.

Ottilie sniffed and blew her nose on a lace-edged handkerchief. 'Thank you, all of you. I can't help but worry. Donald told me once that he was used to this kind of weather. It's just that obviously I lost Marcus in a snowstorm on the mountains and now with Daddy being killed, I couldn't bear for anything else to happen. I simply couldn't bear it.'

'Of course not, darling, we do understand, but Marcus was killed in an avalanche. There is no danger of that here,' Romy replied soothingly and glared around at everyone else to ensure they all agreed.

'Nettie, you are certain? The spirits have come through to reassure you they are safe?' Ottilie looked at the medium as she dried her eyes.

'The spirits have spoken. All is well.' Madam Fortina was calm and unruffled.

'I wish I could be so certain.' Sir Rufus's words were almost inaudible, and Kitty was thankful that Ottilie had not appeared to hear him. Madam Fortina gave him a sharp look.

'It would be good if they have reached the village. They can return tomorrow with the police,' Ottilie said in a slightly brighter tone.

Kitty saw Madam Fortina's hand move to her neck scarf as if to adjust it slightly.

'I'm sure we shall all be relieved to see the police so they can get to the bottom of all of this,' Lady Smythe said.

'How is your stepmother, my dear? Have you seen her this afternoon?' Sir Rufus asked Ottilie.

'She was sleeping when I looked into her room just before I came down. Poor Velma, she and Daddy were very happy together. I know when they married a good many people thought it couldn't be for love, but I really think it was. Daddy adored Velma and she loved him.' Ottilie's face clouded and she looked as if she was about to cry again. 'I just don't know who could have done this or why. I wish Donald were here. What was he thinking to do something so reckless?'

'I'm sure he and Maxfield will be back soon. If not tonight then first thing tomorrow, full of their adventures in the snow and bringing help,' Romy said bracingly. 'We must be brave and stay positive.'

Kitty hoped the actress was right.

. . .

There was still no word at dinner and the two men had not returned. Lady Barlas had remained in her room and Ottilie had also been persuaded to go upstairs to rest. After dinner, Romy tried the wireless in the drawing room, but there was still no power.

'I thought the generator might have provided enough electricity to power the wireless. I'd hoped we might at least be able to check the weather forecast,' Romy said as she finally admitted defeat.

'Stephen once told me the generator mainly powers the kitchen area of the castle. As for the weather, it looks as if it is snowing again.' Sir Rufus had drawn back the curtain to peer outside. 'It's not heavy though so it may stop soon.'

'I hope Donald and Maxfield have reached the village safely,' Matt said as Sir Rufus stepped away from the window and made his way to the drinks trolley.

Madam Fortina was seated next to Romy on the sofa.

'I have told you that the spirits have spoken. They are quite safe.' Her tone was resigned.

'Spirits! I don't know why you persist with this nonsense. It may have worked on Velma and Ottilie, but Stephen could see through you. Don't you think you've done enough damage with your hokey warnings and talk of spirits and ghosts?' Sir Rufus rounded on the medium.

'You may believe what you will. I am not forcing you to believe that I am speaking the truth.' Madam Fortina appeared unmoved by the older man's outburst.

'If it weren't for Velma and Ottilie, Stephen would have sent you packing ages ago,' Sir Rufus continued, his hands clenching into fists.

'Stop it! Just stop! Nettie has done nothing to you,' Romy cried out. 'So what if you don't believe her. She has given a great deal of comfort to Velma and Ottilie. Why are you saying these things now? And weren't her warnings right? How do any of us know what Lord Barlas intended?'

Kitty could see that although the medium didn't say anything more, she looked a little shaken by Sir Rufus's attack.

'You're right, Romy my dear. I apologise. I think my nerves are somewhat frayed by all that has happened. Stephen was one of my oldest friends.' Sir Rufus's hands unfurled, and he turned to the drinks cart.

He poured himself a shot of whisky and drank it straight down, before refilling his glass.

'All we can do is wait until morning for news of Maxfield and Donald. Perhaps some of the gardening staff can set off after them as soon as it's light,' Matt suggested.

'If this blasted snow hasn't covered their tracks, they might be able to check which route they took. See if they tried to follow the road through the woods.' Sir Rufus sat down and took a sip from his glass. His earlier outburst of anger having seemingly evaporated.

'What do you think will happen when the police do come?' Romy asked.

Sir Rufus blinked and took another sip of his drink. 'I expect they will want to talk to Captain Bryant about what he saw when he found Stephen. Then they'll talk to all of us, looking for alibis and such. After that I don't know really. I mean the gun the murderer used is still missing.'

'Everyone was moving around that night, weren't they? After midnight, I mean, before Stephen went out to do the first-footing thing and we all went to the hall,' Romy said.

'That's true,' Lady Smythe agreed. 'You went to fetch your sheet music and I think Maxfield went to get more champagne, rather than disturbing the servants.'

'Donald went to fetch Ottilie's shawl because she was cold. You went somewhere too, didn't you, Rufus?' Romy asked.

'Um, yes, I believe I fetched some more cigars from my

room. I think I saw you, Madam Fortina, on the landing.' He looked at the medium.

'Velma asked me to bring some sage from my kit ready to cleanse the house after the first-footing.' Madam Fortina picked up the tapestry-covered handbag she had next to her chair and opened it. 'It's still in here.'

Kitty could see there was a small bunch of what appeared to be dried grey grasses bundled together. She could smell the faint herby scent.

'After the séance was interrupted, she was concerned that there might be a bad energy in the house,' Madam Fortina explained.

'There was almost an hour in which everyone was in and out of the drawing room. What time did anyone last see Lord Barlas?' Matt asked.

'He went to get ready just after half past twelve. I remember because Velma was reminding him to wear a hat,' Lady Smythe said.

'It's hopeless, we had all been celebrating and everyone was everywhere. I don't think any of us can be certain about anything,' Romy said.

Kitty thought the girl was right. She and Matt had already tried to recall who had been missing before Lord Barlas was killed but people had been moving around and virtually everyone had been in and out of the room at some point.

'I expect too the police will be looking for motives for his death,' Kitty said, keeping her voice level.

'Very true. They usually check financial reasons first,' Matt agreed. 'For instance, who benefits from his will, that kind of thing.'

Kitty felt rather than saw Sir Rufus and Lady Smythe both stiffen slightly.

'I think Stephen updated his will a few weeks ago, didn't

he?' Lady Smythe came and rested her hand lightly on her husband's shoulder as she spoke.

'I believe so, my dear. His old will was made just after he married Velma and he told me he wished to update a few things,' Sir Rufus said.

'Did he say what kind of things he wanted to change, sir?' Matt asked.

Sir Rufus finished his drink. 'Well, many of the things in it were the same. Ottilie naturally inherits the castle and the estate. She has her trust and her late mother's jewels. Velma gets the London flat and the country house in Norfolk. She also retains her marriage monies and her own jewels. It was really the business end of things. Stephen naturally wished to ensure the controlling shares in the theatrical company and the film studio would be in safe and experienced hands.'

'I presume that would be you, sir?' Kitty asked.

'I think that was his intention, my dear, yes,' Sir Rufus said.

'How did that differ from his original will?' Matt asked.

'Velma would have inherited the controlling shares in the theatre company and the new film studio. I already have a substantial stake, but she would have effectively have taken Stephen's place on the board. I believe Stephen had come to realise that Velma lacked sufficient business acumen to take on such a demanding role.' Sir Rufus set down his empty glass.

'I expect the police will be able to check his will. I take it that it must be kept in the safe in his office?' Matt asked.

'Stephen always kept all his important documents there, yes, so I suppose it must be in there.' Kitty noticed a slight tremor in Sir Rufus's hand as he reached up to pat Lady Smythe's hand.

Romy gave a slight shudder. 'All of this is so awful.'

'I wish we knew where the gun was. That scares me more than anything. The idea that whoever did this still has it hidden away somewhere and could use it again whenever they wished.' Lady Smythe moved around to sit closer to the fire.

'Perhaps the police will find it. No doubt they will conduct another search,' Kitty tried to sound reassuring. Privately she thought it unlikely to be discovered if the servants who knew every inch of the building had failed to uncover it.

After all, they had searched Finnglach Castle several times. Both after the gun first went missing and again after Lord Barlas's death. Yet someone in the castle knew where it was, and that person had already committed one murder.

CHAPTER SEVENTEEN

The following morning dawned grey and dismal. Kitty was relieved to see that the snow Sir Rufus had noticed falling the night before hadn't continued. It seemed to her that something of a thaw had started to set in and the tiny icicles above her bedroom window were beginning to slowly melt, dripping down onto the sill.

She and Matt went down early to breakfast. Matt stopped the butler in the hallway before they entered the dining room to ask if the telephone line was restored.

'No, sir, not as yet. I am still trying every half an hour,' the man assured him.

'And is there any news from Mr Waterford and Mr Cotter?' Matt asked.

The butler looked regretful. 'No, sir. I have dispatched two of the gardening staff to look for them.'

Kitty could only hope that good news would come through soon.

They dined alone, no one else appeared to be up and about inside the castle beyond the servants.

'It looks as if a thaw has begun. If the path is less slippery, shall we try outside?' Kitty asked as she gave Lord Barlas's faithful old dog one half of a sausage from her breakfast plate and Bertie the other half.

'No doubt you would like to see where I found Lord Barlas for yourself?' Matt asked as he finished his cup of tea.

Kitty nodded. 'Of course. There may be something that was overlooked. It was so dark when you found him, and the weather was too bad to go out yesterday.' She was keen to see the spot for herself. No doubt when the police did arrive they would not be permitted to access the circle for a time.

Matt grinned. 'We may as well take a look. Let's hope Maxfield and Donald arrive soon with the police.'

'I hope they made it to the village. A night in the forest in this weather wouldn't be good.' Kitty hated to think of the state the two men might be in if they hadn't found shelter.

They hurried off to the boot room and donned their heavy outdoor clothing. Kitty laced her boots and shivered as Matt opened the door to the outside.

'Brr, the ice might be melting but it's still bitterly cold out here.' She held on to Matt's arm as they negotiated their way past the icy patches and on to the thinner, crunchy layer of snow that covered the path to the circle. Bertie trotted along with them in his bright-red coat.

'My guess is that Lord Barlas asked the servants to prepare this path in readiness for first-footing. If that book you found is to be believed, then that would be why he ventured off the route around to the front door of the castle,' Matt said.

Kitty kept a sharp look out as they walked the short distance to the standing stones. Once again, she was conscious of that feeling of dread filling her as they grew closer to the entrance. She could see where the wind had scoured the short stubbly grass almost free of snow, blowing it along to pile it in deep drifts around the outer bases of the large rocks.

'I found him over here, just shy of that big slab rock in the centre.' Matt raised his arm to indicate where he had discovered Lord Barlas.

Kitty felt a little sick when she spotted the dried red-brown stains on the surface of the exposed frozen grass. The snowman that had been there on their first visit had lost his hat. The wind must have blown it off and had sent it scuttling to rest against the base of the table rock. Bertie gave it an interested sniff.

Automatically, Kitty moved to pick it up and released Matt's arm as she crossed the centre to replace it on the snowman's head. It seemed to her that the snowy figure was leaning and leering at her as she approached. She wondered afresh who might have built him, and why was he in the circle, lurking in the shadows of the trees?

As she pushed the hat down on the snowman's head, the top part of the body crumbled causing the head to topple and roll towards her feet. His black stone eyes staring up at her with his carrot nose now at a strange angle. Kitty squeaked in surprise at the unexpected event.

'Darling, are you all right?' Matt turned from where he had been studying the stains on the grass.

Kitty had recovered her wits. 'Yes, it's just the snowman. I tried to put his hat back on and the head fell off.'

Matt chuckled and came over to her. 'Oh dear, shall we try to fix him?'

Kitty poked at the top of the now headless body with a gloved finger. The snow was now quite soft, and she realised that what little sun there was had already started to melt the back of the snowman.

'There's something hard in here.' Her hand had encountered something much firmer than snow inside the snowman. Surely, he hadn't been constructed around a smaller standing stone?

Her curiosity aroused, she dug down and her fingers wrapped around something that she immediately recognised.

'Matt, it's the gun. Whoever built this snowman hid the gun inside it.' She pulled out the missing firearm, holding the barrel gingerly. 'They must have shot Lord Barlas and then pressed it inside the body of the snowman.'

Matt pulled his woollen scarf from around his neck, and she placed the gun inside it.

'I can't see any footprints,' Kitty said as she peered around at the frozen clumps of grass looking for any kind of impressions in the soil.

'I think the ground is too hard. Look at how the wind has blown the snow clear of this part of the circle to pile it up on the other side.' Matt examined the surface of the ground carefully.

'Do you think this is where the murderer hid to shoot Lord Barlas?' Kitty asked as she turned around to look back at the spot where Matt had said he had found the body.

'The angle looks right. They could have been waiting between our snowy chum here and the big stone there.' Matt indicated a gap between the remains of the snowman and the nearest standing stone. 'They would have had a good line of sight and the snowman to help hide them from view. No one inside the castle would have heard the shot. The walls are too thick and we had music playing.'

'Do you think this is where the gun has been all along? It would explain why it was never found inside the castle, and no one destroys a snowman, do they? Everyone just waits for them to melt. It would have been simple enough to listen to the weather on the wireless in case the forecast changed,' Kitty said.

'I think you're probably right. The amount of planning that has gone into this murder is quite frightening.' Matt's mouth was set in a grim line.

'We had better return to the house and tell them the gun has been recovered.' Kitty slipped her hand into the crook of Matt's arm.

'Yes, there may even be some news of Maxfield and Donald

by now,' Matt said. 'Come on, old thing, let's go inside and get warmed up.'

They left their outdoor things in the boot room and made their way to the drawing room. Matt continued to hold the gun, carrying it carefully hidden inside the scarf. Kitty was certain that there would be no fingerprints. It had been so cold out the killer would have surely worn gloves. Not to mention that the wet snow had probably cleaned it anyway when the gun had been thrust inside the body of the snowman.

Sir Rufus and Lady Smythe were seated beside the fire. Ottilie and Romy had taken over the jigsaw and a rather wan Lady Barlas was resting on the sofa, her head on an eau de nil silk-covered cushion. Madam Fortina, clad in vibrant green with the black scarf around her throat was at her side.

Everyone looked up when they entered the room. Kitty supposed they were hoping to hear news of Maxfield and Donald.

Kitty headed for the fireplace, keen to warm herself back up after their foray into the snow. Lord Barlas's dog raised his head as she approached, and Bertie settled down once more beside him with a sigh.

'Sorry, old boy, no sausages now,' Kitty said as she held her frozen fingers out towards the crackling flames.

'Have you been outside? It still looks terribly cold out there,' Lady Smythe asked as Matt came to join Kitty. She looked at the woollen bundle in his hand.

'We needed some air,' Kitty said. 'And while we were out, we noticed the snowman in the stone circle had begun to melt.'

'A snowman? In the circle?' Lady Barlas raised herself to a sitting position, a look of astonishment on her face.

'We saw it when we first arrived and assumed some of the servants' children may have built it,' Kitty explained.

'No, there are no young children here,' Ottilie said. She too looked puzzled. 'None of the staff would have built something in the circle. They are too superstitious about the stones. They never go there.'

'Whoever did build the snowman built it on purpose to hide the gun used to kill Lord Barlas.' Matt revealed the firearm hidden in the scarf. His face was grim.

There was an audible collective gasp of surprise from the house party guests.

'The gun was inside the snowman?' Lady Smythe stared at Matt. 'However did you find it?'

'The snowman's hat had blown off and when I tried to put it back, I accidentally decapitated him and the gun was inside the body, concealed by the snow,' Kitty answered the question.

Sir Rufus peered more closely at the gun. 'That definitely looks like Stephen's gun.'

'I'll make certain that it is kept securely under lock and key until the police arrive.' Matt covered the weapon with the scarf once more.

Ottilie abandoned her attempt at the jigsaw and paced about the room. 'I wish Donald would come back. I've hardly slept all night worrying about him.'

'The gardeners set off after them early this morning,' Matt assured her.

The sudden and unexpected ring of the black Bakelite telephone on the side table startled them all. Matt acted swiftly to reach it first, narrowly beating Ottilie to lift the receiver to his ear.

'Hello, yes, this is Finnglach Castle, Captain Bryant speaking.'

The others had all risen from their seats and had come to stand around him in a circle.

'Yes, I see. That is correct, sir,' Matt responded to the unknown voice on the other end of the line.

Kitty could hear that it was a man's voice, but the connection appeared poor, and Matt had to ask whoever it was to repeat themselves several times.

'I see, yes, thank you. We shall expect you at some time today.' He replaced the receiver. 'That was the police. Donald and Maxfield reached the village safely and sent a message to the police station in the town first thing this morning.'

'Oh, thank heavens for that.' Ottilie sank down onto the nearest chair as if her legs could no longer support her. 'And they are all right? Donald and Maxfield?'

'I believe so. The man said that the villagers have cleared the fallen trees from the road in the forest and the police will be here in a while,' Matt confirmed.

Lady Barlas had retaken her seat on the sofa and sobbed quietly into her handkerchief.

'Now then, the police will soon be here, my dear, and they will get to the bottom of this ghastly mess,' Sir Rufus assured her as he made his way back to his place by the fire.

Madam Fortina was attempting to comfort Lady Barlas, offering to ring for tea.

'It seems your spirit messengers were correct after all,' Romy observed to the medium as she took her place back at the jigsaw table.

Madam Fortina gave the girl a baleful look. 'Of course.'

Kitty couldn't help feeling relieved herself at the news that assistance was finally arriving. She was also pleased to hear that Maxfield and Donald had made it safely to the village.

'Now the telephone is working let us hope it won't be long before the electricity is also restored,' Lady Smythe said.

The mood in the room had lifted considerably since the unexpected telephone call and everyone appeared much more cheerful. Even Lady Barlas, when she had dried her tears, looked calmer and less distraught.

Kitty wondered how the group would take it when they discovered that she and Matt had been invited to join the party in their capacity as private investigators. They would also have to tell the police and give them all the information they had uncovered so far.

They would have to hand over the note from Lord Barlas's pillow and the one attached to his dagger, with the fragment of the will, the gun and the balloon. It would be very interesting indeed to discover if there was a copy of the will inside the safe, and, if so, which one. The original one made just after his marriage or the later one that Sir Rufus had told them about.

It was after lunch when there was a kerfuffle at the front of the castle. Ottilie had been watching from the windows for any sign of her fiancé and Maxfield returning.

'There is a horse and cart approaching,' she called through the open door of the drawing room.

By the time the horse had jingled to a stop near the front door, everyone had assembled in the hall eager to greet whoever was on board. Kitty waited with Matt to see who entered the castle.

The butler opened the door letting in a gust of cold air and a sprinkle of frozen snow as Donald and Maxfield came in first. Ottilie rushed forward to greet her fiancé as he removed his cap and muffler. Romy stepped up to meet Maxfield who looked quite pleased with himself, Kitty thought.

They were accompanied by three other men. Two of them wore a constable's uniform under their great dark-wool cloaks. The third was a man of medium height in his fifties with receding faded auburn hair and a steely glint in his eye as he looked around at the assembled party.

'I have arranged for tea in the drawing room, my lady,' the butler murmured to Lady Barlas once he had closed the great oak door of the castle against the elements.

'Thank you.' Lady Barlas inclined her head gratefully.

She directed the group once the newcomers had divested themselves of their outdoor things to join them in the drawing room. The constables were dispatched to the kitchen for their refreshments and to warm up, with instructions to return to the hall in thirty minutes.

Kitty glanced at Matt. It seemed the inspector or chief inspector did not intend to waste time dallying about. Once everyone had returned to the drawing room, the formalities of introductions were made.

'Thank you, I am Chief Inspector Innes and will be leading this investigation.' The chief inspector looked around the assembled group with a keen eye. 'Firstly, I would like to extend my sympathy to you, Lady Barlas, and you, Mrs Tremaine, on your sad loss.' He nodded to Velma and Ottilie. 'I appreciate that this may be very difficult for you, and I wish to assure you that I shall do my utmost to discover whoever was responsible for this terrible crime as soon as possible.'

The chief inspector spoke with a soft Scottish burr. He accepted a cup of tea from the maid and sipped appreciatively. 'I shall, of course, need to speak to all of you so I can establish clearly what occurred here on New Year's Eve.'

Kitty saw several of the party exchanging glances. Maxfield and Donald were seated on either side of the hearth while they warmed themselves after the long journey by cart. Ottilie had perched herself on the arm of Donald's chair.

Madam Fortina sat beside Lady Barlas and Romy Fisher on her other side. Sir Rufus and Lady Smythe had taken the seats closer to the window. Kitty had chosen a seat beside Matt where they had a view of everyone in the room.

The chief inspector finished his drink and placed his cup down on the table and turned to Matt. 'Now, Captain Bryant, is it? I understand from Mr Cotter and Mr Waterford that you discovered Lord Barlas's body?' The policeman took out his notebook.

'Yes, sir, that's correct,' Matt confirmed.

'And where is his lordship resting now?' the policeman asked.

'I would be happy to show you, sir. I can fill in some of the information you may wish to know on the way,' Matt said.

Kitty guessed that her husband would probably take the opportunity of showing the inspector Lord Barlas's body to pass on the rest of their discoveries and the background to the murder.

'Very good.' The chief inspector followed Matt from the room, leaving the rest of the group to break out into animated discussion as soon as the door closed.

'What happened to you both yesterday? How long did it take you to reach the village?' Ottilie fired questions at Donald.

'It took ages, we had to alternate between using snowshoes and the skis. More than once we almost turned back as it got dark dashed quickly under the trees,' Donald said.

'Once we reached where the road was blocked, we had to make quite a detour into the forest to try and get around. We got lost for a time but fortunately we came across a cottage in a clearing. They had a light showing so we headed for there,' Maxfield explained.

'Frightened the inhabitants half to death when we appeared out of the darkness. Thankfully they took us in, and we slept in chairs beside their fireside until dawn, when we set off again for the village.' Donald took up the tale.

Ottilie hung on to her fiancé's arm. 'Oh, my poor darling. What time did you get there?'

Donald was clearly enjoying Ottilie's attention. 'I think it was about nine o'clock this morning. We found the carter and he sent his boy off on horseback into the town to fetch the police. There was no telephone there either it seems.'

'Then we had to hold on for a reply and for the police to come before we could get back to the castle. The gardeners arrived while we were waiting, and they helped the villagers to drag the fallen trees from the road in the forest with chains and the farmer's plough horse.' Maxfield too seemed to be relishing the limelight.

'Chief Inspector Innes told us that the telephone line to Finnglach was working again so he had sent a message ahead, but he thought the line might well go down again as the repairs were only temporary.' Donald held Ottilie's hand.

'I was so afraid. I kept thinking you might be hurt or stranded in the forest in the snow and the dark.' Ottilie looked close to tears. 'Thankfully, darling Nettie had a message from the spirits saying that you were safe. If not, then I think I may have lost my mind.'

'Thank heavens for darling Nettie, then,' Maxfield murmured in a barely audible tone. Making Kitty wonder what that was all about.

CHAPTER EIGHTEEN

Matt accompanied the chief inspector and the butler down to the farthest of the extensive cellars which lay under the castle. Although the spaces were used now primarily for storage and wine, Matt suspected that many years before they would have been utilised for much darker reasons, such as torture and imprisonment of the lord's enemies.

Since the electric power had not yet been restored the flickering light of the lantern carried by the butler made the stone walls and dark shadowed corners even more atmospheric. The air was cold, and Matt could see his breath in front of his face as they descended the last step.

Matt and Chief Inspector Innes waited for the servant to find the key to the cellar from the large bunch he carried about his person.

'I advised that the room be kept locked, sir, until your arrival. We have not touched anything save to carry Lord Barlas inside and lay him on a trestle,' Matt said as the heavy wooden door finally creaked open.

'Thank you, Captain Bryant. You seem very experienced in

these matters,' the chief inspector observed as they entered the small room.

'It's my profession, sir,' Matt confirmed as the butler hung the lantern from a hook in the low barrel-vaulted ceiling above the body of the dead man.

Matt passed the policeman a business card from his silver card case. The chief inspector squinted at it in the lantern light before tucking it away inside his pocket.

'A private investigator. Were you visiting the castle for pleasure, or were you engaged here in your professional capacity?' Chief Inspector Innes asked as he carefully examined the body of Lord Barlas, noting the entry wound of the shot and checking the pockets of the victim for any contents that might seem out of the ordinary.

'We were engaged in our professional capacity, sir, by Lord Barlas himself. You may check our references with Chief Inspector Greville of the Devon constabulary and with Brigadier Remmington-Blythe at Whitehall.' Matt noticed that the small key to the safe was still attached to the late Lord Barlas's gold watch chain. 'You may wish to take that key, sir. It opens the safe in his lordship's office. I believe Lady Barlas and Sir Rufus Smythe both know the combination which accompanies it. I've been told that Lord Barlas kept his will and various other important documents there,' Matt said.

The chief inspector raised his eyebrows at the information Matt had given him, but removed the key from the chain and added it to the contents of his pocket.

'Very good. I think I have seen enough. As soon as the road here is more navigable, I shall request the doctor to call for his opinion, then the undertaker can take his lordship to a more dignified resting place. Would you be so good, Captain Bryant, as to show me where you found Lord Barlas and go through the events that led up to that discovery?' The chief inspector nodded to the butler who then unhooked the lantern before leading them out of the cellar, locking the door once more as they left.

Once back in the hall, the butler was dismissed, and Matt took the chief inspector through to the boot room where they put on their outdoor clothing. Matt quickly explained how he and Kitty had come to be staying at the castle while they prepared to go out once more to the stone circle.

Matt told the policeman the content of the interview he and Kitty had held with Lord Barlas in his office on their arrival.

'I see, and his lordship claimed he had no idea who had left the notes or who had attempted to push the ice and stone onto him?' the chief inspector asked.

They had paused at the point on the path where the fallen stonework was stacked. Now the snow had melted a little, even in the gloomy fading daylight Matt thought he could detect recent chisel marks on the edge of the stone.

'He claimed to have no idea, sir,' Matt said.

'The gun used to shoot him was his own weapon? And you say there had been an attempt on the safe?' The chief inspector stroked his chin thoughtfully. 'Hmm.'

They walked on, bowing their heads against the sharp wind which had sprung up in the last hour. Once more as they reached the stones the atmosphere seemed to change, and the wind lessened.

Matt showed the chief inspector where Lord Barlas had been found and explained the legend Kitty had discovered in the book from the castle library.

'I suppose that would explain why he would have come here in the dark in such dreadful weather.' The chief inspector examined what was left of the now barely visible bloodstain on the tussocky, wind-scoured grass.

'We have been told he was a great believer in upholding tradition.' Matt huddled down inside his greatcoat.

The policeman straightened and looked around at the

standing stones. 'There is something quite eerie in here, isn't there?' He spotted the remains of the snowman, the head lying on the floor where Matt and Kitty had left it.

'Who built that?' Chief Inspector Innes asked.

'No one seems to know, sir.' Matt followed the policeman as they made their way to the decapitated snow figure.

'A perfect spot to hide and shoot Lord Barlas.' The policeman squinted again as he crouched to work out the possible angles for the fatal shot.

'And for the missing gun to be hidden,' Matt said as he explained about how they had discovered the missing weapon.

'Where is the gun now?' the chief inspector asked.

'Locked in my trunk in our bedroom, sir, along with some other evidence you may find useful.' Matt told the inspector about the séance and the fragment of a destroyed will that Kitty had discovered in the grate of Lord Barlas's office.

'You and Mrs Bryant have certainly been busy,' Chief Inspector Innes observed in a somewhat dry tone.

They had reached the arch-topped exterior door leading into the boot room.

'We haven't disclosed to the other guests that Kitty and I are private investigators. Lord Barlas thought it best if we claimed a distant relationship. I would prefer, sir, if that could continue. Whoever did this is clearly a clever and dangerous individual and I have no wish to potentially endanger either myself or my wife,' Matt said as they prepared to re-enter the castle.

The chief inspector nodded. 'I think you may be right. Once we are inside if you and Mrs Bryant could gather the evidence you have obtained and come to Lord Barlas's study, I should like to talk to you both and make some notes.'

Matt changed quickly and went to fetch Kitty while the chief inspector spoke to his constables. Fortunately, he was able to attract Kitty's attention without causing too much of a stir amongst the other guests. They all seemed to be arguing with Donald Waterford and Maxfield Cotter about something.

Kitty slipped out of the room and met him in the corridor.

'How did it go? Have you told the chief inspector what we've found so far?' she asked.

'He wants us to bring all the evidence we have and hand it over to him in Lord Barlas's study. I expect he will then want to open the safe to look for the will. You go on ahead, I'll nip upstairs and get the gun and the other things,' Matt said.

* * *

Kitty left Matt to head upstairs and hurried along to Lord Barlas's study. Buster followed on her heels as if anxious to see if his master had returned. Chief Inspector Innes was sitting behind Lord Barlas's desk when Kitty knocked and entered the room.

It was clear that he had already begun to sift through the piles of papers which were on the desktop. A glance at the fireplace showed her the grate had been cleaned and a small new fire had been started in the hearth. No doubt to try to dispel the chill of the now unoccupied room.

An oil lamp had been placed on top of the mantelpiece in an attempt to cast some light into the gloom of the late afternoon. Buster looked around sadly and threw himself down beside the fire with a heavy sigh.

'Ah, Mrs Bryant, good afternoon. Please take a seat.' The chief inspector shook her hand and indicated one of the seats they had occupied during their previous visit to meet Lord Barlas.

Kitty sat down and waited for Matt to join them. While they waited, she answered some questions from the policeman about the events that had preceded the murder. Chief Inspector Innes made notes in a small pocketbook. She had just finished when Matt entered the office and joined her in front of the desk.

Matt placed the gun, still carefully wrapped in his scarf, the scrap of pink rubber, the threatening messages and the fragment of the will that Kitty had discovered in front of the chief inspector. The policeman examined the notes first.

'I take it you don't know where the words were taken from?' he asked.

'No, sir, the library here is extensive and as you can see Lord Barlas himself kept a good many books in here and also around the castle.' The question was directed at both of them, but Kitty was first to reply.

Chief Inspector Innes nodded and read the letter that Matt and Kitty had first received inviting them to Finnglach. Matt had brought it with them in case it was needed at any point.

'This Mrs Parsons who recommended you? Who is she?' Chief Inspector Innes raised his gaze from the letter and looked at them.

'My great aunt, sir. She lives some forty or so miles from here closer to the town,' Kitty explained.

'And neither of you had met Lord Barlas or any of his family before you came here? You had never been here on a previous visit?' the policeman asked.

'No, sir,' Matt answered. 'Kitty's aunt Livvy usually comes south to Devon. The climate is kinder to her health.'

'I last visited her when I was a child,' Kitty said.

The chief inspector sighed heavily and refolded the letter, passing it back to Matt. 'Thank you, sir. I'm sure you'll appreciate that I must ask these questions. This is not a straightforward murder.' He leaned back in his chair and templed his hands together to survey them shrewdly.

'I agree, a victim is not usually forewarned of his murderer's intentions,' Matt said.

'Which brings us to these notes and, of course, to Madam

Fortina and her spirit warnings.' Chief Inspector Innes frowned. 'This strange business at the séance and dashing away a whisky glass. What can you tell me about her?'

Kitty told him all they had learned so far about each member of the family and of the guests. The policeman took notes throughout, in tiny, crabbed handwriting inside his pocketbook.

'I see, thank you.' He looked at the fragment of rubber balloon that they had surmised had been used to extinguish the lights at the séance. 'Most ingenious.'

'We assumed it must have been concealed either under the tablecloth or close by,' Matt said. 'We all entered the library straight from the dining room so it couldn't have been concealed on anyone's person. It would have been too bulky when inflated.'

The chief inspector nodded. 'That leaves this last item.' He looked at the fragment of parchment, charred at the edges. 'How did you discover this, Mrs Bryant?'

Kitty explained that she had been concerned that someone may have opened the safe or searched the office and she had noticed the paper in the grate. She also told the chief inspector about Sir Rufus's visit to search the room.

Chief Inspector Innes's sandy eyebrows rose upwards quite considerably when Kitty confessed to hiding behind the curtain at the far end of the office.

'Very well, thank you, Mrs Bryant. You appear to have been most enterprising.' Kitty blushed at the chief inspector's comment. She suspected that he was slightly amused by her nosiness.

The policeman placed the evidence, apart from the gun, inside a large empty manila envelope that he took from a pile inside Lord Barlas's desk. 'I think it would be wise for me to see Lady Barlas now. I should very much like to know about his lordship's will and if Lady Barlas knew of any changes. If she knows the combination, then we can see if the old will or the new will, or indeed either of them, is inside the safe. Depending on what we find it may provide an insight into a possible motive for his murder.'

'Perhaps you might let us know what you find, Chief Inspector?' Matt asked as he stood to leave the office.

'Yes, I appreciate all of your assistance so far with this case. It will be very useful to my investigation if you could continue to observe your fellow guests. I shall have to trespass on Lady Barlas's hospitality myself since it isn't possible to travel from here to the village every day.' The chief inspector rose and extended his hand first to Kitty and then to Matt.

'Would you like us to send Lady Barlas to you?' Kitty asked as she somewhat reluctantly followed Matt to the door.

'Thank you, yes, that would be most helpful.' The chief inspector smiled at her.

Kitty couldn't help but feel slightly annoyed that they had been dismissed before discovering what was or wasn't inside the safe. She was a little vexed that Matt had not made some kind of a protest or argument for them remaining in the room. It was, she felt, the least the chief inspector could have done after all the evidence they had managed to find for him.

Matt took hold of her arm as they approached the door to the drawing room. 'Kitty, wait for a moment. Listen, I asked the chief inspector not to reveal why we were invited to Finnglach. So far as everyone knows we are sticking with the story Lord Barlas provided.'

'Is that why we were sent away back to the drawing room?' Kitty asked.

'I expect so. It would have been odd to have us there while he questioned Lady Barlas and opened the safe to look at the will,' Matt explained.

She supposed he was right; it would have aroused suspicions if they had remained in the study while Lady Barlas was interviewed. Some of Kitty's annoyance dissipated but she couldn't help but still feel frustrated.

'Let's hope that he keeps his word about telling us what he finds then.'

They re-entered the drawing room to discover that Ottilie and Donald had apparently gone to the library. Madam Fortina was still seated with Lady Barlas, Romy was trying once more to get the wireless to work and Maxfield was smoking a cigarette while looking through the window at the melting snow. Bertie was still snoring comfortably in front of the fire.

'Chief Inspector Innes has asked if you might go to the study, Lady Barlas,' Matt asked.

Sir Rufus who was seated with Lady Smythe back at the jigsaw table immediately leapt to his feet. 'Would you like me to accompany you, Velma? These policemen can be devilishly tricky fellows and it may be distressing.'

Lady Barlas blinked and seemed surprised by his outburst. 'No, thank you, Rufus, that's very kind. It may be that he wishes to ask me about some personal matters to do with Stephen. I shall be quite all right, I assure you.'

She stood gracefully from the sofa after lightly pressing Madam Fortina's hand and slipped out of the room. Sir Rufus remained on his feet for a moment longer before taking his place once more beside his wife.

'I hope she doesn't come to regret refusing my offer,' he muttered to no one in particular.

'Why should she, sir? I know she is obviously very upset over her husband's death, but Lady Barlas seems a very level-headed woman. You surely do not suspect that she had a hand in his murder?' Matt asked as he took a seat on one of the fire-side chairs.

Sir Rufus promptly grew quite red in the face and began to bluster. 'No, don't be ridiculous. Of course Velma wouldn't have harmed Stephen. Good heavens, man. No, it's just the police always like to fit these kinds of crimes on a family member, don't they? And as you said, Velma is quite vulnerable at the moment. They may misinterpret something she says, for instance.'

'Dear me, old chap, it sounds rather as if you are afraid that she may say something that could put you in the frame for the murder,' Maxfield drawled as he turned away from the window to extinguish his cigarette in one of the large crystal-glass ashtrays.

'Now see here, you jumped up whippersnapper.' Sir Rufus leapt to his feet once more, his hands curling into fists by his sides.

'Oh, Rufus, do sit down. You will give yourself an apoplexy. Don't you see he is just trying to provoke you?' Lady Smythe said.

Kitty thought Maxfield may have had a point. Sir Rufus did appear to be quite perturbed by the idea of Lady Barlas attending her late husband's office without him.

'Chief Inspector Innes strikes me as a very sensible man. I'm sure his investigation will be most thorough,' Matt said in a mild tone.

Sir Rufus hmphed at this remark and resumed his place beside his wife while glaring at Maxfield.

'I suppose we are all to be sent for in turn, are we?' Romy abandoned the wireless and came to join in the conversation.

'I suppose so,' Kitty said. 'I think that's what usually happens.'

She knew full well that the chief inspector would talk to all of them in turn, including herself and Matt since they hadn't accounted for where everyone was in the crucial thirty minutes leading up to Lord Barlas's murder.

'Well, I for one, have nothing to hide.' Romy gave a careless shrug. 'Everyone knew I was cross with him for refusing to tear up my contract but since he intended me to star in the films he planned to make, then it didn't matter so much. And, I certainly couldn't have dived out of the castle in that terrible weather dressed in my favourite evening gown to shoot him.'

Kitty agreed with the latter part of Romy's statement, but she wasn't wholly convinced about the girl being resigned to having to work out her contract when she could have returned to America.

'You could still have persuaded lover boy there to shoot Stephen on your behalf,' Lady Smythe said. 'Hypothetically speaking, of course.'

'And Sir Rufus could equally have gone outside and killed him, hypothetically speaking, of course,' Maxfield said with a mocking half-bow in Lady Smythe's direction.

'Please stop. This kind of bickering is not helpful. The police will no doubt get to the bottom of the matter. We must just tell the truth and allow them to get on with their job.' Madam Fortina's calm tone was decisive and had the desired effect of quelling the arguments.

Before anyone else could speak a constable entered the room and requested Sir Rufus to attend Chief Inspector Innes in Lord Barlas's office.

'Velma must need my assistance after all.' Sir Rufus sprang to his feet and left with the policeman.

'Or they found something in Velma's statement that they wish to question him about,' Maxfield said.

'My husband has done nothing wrong. He wishes to support the widow of his dearest friend,' Lady Smythe snapped fiercely. 'Honestly, I don't know why you are being so aggravating, Maxfield.'

Ottilie and Donald rejoined the group.

'Where are Velma and Sir Rufus?' Ottilie asked.

'They are being questioned by the chief inspector. What were you two lovebirds up to?' Maxfield asked.

'A little privacy, that's what we wanted,' Ottilie replied.

Donald settled himself on an armchair with Ottilie perching herself on the arm beside him.

Lady Barlas returned looking pale and wan to resume her seat beside Madam Fortina.

'Is everything all right?' the medium asked her.

Lady Barlas raised her shoulders in a helpless gesture. 'I don't know. The chief inspector has opened the safe and Stephen's will is all wrong. It doesn't say what Stephen told me it would say.'

CHAPTER NINETEEN

'I don't understand. What do you mean Daddy's will is wrong?' Ottilie asked.

'Rufus is talking to the chief inspector about it now. He says there was another will. He said the one in the safe is the old one. I know Stephen wrote a new one a few weeks ago, he had his solicitor in London draft it for him. He told me about it himself. I don't understand, it's something to do with the shares of Stephen's companies.' Lady Barlas placed her hand to her head and massaged her temple.

Kitty caught Matt's gaze. The fragment of parchment that she had found must have been that of the new will where Sir Rufus would have taken control of the film studios and of the theatres and their productions. Now the original will would stand which left that control in Lady Barlas's hands.

'But Stephen had said he had drawn up a new will only a few weeks ago. He told Rufus that he wished to clarify how the businesses would run should anything happen to him. You said his solicitor drafted it.' Lady Smythe narrowed her eyes as she looked at Lady Barlas.

'I thought there was a new will too,' Ottilie said. 'Perhaps it's elsewhere in the office and that's why they found the old one in the safe.'

Lady Barlas shook her head. 'It seems not. They looked while I was there, and the chief inspector said he had evidence that a will had been destroyed. Burnt in the fireplace the night Stephen was murdered, most probably by Stephen himself.'

Maxfield let out a long low whistle, startling the group. 'Well then, that doesn't look good at all for Sir Rufus, does it? I presume the new will would have been more to his benefit than this old one. Why would Lord Barlas have burnt the new one? Perhaps he had found out who was behind the threats.'

'Really! That is quite absurd. Do stop with your ridiculous insinuations. The changes Stephen intended were of no great import. They were merely to make things smoother for the board of directors. He must have discovered some kind of error in the new version.' Lady Smythe looked quite furious.

'I can't understand why Daddy would destroy the new will?' Ottilie looked confused. 'That wouldn't be like him at all.'

'Perhaps there was some mistake in the way it had been drawn up, like Lady Smythe suggested? An error he spotted only when he was reviewing it?' Donald suggested.

Ottilie shook her head. 'No, he was very precise with his paperwork. His contracts were always watertight, and he would have checked the draft thoroughly before it was all signed.'

'Which means he must have changed his mind about something in the contents,' Romy said.

'If he burnt it on the fire on New Year's Eve it must have been something that he really wished to ensure was never enacted. Perhaps after those warnings he had decided to revisit his will again.' Ottilie frowned. 'I just can't think why he would have changed his mind.'

'I suppose this means that you are now in charge of my contract, Velma darling,' Romy said.

Lady Barlas looked shocked. 'I don't know. I hadn't thought

about it. I suppose if the new will has been destroyed then I must be. I know the original will placed me as the controlling shareholder. Stephen worried that it might be too much for me.' A tear rolled down her cheek.

'Rufus will support you,' Lady Smythe said and fired a sharp glance at Maxfield Cotter as if daring him to contradict her.

The constable reappeared in the doorway and requested Ottilie to accompany him to see the chief inspector.

'Shall I come too?' Donald asked, preparing to stand.

'Not yet, sir. The chief inspector will send for you in due course,' the constable replied and left with Ottilie.

'No doubt Ottilie will confirm everything that Rufus has probably told the police about the wills,' Lady Smythe said.

'Perhaps.' Madam Fortina's tone was weary. 'Velma, my dear, this must all be very difficult for you, shall I ring for some refreshments?'

Lady Barlas glanced at the clock on the mantelpiece. 'Oh dear me, yes, it's been an age since Donald and Maxfield came back. Tea would be very welcome. I have the most terrible headache from all of this.'

Sir Rufus arrived back in the room at the same time as the late afternoon tea trolley. He looked quite clammy and out of sorts Kitty thought as he sat down again beside Lady Smythe.

'What did the police want to know? What's all this business about the new will being destroyed?' Maxfield asked as Madam Fortina quietly dispensed tea and slices of Christmas cake.

'Really, is it any of your business what Stephen's financial arrangements were? Or what he did with his will?' Lady Smythe asked Maxfield with some asperity as she accepted her tea from Madam Fortina.

Maxfield shrugged. 'Only in that it might be a clue to why he was murdered. Since we are all suspects at the moment, it may be very important.'

'Well, I find it all quite distasteful. You can see poor Velma and Rufus are very upset by the whole affair.' Lady Smythe glanced at her husband.

Kitty thought she was right to be concerned. Sir Rufus certainly appeared unwell since he had returned from talking to the chief inspector. Velma too still appeared to be pale and shaken, although under Madam Fortina's care she looked to have improved a little.

'To answer your somewhat impertinent question, it appears that Stephen, or someone else, has destroyed the later will and unless anything different is discovered then the earlier will, made on his marriage to Velma, is the one which will stand.' Sir Rufus rose from his seat and walked somewhat shakily over to the cocktail trolley to add a shot of brandy to his tea.

Kitty wondered why Sir Rufus seemed so upset by the discovery. Had he suspected the later will had been destroyed? Was that what he had been doing in Lord Barlas's office earlier? She wouldn't have thought the changes to the will would have affected Sir Rufus so drastically. He was already a major share-holder in Lord Barlas's businesses and his friendship with Lady Barlas would probably place him in good stead for any votes the boards might make.

Unless there was something else going on. Something that perhaps Lord Barlas had discovered about his old friend that had led him to change his mind about his bequests. Perhaps financial concerns? Had they argued on New Year's Eve before the party?

Ottilie returned to the room, drawing the attention of the other occupants.

'Donald, the chief inspector wishes to see you.' She subsided gracefully onto one of the vacant armchairs and waved away Madam Fortina's offer of tea.

'Of course.' Donald left for the office.

'Are you all right, Ottilie, my dear?' Lady Barlas asked.

Ottilie nodded. 'Yes, thank you, Velma. I don't think I was much help to them. They asked me a lot of questions regarding my trusts and Daddy's will but, of course, I don't fully understand all of that. Sir Rufus was more use to them there about the terms of the trust.'

Kitty's ears pricked up at this. Was this the cause of Sir Rufus's concerns? He and Lord Barlas were the stewards for Ottilie's money. Had something untoward come to light? Now her father was dead, Ottilie would be in charge once more, if she had understood what Sir Rufus had said earlier correctly.

'I was happy to oblige, my dear. Perhaps we should arrange to sort out your financial arrangements as soon as this business is concluded. You will need to understand your investments,' Sir Rufus said.

'Of course. I can't concentrate on anything right now. My head is all over the place. I'll probably wait until I am back in London, and I can engage an accountant to look at everything with me. Donald too, of course,' Ottilie said.

'Oh, but Rufus can do all of that for you, can't you, my dear?' Lady Smythe replied quickly.

'Indeed, no need to create extra problems and expense for yourself,' Sir Rufus agreed with his wife.

'I think it always a good idea to have a fresh set of expert eyes go over such matters. It protects both the advisor and the advisee,' Matt spoke up.

Kitty thought she saw a fleeting look of consternation at his advice cross Lady Smythe's face.

'I agree, always sensible to get things checked out properly. I'm sure you'll be doing the same thing, won't you, Velma?' Maxfield asked.

Lady Barlas met Maxfield's gaze for a second and then nodded. 'Of course, Rufus understands completely, I'm sure. Ottilie and I are most appreciative of his expertise but there is a lot to take in. My father has some excellent financial people in his employ who can assist us both.'

Sir Rufus swallowed his brandy laden tea in a large gulp before placing his empty cup and saucer down on the side table. 'I shall be delighted to assist whoever you ladies decide to appoint.'

His words didn't match the expression on his face and Lady Smythe looked as if her slice of Christmas cake had been laced with something bitter.

Donald had not returned by the time the tea trolley had been cleared away and the drawing room had grown darker, necessitating the lighting of more of the oil lamps.

'I think I shall go upstairs. I'd quite like a little time to rest before dinner,' Lady Barlas said.

'Very wise, my dear, I think I shall do the same. I'm sure the chief inspector will find us if he wishes to interview any of us.' Madam Fortina rose to join Lady Barlas.

'I wonder if I should wait for Donald. I wonder what can be taking him so long?' Ottilie cast a worried glance at the clock on the mantelpiece.

Romy jumped to her feet, casting aside the magazine she had been flicking through for the last hour. 'I expect we shall know soon enough.'

Maxfield nodded. 'Yes, I'm sure we will.'

Ottilie sighed. 'You're right. Donald can come and find me once he is free.'

The rest of the group left the room, leaving Matt and Kitty with just the dogs for company.

'Sir Rufus seemed very shaken after his interview with the chief inspector,' Kitty said as soon as they were alone.

'Yes, he did, didn't he? He wasn't happy with Ottilie and Lady Barlas saying they intended to seek outside financial advice.' Matt looked at Kitty.

'Lady Smythe seemed most perturbed about that too,' Kitty agreed.

'Hmm, financial shenanigans or something more sinister?' Matt raised an eyebrow as he looked at Kitty.

'It certainly would provide a motive for murder. Do you think Sir Rufus and Lord Barlas argued on New Year's Eve, or did Lord Barlas uncover something while he was working on his papers that led him to destroy the will?' Kitty asked.

Matt frowned. 'It's hard to say. If he confronted Sir Rufus and said he was going to revoke the will, then that would certainly give a motive I agree, but then what of the warnings Lord Barlas received? If Lord Barlas had only just discovered something, then why was an attempt made earlier on his life? And why all the drama with the warnings?'

'Perhaps they realised the discovery of whatever had gone on was inevitable and they wished to deter him or delay him from finding out,' Kitty suggested.

'You say they? I assume you think Lady Smythe is aware of whatever the financial issue is or was?' Matt asked.

'From her reactions earlier, I would say so.' Kitty gave a yawn and stretched. 'We should go and change for dinner too.'

Bertie lifted his head hopefully at the mention of dinner just as Donald opened the drawing room door and peered inside.

'Ottilie has gone upstairs,' Kitty said.

'Thank you, Mrs Bryant.' Donald promptly withdrew.

'I wonder if the chief inspector will wish to interview anyone else before dinner,' Matt said.

Kitty tapped him lightly on the side of his leg. 'I hope it won't be us. We really do need to go and change.'

They stood and went to leave the room only to be met by Chief Inspector Innes in the doorway.

'Everyone else has gone upstairs to dress for dinner, Chief Inspector. Matt and I were about to follow,' Kitty said.

'Then if I may detain you both for a moment longer?' the policeman asked, entering the room and closing the door behind him.

'Of course, sir,' Matt agreed as he and Kitty sat back down on the chairs nearest to the door.

Kitty waited to hear what the chief inspector might have to share. They had learned a great deal from Lady Barlas and Sir Rufus when they had returned from their interviews. With luck they might now hear a few more pointers about who may have murdered Lord Barlas and why.

'I'm glad I caught you both. I'm sure you will have heard from Lady Barlas that the fragment of the will you found appeared to be from the latest version.' The chief inspector looked at Kitty.

'Yes, sir. It seemed to have caused some consternation for Sir Rufus and Lady Smythe,' Kitty said.

'Indeed. Sir Rufus was quite taken aback, insisting we recheck the safe and the contents of the desk drawers,' Chief Inspector Innes said. 'I suggested to Lady Barlas and Mrs Tremaine that they seek outside financial advice regarding their inheritance based on Sir Rufus's reaction. He has denied having any disagreement with Lord Barlas prior to the murder and is adamant he knew nothing of his friend's intention to destroy the latest version of his will.'

'Do you believe him, sir?' Matt asked.

The chief inspector stroked his chin thoughtfully. 'I'm not sure. I believe he was shocked that the will had been destroyed but I think he suspected something was wrong, that was why he searched Lord Barlas's office.'

'How was your interview with Mr Waterford?' Matt asked.

Chief Inspector Innes smiled. 'That young man appeared quite nervous.'

'Lady Smythe said that she believes he is not who he says he is. She knows the Waterford family and does not know of his connection to them, although that is the claim that he has made to Lord Barlas and Ottilie,' Matt said.

'Yes, there were several contradictions in his statement. He has admitted that he has some financial issues at present. He said he didn't wish to trouble his fiancée with his concerns.' The chief inspector gave Matt and Kitty a shrewd look.

'We overheard them arguing over money, he seemed to be trying to persuade her to release some of her trust fund.' Kitty explained about the conversation she and Matt had heard shortly after their arrival at Finnglach.

'Hmm, it sounds as if he was counting on Mrs Tremaine persuading her father to release some of her funds, or to personally back him in some business venture. Now I suppose she is free to use her money as she chooses without recourse to Sir Rufus. Interesting,' the chief inspector said.

'From what we were told by Lord Barlas I think that would be the case. Otherwise Ottilie only resumed full control over her finances when she married,' Matt confirmed.

'And Mr Waterford proposed on Christmas Eve?' The policeman gave a wry smile. 'I had better let you both go. I shall see you shortly at dinner, no doubt.'

Kitty and Matt hurried upstairs. The castle was dark and gloomy despite the many lights the servants had placed around the great entrance hall and stairs.

'I shall be glad when the electricity is back.' Kitty shivered as Matt opened the door to their room. She was pleased to see that both the fire and the oil lamp had been lit in preparation for their return. The curtains were drawn, and the bed turned down.

'I know what you mean. This place is all shadows and strange noises, isn't it?' Matt said as Kitty opened the wardrobe to retrieve her dark-red velvet evening gown.

'Dinner should be interesting with the chief inspector joining us.' Kitty stuck an experimental finger into the jug of water on the washstand and decided it was too cold to do anything other than to quickly freshen her face.

'This whole affair is strange,' Matt agreed, pulling out his evening clothes from the wardrobe.

They changed quickly and made their way back to the drawing room for pre-dinner drinks. The dogs had gone from the fire and Kitty guessed they had been taken below stairs for their food and some exercise. The castle staff seemed to be very good at taking care of the animals. Bertie had certainly made himself at home.

Romy Fisher was perched on the arm of one of the chairs smoking a small cigarette in a green-jade holder. Maxfield Cotter was mixing a cocktail in a silver shaker.

'Drink?' he asked as Kitty and Matt came to join them.

'Maxfield makes the most divine drinks, and I don't know about you, but I could certainly use one after today.' Romy blew out a thin blue plume of smoke.

'Thank you, that sounds lovely,' Kitty said, accepting Maxfield's offer.

'I heard the chief inspector is joining us for dinner.' Romy accepted her drink from Maxfield.

'Yes, he will be staying at the castle, along with the constables, at least until the road is fully open, I believe.' Matt declined the offer of a cocktail and helped himself to a whisky and soda.

'I expect he will carry on interviewing everyone tomorrow.' Maxfield handed Kitty a glass before starting to prepare his own drink.

Romy gave a little shiver. 'Ugh, someone walking on my grave. I declare I shall be so happy to get back to London and civilisation.'

'At least you should be able to talk to Velma about releasing you from your contract now.' Maxfield dropped into the empty space beside the actress. 'After all, she's a close friend. She won't want to stand in your way. You can telephone the movie studio in America.'

Romy smiled. 'Maybe. I expect she may be happy to cancel my contract. Then she can star herself in some of those films that Lord Barlas had planned to make.' She stubbed the remains of her cigarette out in a crystal ashtray and placed her jade holder inside her silver evening bag.

Madam Fortina slipped quietly into the room. She was dressed once more completely in black with a red and black patterned lace shawl around her shoulders and covering her neck.

Kitty wondered if the bruising she had noticed was still visible. There had been no time or a suitable opportunity to discover how that had occurred, or who could have done it. Matt immediately offered the medium a drink and she accepted a small sherry before sitting near to Kitty.

'Any more messages from your ghostly friends?' Maxfield asked. 'No more warnings for any of us? Spooky information for the police?'

Madam Fortina gave him a sour look. 'I suggest you refrain from joking about things that you don't understand.'

Maxfield gave Romy an amused look as if inviting her to share some private joke.

'Perhaps you could try contacting Lord Barlas and ask him who killed him,' Maxfield suggested.

Madam Fortina stood. 'That suggestion is in very bad taste,' she said, and taking her drink with her, she left the room.

CHAPTER TWENTY

'Oh dear, now I've upset the old bird.' Maxfield didn't sound particularly remorseful.

Kitty suspected that Maxfield derived a great deal of enjoyment from stirring up his fellow guests.

'I think you were unkind,' Romy said. 'She takes her work very seriously.'

'Then it was a helpful suggestion.' Maxfield grinned disarmingly at the actress.

Romy sighed. 'You are impossible,' she said.

The rest of the house party joined them. Sir Rufus seemed to have made a full recovery from his earlier upset and appeared intent on charming both Ottilie and Lady Barlas. Donald appeared quiet, almost sullen and Lady Smythe quite sharp.

Madam Fortina had not returned to join them by the time the dinner gong sounded. Instead, both she and Chief Inspector Innes arrived at the dining table a few seconds after everyone else was seated. They took their places at the table, Madam Fortina next to Matt and the chief inspector beside Romy Fisher.

Conversation at the table was somewhat muted and limited to invitations to pass the salt and complimentary remarks about the food.

'I tried the telephone again before dinner and the line is out of service again.' Lady Smythe dabbed daintily at the corner of her lips with a linen napkin.

'Oh dear, I had hoped to telephone my grandmother,' Kitty said. She knew that her beloved Grams would probably be wondering why she hadn't heard from them beyond a quick call when they had arrived.

'Your grandmother?' Lady Smythe looked surprised.

'My mother was killed some years ago and my grandmother brought me up. My father lives in America,' Kitty explained.

'Oh, I'm so sorry, my dear,' Lady Smythe said.

'That's rather like you, isn't it, Donald? Your mother passed away when you were young and a distant cousin took you in.' Ottilie looked at her fiancé.

Donald's cheeks had turned a little pink. 'Um, yes, that's right.'

'Remind me again, Donald, which branch of the Waterfords is your family? Is it the Somerset branch or the Hampshire branch?' Lady Smythe asked, a suspiciously innocent look on her face.

'I, um, the Hampshire part of the family but it is a distant connection.' The colour in Donald's cheeks deepened.

'Really, I know Victoria and Cosmo Waterford very well and I don't recall them mentioning some orphaned relative.' Lady Smythe took a sip from her glass of wine.

Donald now looked decidedly flustered. 'As I said, it's a distant connection.'

'Your mother died too, didn't she, Maxfield? I'm sure you said something like that?' Romy turned her head to look at the racing driver.

He gave a careless laugh. 'She isn't actually dead, darling. I said she was dead to me.'

'Oh dear, that sounds like there was some kind of falling out,' Ottilie said.

'More a gradual drift and a parting of the ways,' Maxfield said.

'What happened to your father?' Ottilie asked, her eyes bright with concern.

Kitty wondered if the recent loss of her own father had prompted the question. Ottilie too had lost her mother as a child and was now an orphan.

'Killed in the war. What about yours, Donald?' Maxfield asked.

'Same.' Donald, however, didn't meet Maxfield's gaze as he spoke, and Kitty wondered if perhaps Donald's mother had been unmarried.

'It seems a shame that you and your mother are estranged, Maxfield. Is there no hope of a reconciliation?' Ottilie asked.

'I think our lives have taken very different paths,' Maxfield said.

Kitty noticed that Madam Fortina had kept her gaze firmly focused upon her plate during this conversation, although she did not appear to be enjoying her dinner. After what the woman had said about her own relationship with her son perhaps the discussion was too painful.

'Well, it's too bad about the telephone line being down again. I expect it will make matters more difficult for you too, eh, Chief Inspector?' Sir Rufus said.

'If the thaw continues then the line will hopefully be restored soon. The electricity too I would imagine. Once the road through to the village is clearer then, we can move forward more swiftly.' The chief inspector looked at the candlelit faces around the table.

Kitty could only imagine that he meant Lord Barlas's body could be collected from the cellar and that the police could complete background checks on the guests at the castle. No doubt he would be able to discover the truth about Donald Waterford, and Madam Fortina.

Once dinner was over, they returned to the comfort of the drawing room for coffee. Maxfield stationed himself near to Lady Barlas and attempted to amuse her with various tales of his racing mishaps. Ottilie and Donald sat nearby joining in from time to time. Lady Smythe and Sir Rufus returned to their jigsaw and Romy made another attempt at the wireless before giving up in disgust.

Kitty and Matt took a seat on the long leather sofa near to Madam Fortina who had removed herself as usual to the edge of the group. The chief inspector had excused himself and had gone to check on the constables who were dining in the servants' quarters.

'Are you all right, Madam Fortina?' Kitty asked the medium in a low voice once she was certain the rest of the group were all occupied. 'Only you seemed rather distrait during dinner, and I wondered if you had found the conversation upsetting.'

The older woman looked up and glanced towards the group near the fireplace. 'Thank you, Mrs Bryant. Yes, it was rather sad. It brought home my own situation. I realised that I had been hoping that perhaps my son and I would find some common ground, but I fear it is much too late for that now.'

'I'm so sorry. It must be horribly distressing,' Kitty said. 'You never know, perhaps a letter or a meeting may bring about a reconciliation?'

A sad smile touched the medium's lips. 'I'm afraid not, Mrs Bryant. Things have gone too far I fear.'

Kitty left the conversation alone at that not wishing to distress the woman further. Madam Fortina finished her coffee and excused herself from the room, stating her intention to retire for the evening.

'I wish this wretched wireless would work.' Romy glared at the offending article. 'The sooner we have electricity again the better.'

'You could always fetch more of the records from the music room for the gramophone in here if you would like some music. It's rather old-fashioned as you have to wind it up to make it play but it's very useful for times like this when the power is out,' Lady Barlas suggested.

'Capital idea. I'll give you a hand to carry them.' Sir Rufus followed Romy out of the room leaving Lady Smythe to scowl at the door of the drawing room.

Maxfield headed for the cocktail trolley. 'Anyone like a drink?' he offered. 'To go with the music?'

Lady Barlas accepted his offer as did Lady Smythe. Kitty was still finishing her coffee as was Matt so they both declined. Ottilie and Donald both opted for whisky rather than a cocktail, which Donald went and poured.

Chief Inspector Innes arrived back in time to accept the offer of a whisky from Donald.

'What are your plans for tomorrow, Chief Inspector?' Maxfield asked as he topped off Lady Smythe's cocktail with a maraschino cherry.

'I have more interviews to conduct which will continue throughout the day. My constables are also interviewing the servants,' the policeman said as he took the chair recently vacated by Madam Fortina.

'You are, of course, welcome to stay here as long as is needed. We are most anxious to ensure that whoever killed my husband faces justice,' Lady Barlas said. She then paused and frowned as if realising something. 'Ottilie, I'm sorry, you should really be the person extending the invitation. Finnglach is yours now.' She looked at her stepdaughter as the alteration in her position dawned.

'Don't be ridiculous, Velma darling. You know Finnglach is your home, Daddy's death doesn't alter that. You will always be welcome here,' Ottilie assured her stepmother, moving to her side and patting her hand.

Lady Barlas pulled out her handkerchief and touched the corners of her eyes. 'Thank you, Ottilie, you have always been so kind to me.'

The drawing room door crashed open again, and Romy and Sir Rufus re-entered, their arms full of records. Romy was giggling at something Sir Rufus had apparently said.

'We're back. Let's have a little music to lighten things up.' Romy headed to the gramophone. She set a record on the machine and put the needle in place before turning the handle at the side to get it to work.

The gramophone crackled into life and the sound of big band music filled the room.

'That's better.' Romy left the gramophone and went to make herself a drink.

Sir Rufus rejoined Lady Smythe at the jigsaw table where he was met by a distinctly frosty glare.

The music did seem to help the mood in the room. Lady Barlas appeared to recover herself and the chief inspector joined in a conversation with Matt about golf and fishing. By the time the record ended everyone appeared to be much more relaxed.

Kitty woke with a start. At first, she was uncertain of what had disturbed her. The room was still dark with only a faint dull red glow emanating from the embers in the fire. Matt remained asleep as she scrambled out of bed and pulled on her thick, red flannel dressing gown and stuffed her feet into her slippers.

The air in the room was freezing and she could see her breath in front of her face as she carefully unlocked and opened the bedroom door. She was certain she had heard a noise out in the corridor. A few oil lamps remained alight in the alcoves, presumably in case any guest wished to find the lavatory in the night.

The faint yellow glow of the lamps cast eerie shadows along the rough stone walls as Kitty set off to try and determine what the sound was that she had heard. It occurred to her as she moved quickly and quietly along the deserted corridor that it might have been wiser to have woken Matt, or found some kind of weapon to take with her.

The corridor curved slightly, and she passed the closed oak doors to a couple of bedrooms. Up ahead the sounds that had woken her seemed louder, a scuffling, shuffling sound and the noise of something falling.

The edge of her dressing gown caught against one of the suits of armour that were displayed at various points along the landing. The clatter of one of her buttons clanging on the hollow metal leg of the armour seemed disproportionately loud in the space.

Kitty winced and paused waiting to hear if she had been noticed. There was a bump like the sound of a door closing and the other noises ceased.

'Hello?' she called quietly.

She listened for a moment; certain she could hear what sounded like someone groaning. The corridor ahead was dark and there was no lamp in the niche on the wall. She crept forward a few more paces. The sound she'd heard grew clearer and more recognisable, and it was definitely someone in distress.

Stepping forward she cannoned straight into another dressing gown clad figure. Her heart thudded against the wall of her chest, and she braced herself ready to scream if whoever it was attacked her.

'Mrs Bryant?' Maxfield struck a match holding it up in the dark space to identify her.

'There was a noise. It woke me. I thought someone was in trouble,' Kitty said.

'I heard it too. Somewhere here,' Maxfield said, extinguishing the match.

They had stopped outside what Kitty could just make out as one of the bedroom doors.

'Help me,' a faint, croaking plea.

'In there,' Kitty said as she opened the door.

'Be careful, Mrs Bryant, look, there's glass.' Maxfield pointed and Kitty noticed shards of a broken glass on the wooden floorboards glinting in the faint light from the dying fire.

'Attacked,' a female voice croaked from the direction of the bed.

'Blast this wretched lack of electricity. Where is the lamp?' Maxfield's slipper-clad feet crunched on the glass shards to reach the oil lamp and light it before they could go further into the room.

By the light of the lamp Kitty saw that Madam Fortina lay half-sprawled across her bed. A large pillow on the floor next to her and the room in disarray as if there had been a struggle.

'Madam Fortina, what has happened?' Kitty picked her way through the debris to try to assist the older woman.

'Someone came in my room and tried to smother me with that pillow...' Madam Fortina broke into a paroxysm of coughing.

'Did you see who it was?' Maxfield asked as he moved the lamp closer to the stricken woman.

The medium shook her head. 'No, I couldn't see anything. I fought for my life. Thank goodness you came when you did.'

Kitty perched on the edge of the bed, her legs shaking as she realised that the woman would have been dead had she not heard the faint sounds of the struggle.

'What's going on? What's happened?' Sir Rufus appeared in the doorway, his grey hair sticking up on end as he tightened the cord belt of his dark-blue dressing gown.

'Madam Fortina has been attacked in her bed,' Kitty said.

'Good heavens, who by?' Sir Rufus was swiftly followed by Lady Smythe swathed a in a red tartan shawl who peered into the room over his shoulder.

'She didn't see who it was. Which room is the chief inspector staying in?' Maxfield asked.

'I think Velma said he was on the other landing, in the room next to Ottilie. I'll go and fetch him.' Sir Rufus disappeared leaving Lady Smythe standing open-mouthed with shock in the doorway.

'Kitty? Are you here?' Matt came to the door. His expression grim as he took in the scene.

'Madam Fortina was attacked. Someone tried to smother her. Sir Rufus has gone to fetch Chief Inspector Innes.' Kitty continued to comfort the medium, ensuring the woman was wrapped in blankets to keep her warm.

'I passed Sir Rufus on my way here,' Matt said.

Even in the poor light of the oil lamp Kitty could see the yellow-green marks of fading bruises on Madam Fortina's neck now exposed by her pink flannel nightgown.

A moment later and Chief Inspector Innes appeared, pyjama-clad like the rest of them. Matt and Lady Smythe stood aside to allow him to access the room.

'Sir Rufus said Madam Fortina was assaulted.' He looked at the woman on the bed.

Madam Fortina explained again what had happened. She had been asleep until the sound of someone trying her door had disturbed her. Before she could move, she had felt the weight of a pillow pressing down on her face, pinning her to the bed.

The ancient feather mattress had given her a little room to wriggle, and she had fought with all her might, knocking her glass of water onto the floor along with her travel clock and several books. She had been reaching the limits of her strength when something had made the intruder stop and leave the room.

'That may have been when I caught my dressing gown on the suit of armour and called out to see who was there,' Kitty said.

'I was woken by the sound of a scuffle, so I came out of my room to see what was happening. I heard a clang and Mrs Bryant call out, then she literally walked into me in the corridor. We came to Madam Fortina's room together,' Maxfield said.

'Neither of you saw or heard anyone else in the corridor?' Chief Inspector Innes asked.

'No, sir,' Kitty said.

'The corridor goes down to the servants' stairs at the end here. It mirrors the grand staircase from the main hall so someone could have either gone down the servants' stairs or across the landing into the other wing of the castle,' Maxfield explained. 'It's a giant loop.'

'So, we must assume the assailant left in that direction, disturbed no doubt by you two coming along the corridor.' Chief Inspector Innes frowned. 'Madam Fortina, are you all right to remain in your room? Do you wish one of the ladies to stay with you? Or I can rouse one of my constables to stand guard outside in the corridor.'

'Thank you, Chief Inspector. I doubt that whoever did this is likely to return tonight after so much furore. I have a key and I shall lock myself in once I have cleared this glass from the floor,' Madam Fortina said in a somewhat stronger voice.

'Let me help you.' Kitty hopped off the bed and carefully

picked up the broken shards of glass, taking care not to cut herself as she stacked them on the dressing table.

Sir Rufus and Lady Smythe both left to return to their room at the bidding of the chief inspector. Maxfield followed them after being assured there was nothing further he could do.

'Are you quite certain you are all right to remain in here?' Kitty asked Madam Fortina as she put the books and travel clock back on the bedside table. It was already three thirty, it would not be long now till daybreak. Matt had occupied himself with making up the fire to restore a cheerful warmth to the room.

'Yes, thank you.' The medium had wrapped herself in a plaid shawl taking care to cover her neck.

'This person that attacked you? Was it the same person who caused the bruising around your throat?' Kitty asked.

The older woman's face blanched as the chief inspector and Matt both turned their gaze to her neck.

'I don't know what you mean,' Madam Fortina stammered, and Kitty could see the fear in her eyes.

'I noticed the bruising the other day. Who did it?' Kitty asked gently.

Madam Fortina bowed her head. 'I don't know. Truly I don't. I was grabbed from the back as I walked along the corridor. They pulled on my scarf until I thought I would pass out or die. I didn't see who was responsible.'

'Why did you not say something about this before?' Chief Inspector Innes demanded. 'You could have come to see me after dinner or when I first arrived at the castle.'

'They threatened me.' Madam Fortina had tears running freely now down her plump cheeks. 'I didn't recognise their voice. I think it was a man and it sounded like they had pulled something over their mouth to disguise themselves. You know, a kind of growly, deep voice.'

'What did they say?' Kitty asked.

'They said I should say nothing to anyone about Lord Barlas's death if I knew what was good for me.' The medium sniffed and looked around for a handkerchief.

Matt pulled a clean cotton square from the pocket of his dressing gown and passed it to her.

'And what is it that you know about Lord Barlas's death, Madam Fortina?' Matt's tone was stern.

CHAPTER TWENTY-ONE

'I can't, I can't say anything.' The woman dissolved into a fresh bout of tears.

'Can't or won't?' Chief Inspector Innes asked. 'The longer you refuse to tell us all that you know about Lord Barlas's murder the greater the danger you personally face. Someone clearly believes that you have seen or heard something that could identify them. They will continue to look for a way to harm you unless you share that information with us.'

Madam Fortina dried her eyes and blew her nose. 'There were a couple of things but truly I don't know how they can possibly help you.'

'I think we should be the judge of that,' the chief inspector's tone was firm.

'I was in the library, leafing through the books as one does. I came across a book entitled *Olde Scottish Superstitions*, it was tucked away, almost hidden. Naturally I was interested in the subject matter. When I opened it, I saw some of the pages had been damaged, words had been cut out.'

Matt exchanged a glance with Kitty. Their guess that the

words of the warning notes had been taken from a book in the library were correct.

'I was frightened and put the book back where I had found it. After the incident with the dagger at the séance I looked for it again, but the book had gone.' Madam Fortina wiped her eyes once more.

'But Lord Barlas didn't tell anyone about the note on his pillow?' Kitty said.

'No, but I pieced together what the words had said, so I kept my eyes open, and I could sense there was something wrong. I am very sensitive to such things. I thought perhaps at first it was some kind of prank designed to scare.' Madam Fortina paused as if trying to recall the incidents in greater clarity.

'Did you know about the gun being taken?' Chief Inspector Innes asked.

Again, Lord Barlas had said nothing to his guests on the matter and the servants had been discreet in their search of the castle. Kitty thought this a good question.

'I noticed that the servants were moving around a great deal, there seemed an unusual amount of activity, cleaning that had already been done before Christmas. It's a tradition in Scotland to have cleaned the house thoroughly before the New Year. Stephen was very committed to upholding traditions. I thought they had to be searching for something. Perhaps something had been stolen, then I overheard one of the menservants telling the butler that he hadn't found the gun.' Madam Fortina blinked as she spoke.

'And you surmised that it had to be one of Lord Barlas's guns that was missing?' Chief Inspector Innes said.

Madam Fortina nodded. 'I was becoming more fearful for his safety.'

'What about the whisky glass that you removed?' Kitty asked. 'Did you see someone tamper with his drink?'

'No, but I had been observing him closely, hoping that I was mistaken in the thoughts I had been having. That night, he had left his glass on the side table. Romy had put some music on the wireless and people were getting up to dance. Stephen was demonstrating a reel movement with Ottilie. The glass was under the lamp. When he put it down the whisky was clear and when he picked it up, I saw it was cloudy. I couldn't risk that something had been placed in it.' Madam Fortina scrubbed at her eyes with the handkerchief.

'So you knocked it out of his hand,' Matt said.

Madam Fortina nodded again. 'Yes, I didn't know what else to do.'

'And what of the incident with the falling masonry?' Chief Inspector Innes asked.

'You cannot see now because it is dark, but this room is almost above the boot room. I heard strange scrapping sounds coming from the empty bedroom next door but thought nothing of it. At first I imagined it must be a servant clearing the grate or something. I knew too that Stephen had charged the staff with removing any hanging icicles from the gutters and ledges around the castle because of the danger to anyone should they fall. Naturally I then thought that it must be one of the staff carrying out just such a task. It was very early in the morning,' Madam Fortina explained.

'Then came the accident that almost killed Lord Barlas with the falling stonework.' Chief Inspector Innes sounded thoughtful.

'The room next to mine is empty, as I said, so anyone could have gone in there, opened the casement window and loosened those stones ready to push them down onto Stephen's head. Everyone knew he went outside with Buster early each morning. Stephen was a man of routine,' Madam Fortina said.

'Did you see anyone go in or out of that room?' Kitty asked.

'No, only the servants and then after the accident, the room was locked.' The medium gave a last dab at the corner of her eyes with the handkerchief. 'I feel so guilty that Stephen is dead, yet I don't know what else I could have done to save him.'

* * *

'The night of the séance, with the note that was on the dagger, do you have any idea at all who could have done that? From what you say, you were not responsible for those warning notes, only for the spiritual warnings and removing the whisky?' Kitty asked.

She had been convinced that somehow Madam Fortina must have been responsible for the notes as part of the other warnings she had given. Now it appeared that this wasn't the case, and it was perhaps the murderer who had been toying with Lord Barlas before his death.

'I promise you, Mrs Bryant, I have no idea who might be responsible for those notes or why they would have sent them. I was not expecting anything to happen during the séance other than messages to come from the Ouija board.' Madam Fortina sounded convincing.

'Then why attack you? Clearly the killer believes that you know something.' Chief Inspector Innes's tone was low, almost as if speaking to himself. 'I shall get a constable to keep watch on your room. I would like you to think very carefully if there is anything else, anything at all, no matter how small or insignificant it seems that you may have neglected to tell us. I shall see you in the morning, after breakfast. For now, I think it best we all return to our beds.'

Kitty would have liked to have lingered and asked a few more questions. Something told her that Madam Fortina was still keeping something back. However, Chief Inspector Innes shepherded them from the room instructing the medium to lock the door.

'Come on, old thing, it's rather chilly now.' Matt placed his arm around her as they walked back to their room. The chief inspector took the servants' stairs to go and wake one of the constables to stand guard over Madam Fortina's door.

Kitty realised she was actually quite cold, her feet felt like blocks of ice, and she was relieved to jump back into bed and snuggle down beneath the blankets.

'You should have woken me, Kitty,' Matt reproved her as he clambered back into bed beside her. 'You could have been in serious trouble.'

Kitty knew he had a point, but she hadn't wished to disturb him if the noise had turned out to be merely the wind outside the castle. 'I'm sorry. I wasn't sure what I heard.'

'Just keep in mind that whoever committed this murder is a ruthless individual.' Matt pulled her closer and kissed her cheek.

He was soon asleep again, but Kitty lay awake in the darkness for quite a while puzzling over the night's events.

Matt woke before her and had rung for hot water to shave and for a tray of tea before Kitty even had chance to gather her wits. A small fire blazed in the hearth and Matt had drawn back the curtain to allow the weak, wintry sunlight into the room.

'What time is it?' Kitty looked around for her leather-cased travel clock.

'Almost nine o'clock.' Matt grinned at her as he opened the door at the maid's knock to accept a tea tray and a jug of hot water.

'Oh dear.' Kitty felt quite vexed, she had hoped to be up in good time so she could talk to their fellow guests over breakfast. She wanted to find out exactly what they had heard and seen during the night.

Matt set the tray on the dressing table and poured her a cup of tea. 'Don't worry, I'm sure everyone will be late rising this morning.'

Kitty accepted the tea gratefully; she supposed her husband

was right. Lady Barlas would probably take her breakfast on a tray, as would Madam Fortina and Lady Smythe. The chief inspector had said he intended to resume his interviews after breakfast so their fellow guests would probably gather in the drawing room.

She washed and dressed quickly so that Matt could complete his shave and his own preparations for the day. They arrived in the dining room just in time to eat before the breakfast things were cleared away.

Donald was seated at the table, the remains of his boiled eggs before him.

'Good morning, we thought we would be too late for breakfast,' Kitty greeted him cheerfully as she helped herself to the last of the sausages, leaving the bacon and eggs for Matt.

'No, everyone was late. There's no one around except for Romy and she didn't stay in here for long. She said something about Madam Fortina being attacked in her room last night. Is it true?' Donald asked.

'Yes, I was woken by a strange noise, so I went to investigate. I met Maxfield on the landing and we discovered poor Madam Fortina had been assaulted,' Kitty said.

'Romy said that was what Maxfield had told her. He told her that Nettie didn't know who it was. Did you see anyone?' Donald frowned.

Kitty applied herself to her sausages and toast. 'No, no one at all. Only Maxfield who had heard the noises the same as I did. Then Matt, the chief inspector and Sir Rufus and Lady Smythe arrived,' Kitty replied before taking a large bite of her breakfast.

'How extraordinary. I always lock my door now, ever since Lord Barlas was killed. One doesn't know, does one, who to trust.' The worried frown on Donald's brow deepened.

'I suppose not,' Matt agreed.

'Why Madam Fortina? That's rather peculiar. Do you think she knows who killed Lord Barlas?' Donald asked.

Kitty shrugged. 'She says she has no idea.'

'Really? With all those warnings she kept giving? It was very odd.' Donald seemed surprised.

'Perhaps that's what the killer thought and why she was attacked. They may have believed she knew something that could identify them and was about to tell the police.' Matt looked at Donald.

Donald appeared to consider this. 'But surely she knew something important, I can't see why else someone would attack her.'

Kitty shrugged. 'It doesn't seem as if she did. The chief inspector is continuing his interviews this morning so maybe he will learn more then. You had yours yesterday though, didn't you?'

She was keen to hear what Donald had to say about his conversation with the chief inspector. He had certainly been in the office for quite some time.

'Um, yes. It was just the usual kind of thing, I suppose. Where was I on New Year's Eve just before Stephen was killed? Did I know anything about the gun being taken, that kind of stuff.' Donald's cheeks had taken on a slight pink tinge.

'I expect he wanted to know about you and Ottilie too, with her inheritance and the money she has in her trust.' Matt made his statement sound casual and matter-of-fact.

Kitty noticed Donald's ears were turning a similar pink hue to his cheeks.

'Oh yes, of course. He asked a load of impertinent questions about our relationship. Dash it all, basically implying I was some kind of gigolo. I'm sure Sir Rufus had probably given him that idea.' Donald scowled at the remnants of shell in his silver egg cup.

'Sir Rufus?' Kitty asked mildly, well aware that Sir Rufus had made several disparaging remarks about Donald Waterford.

'He's Ottilie's godfather you know and takes far too much interest in her affairs if you ask me. It's not as if she's a child. She's a grown woman and is quite capable of managing her own money. She had to beg her father and Sir Rufus for virtually every penny. That was all set to change on our marriage anyway.' The pink on the tips of Donald's ears had deepened to red and he stared belligerently at the table.

'I thought Lord Barlas had no problems with allowing Ottilie access to her money?' Kitty asked. She wasn't sure if this was true but when Lord Barlas had spoken of his daughter's financial affairs it hadn't sounded as if he impeded her access.

'It's Sir Rufus that has always been the sticking point. When Ottilie lost her first husband she was in quite a state, so I think her father wished to protect her. Marcus left her well provided for, in addition to the money she had inherited from her mother. It was all in a trust and her father and Sir Rufus controlled the capital. Sir Rufus likes to take charge of everything to do with financial matters and usually Lord Barlas would take his advice, but I think things had started to change recently.' Donald sounded thoughtful.

'What gave you that impression?' Matt asked.

'When we came back to Finnglach before Christmas, Lord Barlas said he wished to review all of his companies' financial statements. I think he intended a programme of works on the estate and was looking to draw money. He also said he wanted to go over Ottilie's investments so that they would be ready to hand over to her on our wedding. He knew a proposal was in the offing, as naturally I had asked him for his blessing,' Donald said.

'How did Sir Rufus take that?' Kitty asked.

'He seemed quite put out, kept saying there was no hurry and to leave it until the New Year.' Donald's brow furrowed.

'Dashed annoying for Ottilie and me. We had plans we wished to make ahead of our wedding and a cash injection would have been very useful.'

'You have a business?' Kitty's curiosity was aroused. After the quarrel she and Matt had overheard before the murder it would be interesting to hear what Donald had to say.

'I have a number of irons in various fires and then some investment opportunities that were coming up. You know how it is.' Donald appealed to Matt clearly assuming that he would have a better understanding of business affairs than Kitty.

'Stocks and shares?' Matt asked.

'Better. Mining in the Argentine. An old chum of mine. A real opportunity to get in on the ground level so to speak. The initial surveys and samples are very promising,' Donald said.

Kitty's brow raised. She was quite familiar with some of these mining schemes from articles Matt had shown her in the newspapers. They seemed to her to be the latest get rich quick schemes for the gullible. To her, the only people getting rich from the mines seemed to be the ones who had persuaded people like Donald to invest in them. For every successful mine it appeared there were at least ten failures.

'Did you discuss the opportunity with Lord Barlas?' Matt asked.

'Briefly. He asked me for all the details, and I think he was quite interested. I already have a small stake in the company and like I said the initial survey results are very promising.' Donald was more animated than Kitty had ever seen him.

'And is Ottilie keen on the mining opportunity?' Kitty wondered how Ottilie viewed Donald's ideas for spending her inheritance.

'Well, she has a few reservations, naturally, but I'm sure she would come around. After our wedding we plan to go out there to take a look ourselves.' Donald beamed at them.

'Sir Rufus was less keen on releasing any capital?' Matt asked.

Donald's face fell. 'The blighter kept pouring cold water on the idea. He persuaded Lord Barlas not to release any funds. By the time the money would have been available the window of opportunity would have gone. I asked Ottilie to talk to her father but she didn't get anywhere.'

'That's unfortunate.' Kitty privately thought it was probably a good idea that Ottilie's money had been protected. 'I suppose that your family may have assisted you to make the investment though?' She suspected that Lady Smythe had been correct that Donald did not have the connections to the wealthy and influential Waterford family that he had claimed.

Donald's ears once more turned a very telltale pink. 'Um, well my connection is quite distant, you know. My mother was estranged from them when she married my father. I have no contact really with them now.'

'Oh dear, that's very sad when that happens,' Kitty said sympathetically.

The servants began to clear some of the covered dishes from the sideboards, extinguishing the burners that had been keeping the food warm.

'I think we should wait in the drawing room. I expect the chief inspector will keep us all informed with any progress in the case,' Matt said.

'I expect so. I should go and see if Ottilie is up and about.' Donald excused himself and Matt and Kitty walked to the drawing room where they were greeted by an enthusiastic Bertie.

Lord Barlas's dog raised his head hopefully when they entered the room only to lie back down with a disappointed sigh when he saw it wasn't his master.

'The poor thing is pining.' Kitty gave the elderly dog lots of fuss and was rewarded by a wag of his tail.

Romy Fisher was seated in the chair beside the fireplace. 'I say, Maxfield told me what happened last night,' she said as they approached.

Kitty gave the actress a brief recitation of events.

'Golly, poor Nettie. I wonder why she was attacked? It's very frightening. I must admit I have been keeping my door firmly locked every night.' The girl gave a dramatic shiver.

'Yes, it was quite awful. I think she was lucky we heard something and came along when we did.' Kitty thought it had been very fortunate that the noise had disturbed her.

'And Maxfield heard whoever it was too?' Romy said.

'Yes, I met him on the landing just before I reached Madam Fortina's room. We went in there together and discovered her,' Kitty said.

'I never heard anything until a little later when I was woken by voices and footsteps. Then I realised Kitty was missing,' Matt added.

'How awful, and you didn't see who did it?' Romy asked.

Kitty shook her head. 'No, I can only assume that whoever attacked Madam Fortina must have escaped to the other landing or had gone down the servants' stairs.'

'The poor woman, and she doesn't know who it was either?' Romy's eyes were bright with curiosity.

'Apparently not,' Matt said.

'I rather think she is in Lord Barlas's office now with the chief inspector. I expect she will have to give a statement or something. Do you think she knows who the murderer might be? And that was why she was attacked?' Romy sat up a little straighter in her seat.

'I don't think so. I'm sure she would have said something to the police already if she did know anything,' Kitty said. Romy clearly thought the same as Donald.

The actress frowned and pulled her cigarette holder from her bag. 'Yes, I rather think she would have.'

'You've known Madam Fortina for a while now? You introduced her to Lord Barlas and Ottilie?' Kitty asked.

Romy offered her cigarettes to Kitty and Matt before inserting one into her jade holder. 'Yes, Velma and I have known each other for a few years, since we were in a production together. Then she met Stephen and they married. Not long after that Ottilie's husband, Marcus, was killed in an avalanche and poor Ottilie was devastated.' Romy leaned forward to accept a light from Matt for her cigarette.

She blew out a thin stream of smoke and continued her story. 'I had seen Nettie at one or two friends' places, and I knew how good she was, so I introduced her to Velma and Ottilie. I think Lord Barlas was quite sceptical about the whole idea, but she really helped Ottilie enormously.'

'And did you meet Lady Smythe and Sir Rufus at the same time?' Matt asked.

Romy flicked a small piece of ash into the ashtray on the side table. 'Yes, I think so. I've known them for ages. Lynette is rather a pill, but Rufus can be quite fun when he escapes her eagle eye.' Her lips curved up into a smile. 'He can be quite the goer.'

'So everyone here has known one another for quite some time?' Kitty decided not to ask Romy to elaborate on what she meant by Sir Rufus being a goer. It was clear from her inference that the two shared some kind of history that Lady Smythe would not approve of.

Romy took another pull from her cigarette as she considered Kitty's question. 'Yes, Donald obviously only met Ottilie about seven months ago. At a party in town at one of the clubs.'

'And Maxfield?' Kitty prompted.

'He's known Velma for almost as long as I have. He was quite sweet on her before she married Stephen but, of course, Maxfield doesn't have the financial or social cachet that Velma's father wanted for his darling daughter.' Romy flicked more ash into the ashtray.

'I thought Lord and Lady Barlas's marriage was a love match?' Kitty said.

Romy stubbed out her cigarette. 'Oh, darling, it was. Velma adored Stephen and he loved her, absolutely. I think that has always irked Maxfield a little. He doesn't like to lose out in anything. He can be very single-minded about getting what he wants. I suppose in his career that can be a good trait, ruthless you know. It just makes him rather difficult to live with.' The girl grimaced.

'Is that why you and he have an on-off relationship?' Kitty probed.

Romy gave her an amused smile. 'Absolutely, and, of course, I am not wealthy enough to buy Maxfield the toys he so desperately would like. He wants his own racing team, that's why he's considering this film option. It would raise his profile and bring in the dollars. I suppose that's why I was surprised when he agreed to accompany me here, unless he wanted to try and persuade Velma to back him. You know, use his charm on her.'

Kitty was forced to drop the conversation then when one of the constables appeared to invite Romy to see the chief inspector. However, she would have liked to know whether Maxfield had tried to obtain money from Lady Barlas. It would explain his attentiveness towards her since her husband's death. It also explained Kitty's feelings that the racing driver admired Lady Barlas.

CHAPTER TWENTY-TWO

'It seems we shall probably be the last to be interviewed,' Matt remarked once Romy had left the room.

'I suppose that makes sense since we have given a lot of information already. After all, as far as we know we are not considered suspects and it appears that the others all have quite a lot of information to give,' Kitty replied in a thoughtful tone.

'What do you make of what Donald and Romy have told us this morning?' Matt asked.

'It's so confusing, every time I start to think who it might be something else comes up that makes me reconsider everything. I can see why certain people could have had a motive for murdering Lord Barlas and why Madam Fortina gave warnings. What I don't understand are the threats? Why leave notes? What was the last chance referring to in the notes?' Kitty stood and wandered over to the French window to look out at the grey landscape that was slowly appearing as the snow cover continued to thaw.

Matt knew what she meant. He had been convinced that Madam Fortina held the key to whoever had murdered Lord Barlas. The attack last night would have seemed to confirm it, but unless the medium had revealed something fresh to the chief inspector this morning, then that idea was yet another dead end.

'It sounds as if Donald and Maxfield are both after money, for different purposes and from different members of the family but Lord Barlas was the main obstacle in both their paths.' Matt watched as Kitty paced back and forwards in front of the window. 'Sir Rufus too seems to have something to hide.'

'Absolutely. I hope the chief inspector will share anything he has discovered when it's our turn to be seen,' Kitty said.

The telephone suddenly rang out, startling them both and then was promptly silenced. 'It seems the telephone line is back again.' Kitty crossed to one of the table lamps and tried the switch to be rewarded with the welcome sight of a soft pool of yellow light. 'And the electricity, thank goodness.'

'This thaw should make the road passable too and Romy might even manage to get the wireless signal she's been trying to obtain.' Matt couldn't help feeling relieved that their period of isolation at the castle would soon be at an end.

'Was that the telephone I heard?' Lady Smythe entered the room.

'Yes, the electricity seems to have been restored too,' Kitty confirmed.

'Oh hurrah, one might even be able to bathe again by tonight once the hot water is back. Such a nuisance having to ring for water to wash oneself.' Lady Smythe tutted as she joined them. 'Have you been seen yet by the chief inspector?'

'I think we are probably the last of the guests to be interviewed. Miss Fisher is with the chief inspector at the moment.' Kitty sat back down beside Matt.

'I have yet to be summoned too. I thought the chief inspector might have seen me yesterday with Rufus.' Lady Smythe sounded quite put out by the policeman's decision to see her husband without her.

'I suppose he has his reasons for the order in which he is interviewing people,' Matt remarked in a mild tone.

'Well, he certainly has not followed any kind of social protocol,' Lady Smythe declared with a sniff.

Matt bit back a smile. Lady Smythe clearly believed her title gave her a higher status than Romy Fisher.

One of the constables appeared in the doorway. 'Lady Smythe? The chief inspector will see you now.'

Lady Smythe followed the man from the room.

'And then there were two.' Matt grinned at Kitty.

'Indeed. I wonder where everyone else has gone today? I really thought that after last night they all might feel there was safety in numbers and would wish to gather in here.' Kitty looked thoughtful.

'Perhaps it has had the opposite effect and they are keeping apart not wishing to mingle with a murderer,' Matt suggested. 'The castle is certainly large enough if one wishes to avoid people.'

'And for anyone to be attacked or knocked over the head without a witness,' Kitty replied.

'Who else would be at risk though? Madam Fortina was an obvious target after giving all those warnings. The murderer obviously believed she knew their identity or why attack her?' Matt leaned back on the sofa and looked at Kitty.

'I don't know. I've tried to think of people who had motives to murder Lord Barlas and then which of those could physically have done so and I keep getting stumped. Everything appears to be pure conjecture with very few hard facts.' Kitty's brow furrowed and Matt could see she was as perplexed as he was at the moment.

'Captain Bryant, Mrs Bryant, Chief Inspector Innes would like to see you,' the constable said on his return some fifteen minutes or so later. They left the dogs to continue their slumbers and followed the man to the study.

'Captain Bryant, Mrs Bryant, please do sit down.' Chief Inspector Innes had risen to greet them, shaking hands before indicating the vacant chairs in front of the desk.

Once they were both seated the chief inspector dismissed the constable to wait outside the door so they wouldn't be disturbed.

'The telephone lines are operating once more so I have checked those references you provided, Captain Bryant.' Chief Inspector Innes viewed them shrewdly. 'It would appear that you are both well thought of in both police and government circles. I don't mind telling you both, in confidence naturally, that this case is proving quite tricky.'

'We were both saying just the same thing, Chief Inspector. Why would a murderer forewarn his intended victim?' Matt asked. 'Madam Fortina insisted she did not leave either of the notes, despite her other warnings to Lord Barlas.'

The chief inspector drummed his fingers on the desk. 'Perhaps to scare his lordship into a more amenable frame of mind and therefore avoiding the need to kill him?'

'Or because whoever did this enjoyed frightening him. They wanted to make him squirm to provide some sort of perverse pleasure,' Kitty suggested.

'But then who disliked him enough for that? Everyone so far, although many of them may have had a motive for wishing him dead, did not appear to have actively hated the man. That kind of mindset would surely require a level of spite that I have not yet uncovered.' Chief Inspector Innes frowned.

'Has any more information come to light, sir, now that you have spoken to everyone?' Kitty asked.

'I looked at the papers in the safe and surmised that Sir Rufus has been sailing rather close to the wind with some of the financial matters relating to Mrs Ottilie Tremaine's trust fund. He also admitted to having a liaison with Miss Romy Fisher, something the young lady herself has just confirmed.' Chief

Inspector Innes rubbed his face with his hand. 'Apparently Lord Barlas was very traditional in his views about extramarital affairs. He did not approve of Sir Rufus's conduct. I surmise that his disapproval, coupled with his closer examination of some of the decisions that Sir Rufus had made regarding both the businesses and his daughter's finances, may have led him to destroy the later will.'

'That would give Sir Rufus quite a strong motive for killing his friend,' Matt said.

'Yes, but he's not the only one. Donald Waterford's claims to be part of the Waterford family are spurious at best. I have started enquiries but so far all I have learned is that he appears to have come onto the social scene some twelve months ago and has a series of failed ventures behind him. All funded by various ladies with whom he had become acquainted.' The chief inspector leaned back in his chair making the leather squeak.

'Sir Rufus had said he was awaiting proof about Donald which he intended to share with Lord Barlas. They had felt that Ottilie would not believe anything they said about her fiancé without some kind of evidence. If Lord Barlas were able to convince Ottilie to break her engagement, Donald's hopes of marrying and using Ottilie's money would be finished. With her father dead, Ottilie can take full charge of her own money and he could persuade her to fund his various schemes,' Matt said.

'Like mining in the Argentine,' Kitty murmured.

'So another one with a strong motive for wishing Lord Barlas dead,' the chief inspector said.

'What about Maxfield Cotter?' Matt asked.

'We are investigating his background too. He has been in the press with his racing success and also in the society columns. Miss Fisher was most forthcoming about her relationship, or lack of it, with Mr Cotter. He also appears to be in some financial straits. He wants to raise money for his own racing team, not a cheap process and according to Miss Fisher he had designs on Lady Barlas before she married. He may feel with her husband out of the picture and her status as a wealthy recently bereaved vulnerable woman might give him the opportunity he has been seeking,' Chief Inspector Innes said.

'I suppose too there is the question of Miss Fisher's contract. We know that Lord Barlas was not minded to release her from her obligations. However, Maxfield had hoped to raise his profile and his finances with a film deal, but this appeared to be tied to Miss Fisher being available to star with him. I presume this is because he is untried as an actor,' Kitty said.

'Meaning that Maxfield Cotter also has a motive and may have been working alone or with Miss Fisher as his accomplice,' Chief Inspector Innes said.

'Then we come to last night's attack on Madam Fortina.' Matt looked at the chief inspector. 'I assume, sir, that her background is also being investigated?'

The policeman nodded. 'Yes, I have asked my men back at the station to carry out enquiries. She has provided me with some details of where she lived before moving to America.'

'I suppose too we might consider that Lady Smythe could be willing to assist her husband if he were the guilty party. They arrived on the scene quite quickly last night.' Kitty sounded thoughtful.

'Lady Smythe is certainly not a friend of Miss Fisher's. She seemed quite aware of her husband's dalliance. I gained the impression that Sir Rufus is fond of the company of ladies.' The corners of Chief Inspector Innes's mouth quirked upwards in a wry smile.

Matt could see from her expression that Kitty was thinking about everything the chief inspector had said.

'And Madam Fortina could add nothing further about the events last night?'

'No, she said the room was dark and the fire almost out. She had opened her eyes when the click of the door woke her, but she had no time to turn or react before the pillow was pressed over her head, forcing her down against the mattress. It was fortunate, Mrs Bryant, that you and Mr Cotter heard the sounds of the struggle and came along when you did.' The chief inspector gave another sigh. 'My constable is keeping a close watch on that lady for now. I can only hope that when all the results of the background searches come in, I may have a better idea of who killed Lord Barlas.'

There was a tap on the office door and the constable opened it and looked in. 'Sorry to disturb you, sir, but the doctor is here, and you wished to see him.'

'Thank walk, yes. I'll be right there.' Chief Inspector Innes stood and shook hands with them once again. 'Thank you for your assistance. It's most helpful. I must go and speak to the doctor now as he and the undertaker have come to collect his lordship. Please, if you find anything else that may be helpful do come and see me.'

Kitty and Matt followed the chief inspector out of the office. The policeman went to greet the doctor and the undertaker, while Matt and Kitty made their way back to the drawing room.

Bertie and Buster greeted them enthusiastically on their return.

'Shall we take the dogs out?' Kitty suggested. 'It seems to be thawing well now outside and they could do with the exercise. I wouldn't mind some fresh air too.'

'I know what you mean. It's odd to feel claustrophobic in a place the size of Finnglach but it is rather oppressive here right now,' Matt agreed.

They walked down to the boot room and put on their outdoor things. Both dogs followed, their tails wagging with happiness when Matt lifted the leather leashes from the hook on the wall.

Kitty took Bertie's lead, while Matt had hold of Buster. The air outside the castle was still cold but lacked the biting sharpness that had been present each time before when they had stepped outside.

Bertie was eager to explore the clumps of muddy grass that had been exposed by the melting snow and quickly tugged Kitty ahead of Matt. Buster appeared content to plod slowly along at a leisurely pace thoroughly investigating each stone or bush they encountered.

By unspoken mutual choice they walked in the opposite direction to the stone circle, keen to explore part of the landscape they had been unable to see before because of the snow. Before long they discovered that they could reach the stony shore of the loch.

The waters spread much further than Kitty had imagined, the grey semi-frozen surface reflecting the colour of the sky. The loch was fringed by tall, dark evergreen pine trees interspersed with steep scree-covered slopes. Snow-capped mountains framed the view.

'I can hear running water,' Kitty called back over her shoulder to Matt who was some way behind her now. 'I think there must be a waterfall or cascade somewhere ahead.'

She rounded the bend and saw she had reached a point where a small stream gushed and burbled its way over the boulders into the loch. They were beyond the immediate grounds of the castle now and the ground beyond the ancient fortress rose up quite steeply.

A narrow path with several steps, made of logs followed the stream upwards into the trees. The snow had almost gone from this side with only a few pristine frozen pockets remaining at the edges of the path.

Kitty noticed that someone else had obviously walked in this direction since the snow had cleared. There were several footprints in the soft soil surface between the steps. Some looked as if they had been made by a pair of men's boots and there was another set of smaller, more feminine prints.

Bertie bounded on further up the steps, clearly eager to see where the path led. Kitty glanced behind her but could see no sign of Matt. She presumed that Buster must still be taking his own sweet time on his walk.

'Matt, I'm just going to follow the steps for a little way,' she called back.

She decided to see where the path went as she could hear the rush of the tumbling waters cascading down the hillside more loudly now. The path was narrow, and the view ahead was limited as it followed the curve of the hillside, sometimes straying away from the water's edge.

Bertie tugged at his leash, his nose to the ground and she guessed he must have scented a rabbit or a squirrel on the track. Kitty paused for a moment to catch her breath and to assess how much further she intended to climb.

The tall pine trees suddenly enclosed the path and the sound of the waterfall drowned out any hint of birdsong from the forest. Kitty was sure the increase in volume from the water must mean that she was almost at the falls and pressed on.

She had climbed three more of the rustic steps when Bertie suddenly veered from the path, catching her off guard as he plunged through a clump of bedraggled bracken and into the scrubby bushes beneath the trees.

'Bertie!' Kitty tugged at his leash and took a few steps into the forest hoping her dog had not got himself tangled on brambles.

The dog had stopped and was seated next to a large bush looking extremely pleased with himself.

'I hope you haven't found a dead bird or something,' Kitty warned, well aware of her dog's ability to discover offensive smelling objects that he liked to roll in if not caught in time.

She picked her way carefully around a bramble, taking care

not to snag her stockings only to discover that Bertie had discovered something far worse than a dead animal. Instead, she found the recumbent body of one of the police constables who had accompanied the chief inspector to the castle.

Kitty immediately bent to try and discover if the man had a pulse. Her own heart raced as she fervently prayed the man had not been killed. His helmet lay to the side and there was a large contusion on the back of his neck leading her to believe he had been struck from behind.

Thankfully she discovered a weak flutter of life beneath her fingertips, and she realised he was not dead but unconscious. She pulled off her scarf and folded it into a pad, placing it under the man's head. Kitty looked around for any sign of the man's assailant, but her view was limited by the trees. From the marks on the ground and the mud on the constable's boots she guessed he must have been struck on the path and dragged just out of sight.

Satisfied the man was not dead she made her way back onto the path, dragging the reluctant Bertie with her. She was unsure if she should return the way she had come to alert Matt and get the man some help, or if she should continue up a little further. The feminine footsteps she had seen earlier continued onwards and there were other deeper, larger prints accompanying them in the softer parts of the mud.

The constable had been charged with protecting Madam Fortina. Had they come this way together, then the policeman had been assaulted? Did that mean that Madam Fortina was once more in danger? Or was she a co-conspirator with another of the house party? Had she assaulted the constable herself?

Kitty decided quickly that the constable appeared safe for the moment and if Madam Fortina was in danger then she needed to know where the medium had gone. She had to be close to the waterfall now as the noise was so loud. If she reached the falls and no one was in sight, then she would go back down the hill and find Matt.

Her mind made up, Kitty tugged Bertie closer to her and continued upwards. A minute later she discovered the path opened out onto a narrow, open viewing platform. Large grey stone boulders stood on the edge of the forest at the side of the clearing furthest from the waterfall.

Kitty hurried to hide behind them, taking Bertie with her as she looked around for any sign of Madam Fortina or the mystery assailant. It seemed wise not to make herself a target as she had no desire to become the next victim. She had scarcely hidden herself when she spotted Madam Fortina.

The older woman wore a black coat, but her distinctive bright orange scarf made her obvious. She was accompanied by a man. His back was towards Kitty, and she couldn't determine who it might be at first as he was dressed in a dark grey overcoat and his hat was pulled down low on his head.

The man had a tight hold on the medium's upper arm and Kitty could see that there was some kind of altercation taking place. Madam Fortina appeared to be attempting to extricate herself from his grip, while her assailant looked as if he wished to drag her closer to the waterfall.

Kitty realised the falls were on two levels; above the strug-gling couple the waters cascaded down from the hillside, the volume of water swollen by the melted snow, whilst below, this platform marked the spot where the waters took another sheer drop down before continuing on down the hill to the loch below.

Madam Fortina continued to try to pull herself free from the man holding her arm and the struggle intensified. As they fought, the medium succeeded in knocking the man's hat from his head. Kitty drew in a sharp breath when she realised it was Maxfield Cotter who was with the older woman.

Kitty's heart hammered in her chest as she tried to assess the scene. Was Madam Fortina the killer? Had she assaulted the constable and was somehow attempting to escape and Maxfield had caught her? Had she staged the assault in her room to throw them off the scent?

Or was it Maxfield who had attacked both the policeman and the medium? Had he been the one who had killed Lord Barlas? Why was he attacking Madam Fortina?

CHAPTER TWENTY-THREE

Kitty watched in horror as Madam Fortina continued to try to break free. The older woman appeared to collapse down to the floor. Maxfield kept a tight hold of her arm and Kitty realised he was trying to pull the medium to the edge of the falls. Everything suddenly fell into place and she could see the woman was in mortal danger.

Kitty looked around her hiding place for a weapon. There had to be something near to hand that she could use. She spotted a short, stout stick and picked it up from the floor before stepping out from behind the rocks. There was no time to lose.

With luck, Matt would have followed her up the path and would not be too far away. Providing, of course, that the elderly Buster had been able to make the ascent. She could only hope that assistance was coming and coming quickly.

'Maxfield!' The sound of her shout was almost drowned out by the noise of the tumbling water.

Madam Fortina, however, saw her approach and called out, 'Kitty! Help me!'

Bertie added his voice to Kitty's and the sound of his barking caused Maxfield to finally turn to face her.

'Mrs Bryant, what are you doing here?' Maxfield kept the thin veil of civility on his handsome face as Kitty tightened her grip on her weapon.

'Let go of Madam Fortina.' She had edged closer to the two combatants and could feel tiny droplets of icy water on the skin of her face from the spray off the falls.

'Oh, I don't think so. That wouldn't be a good idea. After all, she could so easily fall off the edge here and injure herself.' Maxfield pulled at the fallen woman's arm.

'Kitty, Mrs Bryant, get away and save yourself. He has lost his mind, he doesn't know what he's doing,' Madam Fortina begged.

'Matt isn't far behind me. He'll be here in a minute.' Kitty moved nearer, circling as she did so to try and place herself closer to the older woman.

'I would keep still if I were you, Mrs Bryant. I would hate there to be a double tragedy.' Maxfield tugged Madam Fortina closer to the brink while the woman frantically tried to regain her balance on the muddy surface.

'Let her go!' Kitty slipped the loop of Bertie's leash around her wrist so she could wield the stick with both hands. 'I know you were the one who killed Lord Barlas.'

A sneer lifted the corner of Maxfield's lips. 'I told you and your nosey husband before. I had no motive to murder him. Did I, Mother dear?' He glared at the terrified woman at his feet.

Kitty swallowed hard as she tried to take in this new revelation. 'You had more than enough motive. You want money and Lady Barlas is the key.'

Maxfield referring to Madam Fortina as his mother explained a great deal of the reticence that Kitty had observed whenever the woman had been questioned.

'Mrs Bryant, run, fetch your husband.' Madam Fortina flinched and raised her free arm to protect herself as Maxfield drew back his foot and kicked her.

Instead, Kitty raised the stick she was holding and aimed it squarely at Maxfield. There was a sharp crack as the wood made contact on the side of his head and broke on his shoulder, leaving her holding a much shorter weapon.

Enraged by the attack Maxfield released his mother and turned on Kitty. Blood poured from a cut on the side of his head as he lunged towards her.

'That was very foolish of you, Mrs Bryant.' He made a grab for her as Kitty skipped backwards out of his reach.

Madam Fortina crawled along the ground desperate to get away from the edge of the waterfall. Bertie clearly considered this all to be some kind of threat and capered between them all barking. Kitty held on tightly to his lead trying to prevent her dog from being hurt.

'You were the one who left the note on Lord Barlas's pillow and arranged the business with the dagger at the séance.' Kitty dodged his outstretched hand while she tried to protect Madam Fortina.

'It was most enjoyable seeing the old fool squirm.' Maxfield dived for her again and almost succeeded in catching hold of the sleeve of her coat. 'Velma should have married me. With Stephen now gone, Velma will be mine again and together we will build the greatest racing team.'

Behind him, Kitty saw that Madam Fortina had managed to stand and was looking about her for a weapon.

'You tried to kill him with that stone falling from the castle. Did you put something in his whisky too?' Kitty asked. She wanted to keep his focus on her and not on his mother who had picked up a large stone from the ground.

'The man had more lives than a cat. It didn't help that Mother dearest was trying her best to thwart me, although she thought my campaign was just about scaring the old fool. She never thought I actually would kill him,' Maxfield finished with a cruel smile as he made another dive for Kitty.

He succeeded in catching her arm which caused Bertie to race around them, his long leather leash tangling around the man's legs.

'Let go of her.' Madam Fortina rushed up behind her son, hitting him with the piece of rock she had in her hand.

Maxfield howled with pain and rage and attempted to turn on his mother once more. The struggle had taken them all back closer to the edge of the plateau and Kitty's blonde curls clung damply to the sides of her frozen face.

'Madam Fortina, look out!' Kitty tried to make herself heard over the noise of the water as Maxfield released her arm and lunged for his mother.

The medium stepped sideways as Maxfield reached for her. His feet tangled in Bertie's lead as he did so, tripping him. He teetered for a second arms flailing before the momentum carried him over the edge of the precipice. Kitty gasped in horror as Maxfield Cotter vanished from sight, leaving her standing beside Madam Fortina at the edge of the falls.

Kitty looked straight at Madame Fortina as the two women clung onto each other in shock. Bertie rubbed himself against Kitty's legs seemingly happy that his mistress was now safe.

'Is he...?' Madam Fortina seemed unable to frame the question that was racing through both their minds.

Kitty peered cautiously into the mist obscuring the rocks far below. 'I don't know, I'm so sorry. I can't see. It's such a long way down. I'm so sorry.'

Bertie seated himself by Kitty's side as she tried to gather her wits. 'Matt was behind me, he can't be far away. We need to go and find him and get help. The constable is lying injured just off the path.'

Tears poured down the older woman's face. 'Oh, thank God. I thought he must be dead.'

Kitty placed her arm around Madam Fortina's waist to support her and together they started to stumble back down the path to the place where Kitty had discovered the injured constable.

The man had moved slightly, and they heard him groan as they approached. Kitty's scarf was still in place to cushion him from the cold, hard ground under his head and she was relieved to see that he seemed to be regaining his wits.

'Can you stay with him, while I find Matt?' Kitty asked Madam Fortina.

Returning down the hillside whilst supporting Madam Fortina would take too long otherwise and she was anxious to secure medical attention for the constable. She was also desperate to find her husband to tell him what had happened on the plateau.

The older woman sat down heavily on a nearby fallen log, as if all her strength had gone from her legs. 'Yes, go, the sooner a doctor is fetched the better.'

Kitty thought that Madam Fortina herself could also use some medical attention after her ordeal. The woman's face was almost as grey as the shale on the ground.

'I'll be as quick as I can,' she assured her and hurried away leaving Bertie tied up nearby.

She had not gone far when Matt and Buster met her on the path.

'Kitty? What's wrong? We were coming to find you.' Matt could obviously tell from her demeanour that something had happened.

'Madam Fortina and the constable have been attacked. The constable needs medical assistance,' Kitty gasped a brief explanation. She was out of breath from her hasty descent down the hillside.

'Are you all right? Where are they now? What's happened?' Matt placed his arm around her, concern written on his face.

'I'm quite all right, really. Madam Fortina is with the constable, he is just regaining consciousness. Maxfield Cotter hit him over the head. Bertie is there with them.' Kitty leaned on her husband and tried to recover her breath.

Although she had reassured Matt that she was unharmed the shock of what had just occurred was starting to affect her. She realised that she actually felt quite shaky.

'Cotter? Where is he now?' Matt asked, looking around as if expecting to find the man lurking somewhere in the forest.

Kitty's teeth started to chatter. 'He fell over the precipice at the waterfall. I think he must be either badly hurt or dead, the drop is very steep and there are rocks.'

Matt gathered her to him, and Kitty was comforted by the strong circle of her husband's embrace and the reassuring scent of his overcoat.

'That's awful, my poor darling. I can see there is a lot more that you have to tell me. Are you all right to take me to Madam Fortina and the constable? If he can walk at all it would be better if we could at least get him down this hill.' Matt looked at her with a concerned frown.

Kitty nodded. 'Yes, of course, it's not very far.'

'I'll leave Buster here and we can collect him on the way back.' Matt tied the elderly dog's leash to a tree and the Labrador lay down with a sigh.

Madam Fortina was still seated on the log where Kitty had left her. The constable was now sitting up, his head in his hands and a dazed expression on his face.

Matt immediately went to the injured man and started to assess if he could assist him to make the journey down the hill with some help. Kitty went to Madam Fortina who seemed to have shrunk inside her coat, her eyes still betraying the horror of what she had just been through.

'Kitty, old thing, can you aid Madam Fortina, if I take the constable?' Matt asked.

'Are you able to walk with me?' Kitty asked the older woman.

Madam Fortina gave a stiff nod of her head. 'Yes, I think so.'

Kitty helped the medium to her feet, staggering a little as the woman leaned upon her. She untied Bertie's leash. Matt had the constable's arm around his shoulders and his own arm around the man's waist. Kitty thought they must have made a very strange party as they slowly stumbled their way back to where Buster was waiting patiently for them.

They collected the other dog and walked towards the loch. Thankfully Madam Fortina managed the remaining steps with minimal support. Before long they were at the bottom of the path where the waterfall flowed into the stream leading to the loch.

Matt set the injured policeman down on a nearby stone where he could sit and rest for a few minutes. Kitty's gaze was drawn to the pool where the waterfall fell in a noisy rush of spray. Madam Fortina placed her hand on Kitty's arm, and they peered together at the rocks above the pool looking for some sign of Maxfield.

Kitty could feel the older woman trembling as she clung to Kitty for support.

'Is there any sign of him?' Matt came to join them, posing his question in a low voice, barely audible over the sound of the water.

'Not at this level. The water is moving quite quickly though. I think where the snow is melting on top of the mountain it's sending a lot more water into the river. He could be in the pool higher up or he could have been washed down already and carried out into the loch.' Kitty too kept her voice quite low, not wishing to distress Madam Fortina further. 'Madam Fortina is his mother,' she explained to Matt.

She saw recognition of the situation dawn on her husband's face accompanied by surprise at this unexpected revelation.

'I see. That puts a whole new complexion on the matter. We

need to get her back to the house.' He looked over his shoulder at the policeman. 'The constable too, for that matter. A search party will need to be dispatched urgently to find Cotter. At least we are on more even ground now so the going should be better.'

Matt returned to the constable to determine if the man would be able to walk on a little further.

Madam Fortina shivered. 'I'm so very sorry, Mrs Bryant. I truly never thought that my son was capable of such cruelty. I knew he was no good, even from boyhood, but I never believed him capable of this. Never.' Her gaze was still fixed on the waterfall and the pool.

Kitty placed her arm around the woman once more. 'Come, let's get back to the castle. We can discuss matters further once we are inside and warm again.'

Madam Fortina complied with Kitty's urging, and they set off once more towards Finnglach. The pale-grey walls of the castle were in sight when Sir Rufus and Lady Smythe came towards them.

'Captain Bryant, Mrs Bryant, what has happened?' Sir Rufus quickened his pace to meet them on the path. Lady Smythe hurried behind him.

'Nettie, you are covered in mud!' Lady Smythe exclaimed.

'Sir Rufus, if you could assist me with the constable, he has been injured.' The wounded man's knees suddenly buckled throwing all his weight onto Matt.

Sir Rufus stepped forward giving his silver-topped cane to Lady Smythe so he could assist Matt in supporting the wounded policeman. The two men worked together to hold the constable up as they continued on to the castle.

Lady Smythe clucked and fussed around them as Kitty held on to the dogs' leashes and supported Madam Fortina, who looked as if she was about to collapse. Kitty was relieved when they reached the path that ran around the perimeter of the castle and Sir Rufus sent Lady Smythe off to fetch more assistance.

Within minutes, servants appeared and helped to take the constable inside and to escort Madam Fortina into the drawing room. Chief Inspector Innes was summoned and the rest of the house party assembled near the fireplace.

'Where is Maxfield?' Lady Barlas asked once Madam Fortina was settled in a seat on the sofa and a generous glass of brandy pressed into her hand.

Kitty looked at Matt. She had already taken a reviving sip of brandy herself thanks to Sir Rufus who had taken on the task of ensuring that all those who had come down from the hillside received a medicinal drink.

'I think my son is dead. He fell from the top of the waterfall and I don't know where he is.' Madam Fortina's words stunned the room into silence for a moment before a babble of questions broke out.

Chief Inspector Innes looked at Matt and Kitty for an explanation.

'Maxfield Cotter is Madam Fortina's son. You may wish to send your other constable out with the servants to look for his body,' Matt said. 'Kitty says he fell at the highest point of the waterfall. There was a struggle where he attempted to murder Madam Fortina and then Kitty. We are unsure if he is somewhere in the pool below or if he has travelled down the second cascade and out into the loch itself. It may even be possible that he has survived. We looked but couldn't see him.'

Chief Inspector Innes immediately instructed his man to set off with some of the castle staff to search for Maxfield.

'Do you think that the fall would be fatal?' the chief inspector asked Kitty.

'I think it highly likely, sir, at the very least he must be badly injured. The drop was sheer and although there was a lot of spray and mist it appeared that there were some very jagged rocks below where he fell.' The memory made Kitty feel nauseous and she had to stop and gather herself before taking another sip of brandy.

'Nettie, I don't understand.' Lady Barlas sat beside the medium. 'Maxfield is your son? The one you said you were estranged from?'

A single tear rolled down the medium's cheek. 'I'm so sorry. I didn't know what to do. He threatened me that I was not to tell anyone. I never thought that he would go so far, never...'

It appeared to dawn on Lady Barlas that Maxfield had been responsible for the murder of her husband, and she shrank away from the medium, pressing her fine lawn handkerchief to her mouth.

'Maxfield killed Daddy? Why? What had my father ever done to him?' Ottilie burst into tears as Donald attempted to comfort her.

'All that business about warning Stephen, the messages you received from the spirits. Did you know that he intended to harm Stephen? Why didn't you say something, for heaven's sake? Tell Stephen privately what you knew?' Lady Barlas turned on the medium.

'Ladies, please. Perhaps, Madam Fortina – or is it Mrs Cotter? – you could start at the beginning and tell us what happened.' Chief Inspector Innes raised his hand for calm.

'I hadn't seen or heard from Maxfield for several years until he appeared at a party in New York. It was after Velma had married Stephen and I had given a few readings for Ottilie. I was unaware at that point that he had known Velma before her marriage and still had feelings for her.' Madam Fortina paused and took a sip of brandy as if needing to strengthen herself for the task ahead.

Lady Barlas buried her face in her hands.

'I could see there was some tension between Maxfield and Velma. She didn't appear pleased to see him, but I assumed it was because she thought it might cause trouble in her marriage.'

Lady Barlas gave a muffled sob. 'I loved Stephen.'

'Maxfield exerted himself to be charming. He could be very charming when he wanted to be. He approached me and told me to keep quiet about our relationship. I meant nothing to him, and he was to be nothing to me. He had a successful new life now, and I was not part of it.' Madam Fortina stared at her brandy glass as she continued her story. 'I had no option but to go along with it. There was nothing to be gained then by revealing that he was my son.'

'What happened next?' Kitty asked.

'I became closer to Velma and Ottilie. Velma has been very kind to me.' Madam Fortina broke off to dab at her eyes and glanced at Lady Barlas. 'I was invited to join them to support and advise Velma. I knew there was something troubling Velma, but she would never say exactly what it was. I knew it was something that could threaten her marriage, she would ask me for guidance but never give me any details.'

'It was Maxfield, wasn't it? He said you had given him money. He had something on you too, didn't he?' Romy had been sitting like a statue to one side, but now she turned her steady gaze on Lady Barlas.

CHAPTER TWENTY-FOUR

'Miss Fisher, would you care to elaborate?' Chief Inspector Innes asked.

Kitty guessed from Lady Barlas's reaction and the way Romy had spoken that Maxfield had been blackmailing the two women in some way.

'There were a few letters, indiscreet and foolish from before I met Stephen. Maxfield was always so charming. He said he would ensure they were destroyed.' Lady Barlas bit back a sob. 'Stephen had very traditional views, he wouldn't have understood. I gave Maxfield as much of my allowance as I dared.'

'Ha! That sounds typical of Maxfield. He had some artistic photographs of me taken when I was starting out in the industry. I was his ticket into movies and money, so he had no scruples about persuading me to help him. He knew I didn't have money to give him,' Romy said.

Kitty thought that probably explained the odd nature of the actress's relationship with the racing driver.

'When you were attacked in your room and I came in with Maxfield, did you know he must have been the one who had tried to kill you? I met him on the landing and thought he was going to rescue you but in reality, he must have heard me approach and pretended that he had just arrived instead,' Kitty said.

She wondered that she hadn't thought of that at the time. It had been easy to assume that Maxfield was on his way to the room, not that he had just left it and then had turned around.

'Yes, and before then, when someone tried to strangle you?' Matt asked.

Madam Fortina buried her face in her hands. 'I guessed the attack with my scarf was Maxfield, but he was my son. How could I say anything? Besides he was threatening me and not Stephen. I thought his intention was blackmail, not murder. I had guessed that he was the reason why Velma was so anxious, and I assumed he merely wished to scare Stephen into parting with money. That it was all some scam that he was running. I convinced myself someone else was the murderer.'

'And when you were attacked in your room?' Kitty looked at the medium.

'When he came in with you, and seemed so solicitous, I thought I was mistaken. He couldn't have killed Stephen after all. It had to have been someone else. Donald, perhaps.' The woman ceased talking her voice choked with sobs.

'Me?' Donald was clearly affronted by the suggestion that he could have been a suspect.

'You did have a motive, sir. Your need for money,' Chief Inspector Innes said.

'My financial matters were not so desperate that I would have killed my future father-in-law. Ottilie, my love, you didn't think that, did you?' He looked at his fiancée.

Ottilie dried her own eyes. 'No, of course not. I'm fully aware of your true background and your financial situation and I don't care. I love you and I know you love me and that's truly all that matters.' She kissed Donald on the cheek. 'I know you would never have harmed my father. My concern was Sir Rufus.' She looked at her godfather.

The older man spluttered, and Lady Smythe placed her hand on his arm to calm him down.

'Nonsense, utter nonsense. Stephen was both my friend and my business partner, as you well know. I would have never done anything to harm either him or you.' He glared at Ottilie.

'I know, but it was the business with the will. I thought that perhaps the two of you had fallen out.' Ottilie looked at the chief inspector.

The policeman nodded gravely. 'I demonstrated to Mrs Tremaine that there had been some irregularities with her finances. Monies taken out at various points and then replaced at a later date with no explanation that could be found in the ledgers. I suggested she consult an independent accountant.'

'Pish and twaddle. Every penny of Ottilie's money is in her accounts. There may have been one or two small personal loans from time to time, I admit, but everything was paid back.' Sir Rufus glowered at the policeman.

'However, that may be, sir, Lord Barlas had not been aware of those "loans" at the time. Also, as Lady Barlas has told us, he was a very traditional man. Your, ahem, friendship, with Miss Fisher was not something that he condoned.' Chief Inspector Innes phrased the suggestion delicately.

Sir Rufus's expression turned puce and Lady Smythe's lips puckered as if she had sucked on something sour.

'I believe that it was these discoveries that may have led to the destruction of the later version of the will. Something that Mrs Bryant found out.' Chief Inspector Innes nodded at Kitty.

One of the male servants entered the room and spoke quietly to the chief inspector.

'You must excuse me for a moment.' Chief Inspector Innes followed the manservant out of the room.

Kitty shivered. Had they found Maxfield's body? A hubbub

of chatter broke out as soon as the policeman had gone. Lady Barlas moved away from Madam Fortina to sit next to Romy. She accepted the girl's offer of a cigarette with trembling hands.

Donald and Ottilie remained together, with Ottilie seemingly glad of her fiancé's support. Sir Rufus still looked angry, and Lady Smythe was casting furious glances at Romy.

'I cannot believe it.' Lady Barlas rose from her seat and went to stand by the window, looking out as if hoping to see some sign of what might be happening outside. 'I feel as if all this time I have been nurturing a viper in my bosom.' She whirled around to face Madam Fortina. 'My darling Stephen is dead because of your son. You, who knew who he really was, did nothing.'

Romy sprang up and placed her arm around Lady Barlas's waist. 'Velma, darling. This won't help. I know you are angry with Nettie, but Maxfield tried to kill her. If not for Mrs Bryant then she would have been the one to fall over the precipice or have been smothered in her room. And Nettie did warn Stephen.'

Lady Barlas took a pull on her cigarette. 'I'm sorry, Romy, I wish you had confided in me about the photographs.'

'And I wish you had told me about the letters. Some chums we are, uh?' The actress attempted to comfort her friend.

'What happened on the path up to the waterfall? How did the constable come to be injured?' Kitty turned to Madam Fortina. She was keen to discover how the assault could have occurred.

Her enquiry drew everyone's attention back to the distraught woman sitting alone on the sofa.

'I had breakfast early in my room with the constable attending me. I couldn't sleep properly after the attack. Every little sound had me jumping and it felt as if the castle walls were pressing in on me. My nerves were so tattered, and I kept thinking about Maxfield. I saw the weather had improved and my head was aching so I thought a walk in the fresh air would be safe. It would clear my head and help me to organise my thoughts.' Madam Fortina paused to dab at her eyes once more with her handkerchief. 'The constable said he would accompany me, and I remembered Velma showing us the waterfall when we first arrived at the castle.' She glanced at Lady Barlas.

'Yes, we all walked up there before Christmas to gather holly before it started to snow. Maxfield said it reminded him of Austria.' Romy looked distraught at the memory.

'Rivers and flowing water may be a conduit to the things we cannot see, so it felt natural to take the path up the mountainside. We had walked a little way when I thought I saw a deer in the woods just off the path. In my haste to see if I was correct, I took a few steps away from the constable. The next thing I knew, Maxfield had appeared as if from nowhere and had coshed the poor man over the head with one of the rocks that lay on the side of the path.' Madam Fortina trembled as she spoke, and Kitty could see that the woman found the telling of her story traumatic.

'The constable had been dragged from the path to behind a clump of bushes so he would be out of sight,' Kitty said.

'Maxfield made me assist him. I knew I couldn't outrun him, and I thought my only chance was to try to humour him until I could spy a chance to escape,' Madam Fortina explained. 'He took hold of my arm and forced me to continue on up the path to the viewing platform. I begged him to let me go. I didn't know if the constable was alive or dead at that point.'

'What did he say to you? I could see that you were arguing when I arrived with Bertie.' Bertie raised his head at the sound of his name and nestled in closer to Kitty's foot.

'I was crying, beseeching him to go back and check on the policeman. That it wasn't too late, and he could get away from Finnglach. I said I would help him. I don't recall what I was saying.' Tears poured down the medium's face once more. 'He said I was the only witness and once I was gone it would look as if I had killed Lord Barlas and attacked the constable. He tried to force me over the edge of the precipice and onto the rocks. I begged him as his mother to stop.'

'That was when Bertie and I came upon you.' Matt took Kitty's hand and gently squeezed her fingers.

'You have saved my life twice now, Mrs Bryant. I can never repay you.' Madam Fortina sobbed.

'You were lucky he did not kill you,' Matt murmured in Kitty's ear.

'I think we've discovered that I'm actually quite hard to kill,' Kitty quipped back quietly. There had been several of their cases which had placed both of their lives in danger. 'I'm sorry I didn't have time to alert you.'

Matt sighed gently. 'It sounds as if you had no choice. I'll let you off this time.'

Kitty managed a small smile. 'Thank you, darling.'

'The chief inspector has been gone a dashed long time. What do you suppose is going on?' Sir Rufus asked.

Kitty realised uneasily that the older man had a point. Surely if the searchers had discovered Maxfield's body he would have returned by now.

'You're right, sir. I'll go and see if I can find him,' Matt offered.

* * *

Matt left the drawing room and went in search of the chief inspector. He could see no one about in the great entrance hall so walked to the boot room thinking the police would naturally be outside.

'Captain Bryant?' The chief inspector was crouched down on the red-tiled floor of the room.

'Sir? I was sent to see if there was any news.' A prickle of unease ran along the nape of Matt's neck.

He could see the quarry-tiled floor was a mass of muddy footprints and puddles of water. What looked like sodden clothing lay in a heap on one of the wooden slatted benches and where the chief inspector had been kneeling, bright red droplets marked the floor.

'The staff are still searching the grounds in the immediate vicinity of the castle. There was no sign of a body at the water-fall or in the mouth of the loch where it meets with the stream. The gardener and his boy took the rowboat out but there is no sign of Mr Cotter in the loch.' The chief inspector's expression was grim.

'Those wet clothes, and the blood on the floor? You think he is alive and has been back?' Matt asked.

'It's beginning to look as if Cotter has survived the fall and may be injured. I assume he has managed to change his clothes and is possibly hiding out waiting for an opportunity to get away.' The chief inspector indicated the chest of dressing up costumes.

Matt remembered that there had been several men's suits in the box. 'Surely, he can't have gone far? The castle is remote and it's quite a distance from the village. He would need a motor car or horse surely to even get that far. Then it's quite a way again to reach the town or the station.'

His mind worked overtime trying to place himself in the injured man's shoes. How would he try and get out of Finnglach and where would he run to?

'My thoughts exactly, Captain Bryant. Plus, it would seem that he is hurt, bleeding. There is a trail of blood outside on the path. The weather is set to freeze again tonight so he will require shelter.' The policeman stroked his chin in a thoughtful manner.

'Do you think he may already be inside the castle? There are a good many rooms and hiding places,' Matt suggested.

'That is what I'm afraid of. He will need first aid, food,

drink and shelter. He could easily have come back inside while we were all out looking for him. He has clearly been in here.' Chief Inspector Innes looked troubled.

'We were all together in the drawing room,' Matt said. 'I'm the only one to have come out.'

'I suggest you return and ask everyone to remain in there for now. No one should go anywhere unaccompanied until Cotter is caught. He is clearly highly dangerous and will stop at nothing to keep his freedom,' the chief inspector said.

Matt nodded. He could only hope that the police and the castle staff could find Maxfield quickly before anyone else was hurt or killed.

* * *

Kitty placed her empty brandy glass down on a nearby side table and walked over to the window. Lady Barlas and Romy had moved away to sit on one of the sofas together. Her stomach rumbled reminding her that breakfast had been quite some time ago and it was now well past lunchtime.

The promise of the morning had now given way to a dull and cloudy afternoon made more miserable by the dripping of melted snow from the creeper that surrounded the window. She couldn't see any signs of activity on the terrace so she presumed the search for Maxfield must be concentrated around the loch.

A shiver ran along her spine, and she hoped the man would be found soon and brought back to the castle. It had been impossible to see if he had survived the fall, but she had thought it unlikely.

A movement near the edge of the terrace caught her eye and she moved her face closer to the glass to try and see what it was. Too large for a bird or one of the squirrels that often ventured impertinently along the stone slabs.

No, this was someone moving furtively, someone who didn't

wish to be seen. She caught a glimpse of dark-grey material against the leaves of the evergreen shrub at the side of the path.

Her heart hammered in her chest and her pulse speeded as whoever it was moved just out of sight. It couldn't be a servant, surely? And the police were in uniform and whoever that was wore grey not dark blue.

Kitty glanced back into the drawing room, everyone appeared occupied, no one was missing except Matt. Another look back out of the window revealed no sign of the mysterious figure. Even so, a sense of foreboding filled her, and she decided that she needed to let Matt know what she had seen.

She slipped out of the drawing room and started along the corridor to the main entrance hall. Everywhere appeared deserted and the dullness of the afternoon cast dark shadows in the unlit corridor.

The heels of her boots clicked loudly against the tiled floor reminding her that she had not changed into her indoor shoes. Kitty rounded the corner to enter the cavernous main entrance hall and was relieved to see Matt approaching from the direction of the boot room.

She had opened her mouth to call to him when she was seized from behind. A leather-gloved hand pressed against her mouth prevented her from screaming and something hard and cold was jammed against her ribs.

CHAPTER TWENTY-FIVE

'Not so fast, Mrs Bryant,' Maxfield murmured in her ear. 'Now, I suggest you keep nice and still, I'd hate this gun to go off by accident.'

Kitty struggled to breathe as Maxfield pushed her to walk forward into the centre of the hall. The smell of damp woollen cloth and leather filled her nostrils. Her heels clicked on the floor as they approached alerting Matt to their presence, and she saw his eyes widen in surprise and shock.

'Captain Bryant, how fortuitous. I just ran into your lady wife.' Maxfield's voice sounded laboured as he tightened his hold on Kitty.

'Maxfield, what do you want?' Matt asked.

Kitty could see her husband trying to assess the situation.

'Obviously, I need to curtail my stay at Finnglach and I believe Mrs Bryant here may be able to assist in the arrangements for my departure,' Maxfield said.

'Let Kitty go. You know that it's futile to even try to get away from here. This place is so isolated, and you're injured. You need medical attention.' Matt's tone was calm and reasonable.

'The road through the forest is open. I can take one of the cars. I know there is more than one housed in the old barn.' Maxfield poked Kitty in the rib with the hard, metal barrel of the gun. 'Get one of the servants to bring Lord Barlas's fastest motor around to the front of the castle and make it sharp. I want to be well on the road before the last of the daylight fades.'

'Then will you let Kitty go?' Matt asked.

'What's going on?' Chief Inspector Innes entered the hall behind Matt, his expression tightening when he took in the situation.

'Cotter wants a car,' Matt explained swiftly as Maxfield removed his hand from Kitty's mouth. Instead he now grasped her around her waist, pulling her close to him.

Kitty gulped in air. 'He has a gun.'

'Get Barlas's fastest motor outside the front of the castle or Mrs Bryant may meet with an accident.' Maxfield snarled at the chief inspector. 'And no funny business. I want a full tank of fuel and a can in the boot.'

Kitty could only stand there helplessly pinned in Maxfield's grip while the chief inspector turned to presumably obey Maxfield's instructions.

'Where do you think you can go? You will have to pass through the village and the town before you can even hope to reach any of the cities. You'll be a marked man. Give yourself up now, while you still can,' Matt urged.

'Please don't worry yourself on my account, Bryant. I know a good many people who can assist me once I reach civilisation.' Kitty felt Maxfield wince as he spoke, and she wondered at the nature of his injuries.

Her captor was evidently in some pain. He had survived the plunge into the falls but at what cost?

Maxfield dragged her round as he started to edge closer to the front door of the castle keeping his gaze fixed on Matt as he moved. Kitty did her best to make the movement as difficult as possible, passively resisting her captor and forcing him to exert himself. If she could weaken him then she might be able to break free and escape.

Maxfield's breathing was laboured now in her ear as he forced her to the partially open front door. His grip slackened fractionally, and a blast of cold air hit her as he nudged it open wider in readiness to leave the castle. She heard the dull roar of a car engine and the crunch of tyres on gravel as someone brought a motor car around.

'Keep the engine running with the keys in the car and the door open,' Maxfield shouted out through the open door.

Kitty saw Matt seize the opportunity to move closer while her captor's attention was momentarily diverted to the activity outside the castle.

'Keep still, Bryant. Don't even think of coming any closer or you can say goodbye to your wife,' Maxfield gasped as he turned sharply, the movement obviously catching his eye.

Matt was forced to halt, raising both hands in the air to demonstrate he had no weapon.

'Come along, Mrs Bryant, our transport is waiting.' Maxfield started to pull Kitty through the open door.

She knew that if she allowed herself to leave the castle she would be unlikely to survive.

'Stand clear of the motor,' Maxfield shouted his order to whoever was outside.

Kitty seized her chance to wedge her boot behind the partially open door. She jammed her toes under the ancient door wincing at the pain that sheared through her foot. Her action meant that Maxfield was jerked back, jarring whatever injury he had sustained during his plummet down the waterfall.

He swore loudly in her ear as she raised her elbow and jabbed back against him as hard as she could praying that he did not fire the gun that was still against her ribs.

'Kitty!' Matt shouted a warning as he sprinted towards her.

She grasped the edge of the solid oak castle door as leverage. She then shoved firmly against it to try and free herself from Maxfield's grasp. Unexpectedly, he released her, and she sprawled forwards onto the cold, hard-tiled floor of the hall twisting her foot as she fell. Matt threw himself on top of her to shield her should Maxfield turn the gun on her.

Instead, the racing driver disappeared through the doorway slamming the door shut behind him. The sound of men shouting carried inside and then a shot, horribly loud. A second later the roar of the car engine rose in volume then grew fainter.

'Darling, are you all right?' Matt rolled away up onto his knees to bend solicitously over her as she tried to recover her breath. Her foot throbbed from where she had jammed it under the door.

'Yes, he didn't hurt me. Has he escaped? Was that a shot? Is anyone hurt?' Kitty sat herself up as Matt rushed across to the castle door and opened it.

Chief Inspector Innes and one of the uniformed constables rushed inside.

'Mrs Bryant, are you hurt?' The chief inspector hurried towards her as Matt returned and assisted her to her feet. He placed his arm around her, and she winced as she leaned against him, taking care not to put weight on her injured foot.

'Yes, I'm unharmed, just a twisted ankle and some hurt toes. Has he gone? I thought I heard a shot.' Kitty held on to her husband for support. Her heart was still racing from her narrow escape.

'He fired at one of the servants, luckily he missed. He won't get far, the roads are still not properly clear and the temperature outside has started to drop. If you'll excuse me, I must alert the police stations along the route.' The chief inspector moved briskly in the direction of Lord Barlas's study.

'Come along, old thing. A drop more brandy wouldn't go

amiss.' Matt supported her as they walked back to the drawing room.

Kitty's knees were sore from where she had fallen onto the floor. She suspected she had twisted her ankle too when she had planted her foot behind the door. She certainly couldn't put her weight on her foot properly.

'You're limping,' Matt observed as he guided her to a chair.

'What's happened? What's going on? We thought we heard a car drive off and shouting,' Lady Smythe demanded as Matt requested more brandy for Kitty while he gently unlaced her boot.

'Maxfield Cotter is alive but injured. He attempted to take Kitty hostage and then escaped in Lord Barlas's motor car.' Matt explained what had happened as Sir Rufus poured another generous helping of brandy into a crystal glass.

'I saw someone outside on the terrace behaving oddly. I went to find Matt or the chief inspector and Maxfield captured me and held me hostage. He has a gun,' Kitty added to Matt's story. Her teeth chattered on the edge of the glass as she forced herself to take a sip. The drink she had taken earlier made her head feel quite swimmy.

'The chief inspector is telephoning ahead now to warn the police stations to look out for him,' Matt continued.

Kitty winced as Matt drew up a tapestry-covered footstool and carefully placed her injured foot on a pile of cushions.

'Are you hurt?' Lady Barlas asked her as she came to take a look at Kitty's foot.

'I think I twisted my ankle and hurt my toes when I broke free,' Kitty explained. 'It's just a sprain.'

Lady Barlas rang the servants' bell. A flushed and excited-looking young maid answered, and Lady Barlas requested cold compresses for Kitty's foot. She also asked that tea be served.

'It is far too late for luncheon now. I do hope cook will not be upset,' Lady Barlas said as the maid scuttled away back to the kitchens on her errand.

Madam Fortina had been sitting silently throughout the commotion that Kitty's arrival back in the room had created.

'Maxfield often used to travel with a gun,' Romy shivered. 'He used to say it was his insurance. He must have come back and collected it from his room or somewhere. I didn't know he had it here. When Stephen was killed using his gun I thought... well, I thought it couldn't have been Maxfield. Why steal a gun if you already had one? But I suppose by using Stephen's own gun then it would have put him in the clear, wouldn't it?'

'I regret to say that he would have enjoyed the irony of shooting Stephen with his own weapon. It would have been better if Maxfield had died in the fall,' Madam Fortina said. 'This will not end well for him.'

Chief Inspector Innes entered at the same time as a heavily laden tea trolley was pushed in by the maid.

'Every police station has been alerted along the route from Finnglach on into Edinburgh, Glasgow and Aberdeen.' The policeman's face was stern.

'Do you think that is where he will go?' Sir Rufus asked.

The chief inspector nodded. 'Aye, if he makes it that far. There are road, boat and train connections from those cities and plenty of places to lie low. He has been losing blood though since he made it back to the castle from the waterfall.'

Kitty gratefully accepted a hot cup of tea and a plate of cheese sandwiches from the maid. 'You think he may collapse from his injuries behind the wheel?' she asked.

'He took off out of here like a madman. The roads are bad, and he is seriously wounded. I think the chances of an accident must be high,' the chief inspector said.

As he finished speaking the ring of the telephone startled them all. The policeman hurried over to answer the call.

'I see, yes, no there is nothing further that can be done,

thank you.' Chief Inspector Innes replaced the handset and turned to face them. 'That was the police station in town. Maxfield Cotter has indeed crashed the car into a tree just outside of Finnglach. He has been pronounced dead at the scene.'

There was a shocked collective gasp that the policeman's prophesy had been realised so quickly.

'I am very sorry, Madam Fortina, he was your son,' the chief inspector addressed the medium.

'I lost Maxfield a long time ago, Chief Inspector. His death today has been a long while coming.' Madam Fortina bowed her head and excused herself from the room.

Ottilie set aside her tea. 'I shall go after her. She should not be alone. She has suffered as much in all of this as we have, and she was very good to me when Marcus was killed.'

Lady Barlas inclined her head in acknowledgement, and Ottilie followed after the older woman.

'I must say, Mrs Bryant, you were dashed plucky by all accounts when the bounder grabbed you.' Sir Rufus looked at Kitty.

'And when you rescued Madam Fortina at the waterfall,' Romy added.

Kitty shifted uncomfortably in her seat and looked at Matt. It seemed that now would be an opportune moment to come clean about their presence at Finnglach.

Matt duly took out his silver card case and passed a card to Sir Rufus and one to Romy Fisher and Lady Barlas.

'Private investigators?' Lady Barlas frowned. 'Did Stephen arrange for you to be here? You aren't some distant cousin?'

'No, that was Lord Barlas's suggestion,' Matt continued to explain.

'Were you aware of this, Chief Inspector?' Lady Barlas asked looking at the policeman.

Chief Inspector Innes nodded. 'Yes, they informed me

when I arrived and, naturally, I checked their credentials. Both Captain and Mrs Bryant are very well thought of.'

Sir Rufus looked quite taken aback, setting his cup of tea and his sandwich down on the side table in surprise. Bertie, always quick to spy an opportunity helped himself to the sandwich.

'Bertie is not a member of the agency,' Kitty said as the group broke into laughter at the spaniel's thievery and Sir Rufus's startled face.

'Yes,' agreed Matt, 'he failed dismally on the test for working undercover.'

A week later, Kitty and Matt were at breakfast back in their own house at Churston. The snow and ice of Finnglach already felt like a distant memory. Bertie lay snoozing under the table, his furry tummy full of sausages. Rascal, the cat, lay next to him clearly happy for them all to be home.

Matt had some of the morning's post in front of him and was occupied in slicing the envelopes open with a clean butter knife.

'A letter from Lady Barlas, thanking us for our services and enclosing a cheque. She says that she intends to return to America with Miss Fisher after Lord Barlas's funeral. They will return to London in March for Ottilie and Donald's wedding,' Matt said.

'Does she say anything about the others?' Kitty asked as she gathered up the used crockery.

'Sir Rufus and Lady Smythe are also gone to London. Oh, Madam Fortina has gone to stay at Eastbourne where she has a friend.' Matt skimmed the neat handwriting.

A shiver ran along Kitty's spine. 'I can't help feeling rather sorry for Madam Fortina.'

Matt raised his eyebrows. 'Yes, I know what you mean. I'm

just thankful, however, that you escaped unharmed. That we both did, in fact.'

Kitty wholeheartedly agreed with that statement. She could do without any more excitement for a little while. The post had also included a note from her grandmother asking her to take on some of her roles in the local hotelier association.

Looking over some of the new applications for membership to the organisation should keep her out of mischief for the next couple of months at least. A few nights away and enjoying dinners in some top hotels was a safe occupation, surely? Kitty smiled to herself and hoped so. She'd had quite enough of murder for now. This new job sounded much more pleasant.

A LETTER FROM HELENA

Dear reader,

I want to say a huge thank you for choosing to read *Murder at the Highland Castle*. If you did enjoy it and would like to keep up to date with all my latest releases, just sign up at the following link. Your email address will never be shared, and you can unsubscribe at any time. You also get a free short story!

www.bookouture.com/helena-dixon

This book took Kitty and Matt on quite a different kind of adventure, and I hope that you've enjoyed this new story. Hogmanay in Scotland is a very special time of year but usually doesn't involve a murder. There are lots more stories to come with new characters to meet.

I do hope you loved *Murder at the Highland Castle* and if you did, I would be very grateful if you could write a review. I'd love to hear what you think, and it makes such a difference helping new readers to discover one of my books for the first time.

I love hearing from my readers – you can get in touch with me on social media or through my website.

Thanks,

Helena

KEEP IN TOUCH WITH HELENA

www.nelldixon.com

 facebook.com/nelldixonauthor
x.com/NellDixon

ACKNOWLEDGEMENTS

My grateful thanks to my Scottish friends and readers for all their information about Hogmanay and the traditions involved. Especial thanks to my Roller sisters who, as always, give me such fabulous encouragement, especially when it involves all things Scottish.

My thanks as always go to my support teams, the Tuesday morning Zoomers and the Coffee Crew, who keep me sane, help me talk through my plots and make me laugh! All very important.

Hugs and much love to my incredible agent, Kate Nash, who puts up with my wittering and provides sage advice and encouragement.

Finally, and most importantly, love and thanks to everyone at Bookouture. There are so many people all working so hard to make my books the best that they can be and I appreciate every one of you.

9 781837 900640